SILVER REAPER

REAPER'S ASCENSION BOOK THREE

SHELLEY RUSSELL NOLAN

First published 2017. This edition republished 2019.

❋ Created with Vellum

For Grant

CHAPTER 1

A shiver swept over my body as I stared at the reflection of a person a short distance away from me, a grinning skull where their head should be.

Whoever they were, they were about to die.

I turned around to see who the death portent belonged to, matching the green singlet and khaki shorts to a young man barely out of his teens. Fit, healthy, he gave no indication of his impending demise. Instead, he joked with two friends while they checked out a poster for a new Xbox game in the window in front of me.

I'd been reading about the game myself, wondering if I should order a copy for my younger brother's upcoming birthday. The game was due for release in a week's time, but the young man standing next to me would not live long enough to play it. He had less than twenty-four hours to live.

Unless I could somehow stop him from dying.

He looked over at me, a wide smile on his face as his gaze skimmed my body before settling on my eyes. 'Hey, gorgeous, how you doing?'

'Busy,' I said, tempering my rejection with a smile before I fished my mobile phone out of my handbag and moved away. I pretended to check something on my phone while surreptitiously watching as he and his friends entered the electronics shop.

I had no idea what form his death would take, so I didn't know what I could do to save him. He didn't appear to be sick, unlike the elderly woman whose soul I had reaped the week before. She'd been in the palliative care unit in the same hospital as a client I had been called for. When I first entered the room, she had not been marked with the death portent. It appeared just before I left, in her reflection in the gleaming stainless steel machine she was hooked up to. I'd been called back to reap her soul exactly twenty-four hours later.

The young man's death could either be the result of an accident or foul play, but I had no idea which. I would have to stick close, hoping when the time came I would be able to do something to prevent his dying. But how was I going to do that without being arrested as a stalker?

I cringed at the idea of using his earlier attempt to flirt with me. Even though I was sure Sam would understand why I was doing it, pretending I was interested in another man would still feel like a betrayal. We had been through so much, overcome more obstacles to our happily ever after in the first two weeks of our relationship than most couples do in a lifetime. But we'd made it.

Six months on from the battle at Killian's compound, with the threat posed by Almorthanos and the Tr'lirians who sided with him vanquished once and for all, we were happier than ever. He'd accepted my role as reaper to the people of Easton and I had grown accustomed to reaping the souls of all those who died.

The worst part of being a reaper was when I knew someone was about to die and could do nothing to prevent it. I couldn't do anything for the elderly woman who'd passed away in her sleep after a protracted illness, or the little boy who had been born with a rare and deadly disease. But at least those reaps had been peaceful transitions to rebirth. There had been nothing peaceful about the reaping of a woman I followed home from the supermarket, after witnessing the death portent in a freezer door as she made her selections. I had been helpless to do anything other than watch as a truck ran a red light and smashed into the side of her small sedan.

I could not sit back and watch another person die right in front of me.

I had to save him.

But how?

The forgotten phone in my hand rang and I jumped, fumbling to answer it, relief flooding me as I saw who the caller was. 'Sam, I need your help.'

In a rush of words, I explained the situation to him. 'I need you to arrest him. If he is locked up for the next twenty-four hours no one could hurt him.'

'Tyler, I can't arrest a guy just because you tell me he is going to die. It doesn't work like that.'

'We'll make it work. I'll say he attacked me or something.'

'Sweetheart, you can't do that to the poor guy.' His voice was calm, reasonable.

I was feeling anything but reasonable. 'That poor guy is going to die if we don't save him.'

'I know. I know. But accusing him of assault isn't going to help anyone.'

I shook my head, gripping the phone tightly. 'What's the point of being able to see the death portent if I can't do anything about it?'

'I'll be there as soon as I can. Sit tight, and do not approach him. I don't want your name turning up in a police report.'

I hung up the phone, nibbling at my bottom lip as I waited for Sam to arrive, hoping the young man and his friends would stay inside the store until he did. I caught glimpses of them as they roamed the aisles, breath catching in my throat when not five minutes later they approached the door.

I had to stop them leaving.

I stepped forward, planning on faking a faint at the feet of the guy who was going to die.

Before I could act, a pained expression crossed his face. He groaned, hands going to his head. A second later his body dropped to the shopping centre's tiled floor.

My eyes stung from unshed tears as the hollow below my throat went cold, and the call to reap his soul hit.

His friends kneeled over his body, shaking him, alarm in their voices as they desperately sought a response that would never come. He was dead, life extinguished in the blink of an eye. All that was left was for me to release his soul and send it on its journey towards rebirth.

I took a deep, shuddering breath and quickly scanned the people who had stopped to see what was going on, relieved when I found only adults. Young children could often see into the astral plane and I tried to avoid reaping a soul in front of them. Death was hard enough for them to deal with at any time, let alone witnessing something no one else could.

I forced my feet to move and soon kneeled at my client's side. I tried to make it look as though I was checking for a pulse as I called his soul. It shimmered in the air in front of me, a thin glimmer of light connecting it to his body. Beautiful, vibrant, so full of potential; it eased some of my heartache at not being able to save him.

I touched his soul with a fingertip to release it before I rose and shuffled backwards. A Good Samaritan quickly took my place and began a futile attempt at CPR. I surveyed the growing crowd of onlookers, and when my eyes met Sam's I gave a wobbly smile. He reached out and took my hand in his, pulling me through the circle of people.

We didn't speak as we walked away.

What was there to say?

A young man had just lost his life and there had been nothing I could do to prevent it. That would not stop me trying to save any others for whom the death portent appeared.

CHAPTER 2

'How is the investigation going?' I asked, before Sam could break the silence.

He ran a hand through his close cropped brown hair, hazel eyes shadowed as he shook his head. 'We still have no clue who the men were or what killed them, and no one has filed a missing person's report fitting either of their descriptions.'

Four days ago, squatters had stumbled across two dead bodies in an abandoned house on Easton's northern outskirts. Both bodies showed evidence of having been restrained and possibly tortured, suggesting it was a double homicide. Sam had been called in to investigate but had been left with more questions than answers.

I had only one question. I was the reaper for Easton, and yet I had not been called to reap the souls of these men.

If I hadn't reaped them, who had?

Goose bumps peppered my skin as I exited the shopping centre. The midday sun did little to warm me as Sam and I walked to where my car was parked.

'I have to get back to the station. Are you going to be okay?'

I nodded, a wry smile curving my lips. 'Of course. Watching people die is an occupational hazard for a reaper.'

'Tyler.' He moved in close, one hand coming up to caress my cheek. 'I know you hate not being able to help people, but you can't save them all.'

'I haven't saved any of them.' That was the problem. But it was my problem, not Sam's. 'You better get going. I'll head home and get an early start on my next assessment piece.'

Studying journalism part-time while working full-time in the office for the *Easton Chronicle* required me to stay ahead of my study commitments. I hated being rushed so was currently up-to-date, which meant I should have been able to spend this month's rostered-day-off relaxing. After what I'd just witnessed, relaxing was the farthest thing from my mind. Much better to delve into the world of digital journalism in the multi-media age than to dwell on a young life cut short.

I kissed Sam goodbye, fished my sunglasses out of my bag, and got into my car. I gave him a wave and managed a bright smile as I drove away, a smile that faded as soon as he was out of sight. Asking Sam about his investigation had brought back my uneasiness at knowing there was at least one other reaper operating in Easton.

Part of my job at the *Chronicle* was to compile Death Notices.

Up until the discovery of the two deaths Sam was investigating, each notice had lined up with the souls I had reaped. I'd been busy, often called to reap at inopportune times, but had managed to do my duty without making anyone suspicious. It was not an easy task when my body would appear to be unconscious while my astral form was roaming the astral plane to reach my client.

Had the Grim Reaper assigned another reaper to Easton to ease my work load?

When Jonathon Grimm trapped me into becoming a reaper I'd immediately incurred a soul quota of one thousand. What he didn't tell me until after I'd reaped the soul of the wraith that had murdered me was how each illegitimate reaping added another one thousand souls to my quota.

During the weeks when I fought to stop Grimm's master, Almorthanos, escaping from Demania and enslaving mankind, I had been forced to reap the souls of over a dozen wraiths. With such a large soul quota, it would take me years to fulfil my contract and finally get my life back. That task would take even longer if another reaper was called to reap souls I would normally be assigned.

Not that I wanted people to die so I could fulfil my contract sooner. I just didn't want to be a reaper for one minute longer than I had to. Easing the passing of the dying and sending their souls on to rebirth was all well and good, but bearing witness to so much death was not pleasant. As much as I tried to focus on the positives, I was convinced I'd be surrounded by death right up until the day I died.

If my quota wasn't complete, I wouldn't be free even then.

As if to remind me of the chain Grimm had shackled me with, the hollow below my neck went cold soon after I walked inside the house Sam and I had moved into a month ago. I dropped my bag on the floor beside the dark grey chaise lounge and lay down, ready to take astral form. I focused on the draw of my client, wings unfurling behind me as I slipped free of my physical body and into the astral plane.

The call to reap drew me to the northern outskirts of town, and as I neared the street where the unidentified bodies had been found, a tremor swept through me. Relief I wasn't drawn to the house where they had been discovered faded when the call took me into its overgrown backyard.

Rusted vehicle shells and large chunks of machinery were jumbled in among dead tree branches, all of which were virtually obscured by metre high swathes of grass. It was an urban jungle, and my client was somewhere in the middle of it.

Grateful for my astral form, I slipped through the barrier

made of metal and greenery, wings retracting as I floated to the back corner of the yard.

My client lay on his side, half-naked body covered in a bloody mess of grass and dirt. He was facing me, eyes open but unfocused. Blood from numerous cuts obscured his features. His eyelids fluttered to a close as he let out a low moan and rolled onto his stomach. I put out my hand, ready to call his soul, but froze when I saw his back.

Two long scars ran down both shoulder blades.

I'd seen scars like these before, on Tr'lirians who'd lost their wings. Thick and raised, still slightly red, these scars looked too new to have been made years ago.

Had this man been one of the many who'd lost their wings during the fight between Almorthanos and Cade's forces? If so, whose side had he been on?

Not that his allegiance would change the outcome of his reaping. As he took a last stuttering breath I called his soul to me and sent him on the way to rebirth.

Duty fulfilled, I slipped out of the backyard jungle, unfurled my wings and headed back to my body. As I flew over Easton, I thought about the implications of a wingless Tr'lirian dying in the yard of a house where two other unidentified bodies had been found.

Sam was well aware of what happened to Tr'lirians when they lost their immortality. If the two unidentified bodies had had the same scars he would have come to the same conclusion as me.

I had to go to see Killian.

CHAPTER 3

I hadn't been out to the Greenlakes compound since the battle. As I drove up to the large wrought iron gates I fought not to dwell on the heartache and pain endured back then.

My resolve was tested the second I gained access to the compound. When last I'd been here, the grounds had been littered with the wreckage of bodies and buildings. The carnage was the result of an explosion Almorthanos had arranged to distract and disarm Cade's right hand man, Killian, and his men. Though the bodies of the dead had long since been buried, the compound still looked like a warzone.

I had to pass two fenced checkpoints on my way up the long winding drive to the main house, each manned by armed guards stationed in bulky concrete bunkers. Barbed wire ran around the tops of two rings of fencing encircling the main compound, with deep trenches dug either side of the road.

Scaffolding surrounded the main house, not to repair but to build two more storeys and add reinforcement to the existing walls. Bare-chested winged Tr'lirians flew through the framework, aiding those who were doing the actual construction work.

The war had been won. Yet it looked like Killian was gearing up for a massive assault on the compound.

What had I missed by avoiding this place for the last six months?

Two Tr'lirians, wingless and with loose shirts covering their scars, waited in front of the main house for me to exit my car. I did so reluctantly, bombarded with images from the last time I was here. I wrapped my arms around my middle to ward off a chill and steeled my nerves to enter the building. My steps slowed as I walked down the long hallway where I had been captured by Almorthanos's people. I pushed aside the memories of helplessness that threatened to swamp me and focused on the unsettling changes to Killian's compound.

Maybe I should have called Sam, and waited for him to be able to come here with me. No, he was busy with his investigation, and it could be a coincidence that my client had been found in the backyard of the same house as the two homicides he was investigating.

Besides, I was not helpless.

Far from it.

If anything bad happened, I was ready to form a wall of aether around me, or blast my attackers with lightning. It wouldn't kill a winged Tr'lirian, but it should slow them down long enough for me to get away.

I let my arms fall to my sides. Back straight and head held high, I marched inside the large room Killian used as his meeting room, prepared to face anything.

Anything except Chris Bradbury.

'What are you doing here?' I blurted out the words, heart racing at the sight of him.

'Hello, Tyler.' His smile was strained, face shadowed as he stared at me.

He stood in front of Killian's desk, dressed in a dark blue suit that enhanced the colour of his eyes. I took in his unshaven chin and how his dark blond hair looked as if he'd run his fingers through it numerous times. Even dishevelled he had a presence that caught my breath.

I hadn't seen him since the aftermath of the battle in this compound. As far as I was aware he hadn't been back, supervising the completion of Riverside Plaza from Sydney. He'd also been missing from the social pages in the nation's tabloids, after announcing an intention to focus more on the corporate side of the Bradbury Corporation. I hadn't tried to contact him, aware he was hurting because I'd chosen Sam instead of him.

'His business is with me, Miss Morgan, not you, so why don't you tell me why you insisted on meeting with me so we can get back to our work,' said Killian, deep voice roughened with fatigue.

He got up from the chair behind his desk and stalked towards me, not stopping until he was inches away, looming over me. He appeared to be as exhausted and troubled as Chris, though just as impeccably dressed.

'What's going on? What's wrong?'

Killian's nostrils flared. 'It does not concern you. Why have you come here?'

I shook my head, wide eyed. 'This place looks as though you're preparing for another war. How can that not concern me?'

'If your only reason for being here is to critique my architectural project, then I suggest you leave. I do not have time for a social visit or to pander to the whims of a Davilian.'

I stiffened. The derision in his voice cut. I'd thought he'd got over the matter of my Davilian heritage, going so far as to urge the leader of Clan Godden, Cade, to trust me when it came time to go up against Almorthanos. We'd been allies. Now he was looking at me as if I was dirt. Unclean.

'Michael, Tyler obviously has something important to tell you or she wouldn't be here.'

I frowned, the ease with which Chris used Killian's first name suggesting a long acquaintance. Even more startling was the way Killian immediately backed down.

'Very well. She has five minutes.' He took a step back, arms folded in front of him, and glared at me. 'Start talking.'

I took a deep breath, shaking off the increasing feeling of unease building in the room. 'I just reaped the soul of a man, and I think he was Tr'lirian.'

'What did you say?' Killian lunged forward and grabbed hold of my shoulders.

I reacted on instinct, calling up a wall of aether and shoving him away from me. Chest heaving, breath speeding up, I put up my hands to ward him off when he tried to grab me again. 'Touch me and you will regret it.'

Chris launched himself across the room to stand between us. 'Everybody needs to take a step back and calm down.'

After an angry glare my way, Killian moved to his desk and poured himself a drink from a crystal decanter, taking a long swallow of an amber liquid, face averted.

Chris faced me, expression earnest. 'What makes you think your client was Tr'lirian?'

I met his worried eyes and told him what I had discovered.

'Have you told anyone else about the body?'

I shook my head. 'No, I came straight here.'

'What about Lockwood?'

I stifled the guilt that rose within me. I should have called Sam. He was a homicide detective. It was his job to investigate dead bodies in Easton, but…'If I'm right, and the man is Tr'lirian, I thought it best to come here before the police were involved.'

Killian strode to the door and called out a command. Two winged Tr'lirians, a man and a woman, dashed inside the room. Like all the winged Tr'lirians I had ever seen, they both wore dark pants. The male was bare-chested except for a thick strap that secured the sword sheathed between his shoulder blades. The woman wore a vest tied in a way to prevent it from interfering with the large white wings that swept the floor with each step she took. She also had a sword sheathed on her back; the hilt twisted to the left to stop it banging into the back of her head.

The militant way they both moved and the muscles on display in their skimpy attire suggested they were well versed in sword-play. After a hurried conversation with their commander, they were sent winging on their way to the abandoned house.

While we waited for them to return, I examined Killian and Chris. Neither man seemed able to sit still, either pacing across the room or fidgeting with the objects on top of the desk.

'You two are acting like caged lions, all set to pounce only you have no one to pounce on. Will one of you please tell me what the hell is going on?'

Killian didn't even look up. 'I already told you, this does not concern you.'

'Really? Then I suppose you don't want to know about the other mysterious bodies that have appeared in Easton this week?'

Killian moved so fast I had no time to think as he launched himself at me, hands wrapping around my throat. 'What bodies? Was one of them female? Tell me.' He shook me, hands tightening their grip.

I choked, desperate to breathe as I called on aether, ready to blast his soul to shreds. Before I could lash out, Chris appeared at my side and wrenched him away from me.

'Calm down. Let Tyler talk. You don't know that any of these bodies are Rebecca's.'

'Who is Rebecca?' I asked, massaging my throat.

'My daughter.'

'My fiancée.'

Their voices overlapped and it took me a second to sort out what each of them had said.

'You're engaged to his daughter? When did that happen?' I stared at Chris, eyes widening even more at the cautious look in his eyes.

I shifted my gaze from Chris to Killian. 'I didn't even know you had a daughter.' That explained why Chris was using his first name and why Killian listened to him. Still, six months seemed a short time for Chris to have fallen in love and proposed.

'Was one of the bodies that of a young woman?' Killian asked, visibly bracing for my answer.

Understanding at least part of his concern, I shook my head. 'They were both male, but so far the police have not been able to identify them and have no clues as to what killed them.' I quickly recited what I knew of the ongoing homicide investigation.

There was silence after I finished talking; silence in which the two of them shared looks full of hidden meaning. I squared up to Killian. 'All right, I've told you what I know. Now it's your turn. Why do you think your daughter might be dead?'

'Rebecca left the compound two days ago, in the company of

one of my men.' His expression was bleak. 'A good man, who lost his wings six months ago. He would die before allowing any harm to befall my daughter, but no one has seen or heard from either of them since.'

'And you think the client whose soul I just reaped is the man who left here with Rebecca?' That explained the tense and harried expressions both men wore when I entered the room, and the reaction to my announcement of more dead bodies. It didn't explain why Chris was engaged to Killian's daughter. But that really was none of my business. If he had found love then I was genuinely happy for him, and would do whatever I could to help him find his missing fiancée.

'Have you filed a missing person report with the police?'

'I do not want the police involved.' Killian's response was clipped, determined.

'Why the hell not? If you think she's in danger, you have to call the police.'

Chris shared another telling glance with Killian before he responded. 'We don't know for sure if she is in danger, or even missing. She wasn't exactly in the best of moods when she left here. She made it quite clear she didn't want anything to do with either of us. Our inability to contact her could be caused by her simply refusing to answer the phone.'

The woman Killian had sent to check the body of my last client entered the room and strode over to whisper in his ear. I couldn't hear what she was saying but the relief in Killian's eyes was evident. He dismissed the Tr'lirian, back straight, and turned to me with a determined look.

'My soldiers will now travel to the morgue to view the bodies found in that house. We'll soon know if their deaths are connected to Rebecca's disappearance.'

'What about the man whose soul I reaped? Is he one of yours or one of the Davilians who sacrificed their immortality in exchange for being allowed to live? They'd have the same scars.'

My stomach churned just thinking about the agonising cries that had echoed throughout the compound when Cade had enacted his revenge on those who'd fought against him.

Given the choice of death or exile to the physical plane, most of the Tr'lirians who fought for Almorthanos had opted to have their wings ripped from their backs. Doomed to a mortal existence, they would no longer be able to return to their home, Angellin, though they would still be able to access the astral plane.

'He was one of my men.'

'I'm sorry for your loss.'

Killian's eyes narrowed. 'Why? He was nothing to you. I hardly think you would concern yourself with my sorrow, or that of any other member of my clan.'

I recoiled. 'No one deserves to die as he did. Alone and cast aside like rubbish. Just because I didn't know him doesn't mean his death doesn't sadden me. All death saddens me.'

'Then perhaps you had better get yourself a new job, reaper.'

'Michael, that's enough. Tyler came here in good faith. You need to treat her with respect.'

Killian glared at Chris before storming out the door without saying a word.

Chris came forward and laid a hand on my shoulder. 'Don't take his attitude personally. He's just worried about Rebecca.'

'What about you? You seem awfully calm for a man whose fiancée ran out on him.' I wanted to ask him what it was he and Killian had done to make Rebecca flee the compound in the first place, but now was not the time.

He grimaced. 'It's complicated.'

'I'll bet.' My smile was strained as I looked at him. Something was going on here. Something more than a missing daughter and fiancée. 'Does it have anything to do with why this place is turning into a fortress?'

Chris's brow creased. 'A fortress?'

'Come on. You can't have missed all the construction work, or the battleground being prepared right outside the front door. From the looks of it, Killian is expecting trouble.'

He ran a hand through his thick hair. 'When I arrived here two days ago it was in the middle of the night and, honestly, I was so tired I didn't take much notice of anything other than where and when I would be able to sleep.'

'And Rebecca, what did she think?'

'Excuse me?' He raised one eyebrow.

'You said she took off two days ago, so two nights ago she would have been here with you, right?'

'She was already here when I arrived, but I didn't get to meet her until the next morning.'

I frowned, his phrasing confusing me. Before I got a chance to question him further, Killian walked back into the room, a tight smile on his handsome face.

'Tyler, you have a visitor.'

Sam strode in behind him, and from the look he gave me he was not happy. His frown deepened when he spotted Chris. 'Should have known you'd be mixed up in this mess, Bradbury.'

'Pleasure to see you again, too, Lockwood.'

I moved to Sam's side. 'What's going on? Why are you here?'

'I should be asking you the same question, but first I'd like to know what the hell two of your goons were doing running around my crime scene?' He confronted Killian, gaze steady as he waited for an answer.

Killian held his head high, a smirk curving his full lips. 'I'm sure I don't know what you're talking about.'

'Bullshit. Last I checked you were the only man in town with winged minions at his beck and call. Or is there another Tr'lirian arsehole trying to lay claim to my town? From the way you're fortifying this place I'm guessing you're preparing for one hell of a fight.'

'I can assure you that your town is not under threat.'

'Then what's with the makeover, and interfering in a police investigation?'

Killian's smirk never wavered as he raised an eyebrow. 'There's nothing wrong with being prepared. A number of my clan are now stranded on this plane, outnumbered by humans. I'm just ensuring they have a safe place to call home if our presence is discovered. Your lot aren't exactly known for their hospitality towards illegal immigrants.'

Sam stared at him for a moment longer, before shifting his attention back to me. I didn't blame him for being suspicious of Killian's smooth answers. I hadn't missed the way he'd avoided mentioning the reason his men had gone to the abandoned house. But it was something else he didn't say that concerned me more.

'What about the Davilians who lost their wings? Do they have a safe place to call home or did you just cast them out and let them fend for themselves?' I lifted my chin, determined to get answers.

Killian cast a glacial glance my way. 'They have been taken care of and are no longer your concern.'

I frowned. "Taken care of" could mean a lot of things, and not all of them good. 'Where are they?'

'Gone from Easton, and before you threaten to blast my soul to smithereens I can promise you they are all alive, and will continue to stay that way as long as none of them pose a threat to Clan Godden.'

I sucked in a breath. 'Do you think one of them has something to do with Rebecca's disappearance, or the dead Tr'lirian I found today?'

'Whoa. Back up. Who is Rebecca and when did you find a dead Tr'lirian?' Sam clutched my arm, eyes narrowed. 'Is that what his goons were doing at my crime scene? Sniffing out a dead body?'

I nodded, explaining what had happened since I said goodbye

to him at the shopping centre. 'Killian's people confirmed the deceased is a member of Clan Godden, but not the man who was with Rebecca when she left here two days ago.'

Sam grabbed out his phone. 'I'll call in the dead body, and have your fiancée listed as a missing person,' he said to Chris. 'Do you have a recent photo of her I can use?'

Chris shook his head. 'Sorry, I don't have any photos of Rebecca.' He turned to Killian. 'Michael?'

'I'm afraid I have no recent photos of my daughter. It has been some years since we were in contact with each other, and my soldiers have already taken care of the body of their fallen brethren. Once they return from the morgue we will know if the dead men who were found inside the house are also Tr'lirian.'

Sam looked ready to explode. I stepped to his side and put a hand on his arm. 'With any luck, Killian's men will be able to identify them and you'll finally have more to go on.'

Lips thin, nostrils flaring, Sam shook his head. 'I'm supposed to just forget they removed a body from a crime scene, and are breaking into the morgue? Are they going to steal those ones too?'

The conflicted expression in his hazel eyes made guilt fizz through me. 'I'm sorry. I should have come to you first.'

'Yes, you should have.' He tempered his rebuke with a squeeze of my hand. 'But you're right about one thing. This could be the break the case needs.'

The Tr'lirians Killian sent to the morgue wore grim expressions when they returned and marched across the room to report to him. They conferred in quiet tones on the other side of the room from where we waited making stilted small talk with Chris.

After five minutes of this Sam strode forward. 'Enough chit chat. What have you got?'

Killian was not pleased by the interruption but Sam showed no sign of being intimidated by the black look sent his way.

Killian dismissed the Tr'lirians and waited until they had left the room before turning back to Sam. 'Very well, detective, here is what I know. The men are not Tr'lirian, but they are known to me.'

'How, exactly?'

'I had business dealings with them, five days ago. Afterwards I assumed they had returned to New South Wales, where their business is based.'

'What business would that be?'

'Real estate. And before you ask your next question, the details of my dealings with them are not pertinent to your case.'

'That's not up to you to decide. This is my case. I need to know everything you know about those men, starting with their names.'

With Sam in full detective mode, I left him to it. It was time to do my own interrogation. 'What's really going on here, Chris?'

'What do you mean?'

'You. Rebecca. This so-called engagement.'

'There is nothing so-called about it.'

'Really? Then why did you say you only got to meet her the morning after you arrived here? And why would she come here at all? Killian said he hadn't seen her for years. Why the sudden visit to a father she wasn't even in contact with? Don't tell me you had to ask his permission to marry her?'

I caught my breath. 'Is that why she took off? He refused to let her marry you?'

Chris's smile was bitter. 'Do you really think he'd say no to Cade's son?'

'You're not his son. Just because your soul is in the original Chris Bradbury's body doesn't make you family.'

He snorted. 'Tell that to Cade. As far as he is concerned, I am his son in every way that matters. And Michael is his man all the way.'

I shook my head. 'It sounds so wrong to hear you call him that, as if you were friends. He tried to kill us. In fact, that was his and Cade's plan. To kill both of us.'

He grimaced. 'Tyler, this isn't the time to be having this conversation. Right now we need to focus on who is killing Killian's men, and finding Rebecca before she becomes the next victim.'

I wasn't ready to let it go but had to when the call to reap hit, the chill emanating from the hollow below my throat making me shiver.

'Someone is dying,' I said, hoping his last words would not prove prophetic as I moved over to a chair and sat down.

As I slipped out of my physical body and unfurled my silver astral wings I caught sight of panic on Killian's face. For his sake, I hoped it wasn't his daughter's soul I was being called to reap.

I had no reassurance to offer him or Chris as I left the compound, the call taking me back towards Easton. I reached the edge of town, relieved when I was not called to the house where I'd found the dead Tr'lirian. Instead, the call took me to the winding rabbit warren of streets around Easton's Botanical Gardens.

My pace slowed so I knew I was nearing my client. As I prepared myself to reap, a car rocketed around the corner and roared towards me. I instinctively flew higher, even though the car would pass right through my astral form. I caught a glimpse of the driver, his eyes wide with fear, before the car slammed into a lamppost, the force of the collision echoing in the air around me.

A familiar dark shape swirled out of the mangled wreck and swiftly vanished.

A shudder rippled through my astral form.

A dark reaper had been in the car with the man prior to the crash. I had no urge to reap his soul, so either the driver was still alive or the other reaper must have taken it. I couldn't see how anyone could have survived a crash at that speed, but the call to reap was pulling me farther down the road.

I continued on to my client. The broken body of an elderly gentleman was sprawled in the middle of a pedestrian crossing, a mangled walking frame several feet away. It appeared he had been run down by the car. Death had surely been instantaneous. Tears streamed down my cheeks and crystalised as they fell, smashing once they hit the ground.

I hovered over the old man, averting my eyes from his shattered body as I called forth his soul. Its brilliant light intensified when I touched it and sent it on to rebirth. I took a moment to steel myself before flying back to check on the man who had killed him.

The driver was slumped over the steering wheel, blood leaking from numerous gashes in his flesh. His eyes were open, and blank, and it took only a second to determine a hole gaped where his soul should be. The dark reaper had taken it.

I shook my head, struggling to understand what had taken place. The Grim Reaper had taken all the dark reapers with him to the Underworld after I cleared him of Almorthanos's taint. For one to be here, reaping; it had to be on his orders. But at least I hadn't been called to reap the soul of Rebecca Killian. I let that thought buoy up my spirits as I flew back to the compound to reconnect with my physical body.

Sam, Chris and Killian were standing around the chair on which my body reclined, matching expressions of concern on their faces as they waited for me to tell them whose soul I had reaped.

I fought the disconnection I always experienced when I returned to my body and opened my eyes.

'It wasn't her,' I said the moment my vocal cords were capable of producing a sound. The words were croaky but the relief in three sets of eyes showed they understood.

I pushed myself upright, giving Sam a grateful smile when he assisted me, happy to lean on him until my legs felt steady enough to support me unaided. Their relief faded when I told them what I had witnessed.

'A dark reaper? How can that be?'

I shrugged my shoulders; sure the apprehension in my eyes matched what I saw in Chris's. He more than any of them understood what the appearance of a dark reaper could mean. If the Grim Reaper had sent the dark reaper to Easton to reap souls, did that mean his malevolent alter ego, Jonathon Grimm, had resurfaced and was after the nether created when people died violent deaths? Would we soon be fighting to stop him trying to take corporeal form on the physical plane?

The thought of going through the horror of six months ago all over again was daunting, but I would not let it stop me from doing what must be done.

'The men Killian had business dealings with,' said Sam, a pensive twist to this mouth. 'Could the dark reaper you saw be responsible for their deaths? Or do you think the Grim Reaper has sent more of them to Easton?'

I shrugged, struggling to come up with an explanation that didn't involve the possibility of all-out war with the leader of the Underworld. 'We don't know for sure the dark reaper was sent here by the Grim Reaper, or that there are more of them running around the astral plane. This reaper could have been left here when the rest were taken back to the Underworld.'

'Then why have you found only two bodies with their souls missing before today?' Chris asked.

'That's two in Easton. Maybe reapers in other places have encountered the same thing. This happened four days ago. Maybe the dark reaper fled Easton after the battle and has only just returned. This might not have anything to do with the Grim Reaper at all.' At least, I hoped it didn't.

'What is clear is someone has it in for Killian's friends,' said Sam. 'It can't be a coincidence two of his business associates were found murdered four days before one of his Tr'lirians is tortured and left for dead.'

'What about the driver of the car Tyler just witnessed crashing?' Chris rubbed his chin. 'If, as you suspect, someone is targeting Killian's people, could he also be connected in some way?'

'Only one way to find out,' said Sam. He moved away and took out his mobile phone. A short time later he was deep in conversation with whoever had been called in to take charge at the accident scene. He hung up the phone and looked over at Killian.

'The name Vincent Troughton mean anything to you?'

Killian stiffened, providing the answer even before he said, 'He is...was the local representative for the real estate firm, as well as being half Tr'lirian.'

'So it's official. This dark reaper is going after your Tr'lirians or people who work for you,' I said.

Kilian swung around to face me, a fierce glare on his face. 'You need to go to the Underworld. Talk to your boss. Find out where my daughter is, and why his dark reapers are targeting my people.'

'Excuse me?'

'You heard me.'

'I am not going anywhere near the Underworld. Send one of them,' I said, pointing to where his winged lieutenants stood waiting for orders.

'I can't. Ever since we retrieved your body the Underworld has been closed to us.' He peered down at me. 'My men risked their lives so your soul had a chance to return to your own body. You owe us this.'

'Like hell she does,' said Chris, storming over to confront Killian. 'The cost of retrieving her body has already been paid.'

'Not in full, it hasn't.'

I frowned. 'What are you talking about? What cost?' I looked from one of them to the other. 'Will one of you please tell me what's going on?'

'It's nothing. It was a private matter between Killian and me. You don't need to concern yourself with it,' said Chris.

'I wish people would stop trying to tell me what does and doesn't concern me. You're talking about my life here.' My eyes widened, remembering a number of whispered conversations between Chris and Killian after my soul had accidentally been trapped in my cousin's dead body, bringing it back to life.

I'd been unable to reconcile myself to living in Emily's body, and had been determined to die once and for all after Almorthanos was defeated. But then Killian had retrieved my own body and I'd been able to transfer my soul back to it. Emily had not been so lucky; her soul already on its journey towards rebirth. I'd always believed Killian had acted as he had as thanks for my help in the battle.

I looked at Chris. 'Are you telling me you paid them to retrieve my body from the Underworld?' I shook my head, unable to comprehend how mercenary this all was.

'So, tell me, how much was my life worth? How much did you charge him?' I glared at Killian.

'I can assure you, no monetary compensation changed hands. Our transaction was of a more personal nature.'

'What the hell does that mean?' I thought back, trying to think what else had changed when I'd been given my life back. There was only one thing I could think of.

I stared at Chris. 'That was when you started referring to Cade as your father. Is that what it cost? Becoming part of the family?' I clutched the back of the chair in front of me to steady myself.

'Oh my God. That's why you're marrying Rebecca.'

Chris gave me a self-deprecating smile. 'That was the plan. Unfortunately, my future bride wasn't keen on the idea of an arranged marriage, even if it was to me.'

I shook my head as I scowled at Killian. 'You people are insane.'

I rounded on Chris. 'And you, what the hell were you thinking to agree to this in the first place? An arranged marriage? Seriously?'

His brows narrowed; deep blue eyes filled with emotion. 'You were determined to sacrifice yourself, to give Emily's parents closure and a chance to say goodbye to their daughter. What else was I supposed to do? Sit back and let you die, again?'

'Yes. That was exactly what you were supposed to do. Not sell yourself to Cade.'

He shook his head, mouth firming, chin raised. 'No. That was never going to happen. I loved you, Tyler. I would have done anything to save you, protect you. This was a small price to pay to give you your life back.'

I opened my mouth, ready to scream about how crazy this all was, but he cut me off.

'This was my choice. And I'd do it again.'

Sam put his arm around my shoulder and turned me to face him. 'And I'd let him do it. You're alive and in your own body. How that happened is not relevant. We have more important things to worry about.'

'I couldn't agree more, Detective Lockwood,' said Killian. 'Tyler might not like how her resurrection was achieved, but it would never have happened without my help. Now I need her help to find my daughter.'

He strode forward to stand right in front of me, deep blue gaze digging into mine. 'Rebecca is innocent and you are the only one who can find out what happened to her. Don't make her pay for what you see as my sins. Don't do to her what others have done to you. I have overlooked your unfortunate heritage, done what I can to protect you, and stayed Cade's hand when he ordered your death. Save my daughter and I will consider the debt paid in full.'

'Tyler, no. You don't have to do this,' said Sam. I could see in his eyes that he knew how much the thought of returning to the Underworld terrified me.

I shook my head. 'It doesn't matter anyway. I have barely any Tr'lirian blood. I can't just slip into the astral plane anytime I want. I have to wait for the call to reap, and even then I have no idea if I'd be able to cross over.'

'Have you even tried?' Killian asked. 'As I understand it, ever since you gained your astral wings you have not been constrained to return to your body immediately after reaping a soul. What's to say that is not the only change to have occurred? You are unusually gifted when it comes to manipulating aether. I'm sure if you put your mind, and spirit, to it, you would be able to access the astral plane without the need to reap.'

I stared at Killian; aware he was seeking to manipulate me but unable to dismiss his suggestion out of hand. He was right. I had no idea what I was capable of. I hadn't realised I could destroy souls with a blast of aether or use it to create an impenetrable barrier until I'd been attacked and forced to defend myself.

Not only that, but after my soul had been returned to my body I'd soon realised I could hear the songs broadcast by the souls of all those around me if I concentrated. Who knew what else I could do if the situation warranted it? But even if I did manage to take astral form without the need to reap a soul, that didn't mean I was willing to fly to the Underworld and confront the Grim Reaper.

'Let's take a step back and think about this,' said Sam. 'I know you're worried about your daughter, but putting Tyler in danger isn't going to help her. You don't even know if the Grim Reaper has got anything to do with Rebecca's disappearance. If he is behind it, the last thing we should be doing is letting Tyler get anywhere near him.'

'Of course he's behind it. He controls the reapers. None of them would be reaping the souls of my people without his say so,' said Killian.

'He doesn't control me,' I said, shoulders back.

'No, but he does owe you. You freed him from Almorthanos's taint. If you seek to gain entrance to the Underworld, I'm sure he will let you pass through the nether barrier. If not, you can always blast it with aether. You've already proved which is stronger.'

I gave a snort. 'What a fantastic idea. An all-out assault on the Underworld. That is sure to have him eager to spill his secrets.'

'My daughter's life is at stake, and you're making jokes and refusing to do anything to save her.' His brows arched, giving his handsome face a devilish cast.

I lifted my chin and glared at him. 'Enough with the emotional blackmail. If I go to the Underworld it will not be because of your daughter.'

Sam took my hand. 'Tyler, no. You don't have to do this.'

I let go of my anger, managing a rueful smile as I faced him.

'Yes, I do. You're right. We don't know if Rebecca is even in danger. It could be a simple case of a woman pissed at her dad for trying to marry her off to a complete stranger. What we do know is that a dark reaper is operating in Easton. I'm not happy about it, but we need to know now if this is the start of something.'

Terrified or not, while I'd listened to Killian rave on about my responsibilities I'd realised he was right. Not that I owed it to him or his daughter, but to the people of Easton. Their souls were in my keeping and if there was even a chance of Jonathon Grimm making a reappearance it would be my duty to make sure that never happened.

'Of course, saying I'll go is a lot different than getting there. First I have to figure out how to take astral form without needing to reap. Otherwise I'll have to wait for the next person to die and go then.'

Working out how to take astral form with all of them watching on would not be an interesting experience and I had no wish to make it any harder on myself. 'I need somewhere quiet to see if I can figure this out.'

'Of course. I'll take you to one of the guest rooms,' said Killian.

I winced. It had been in one of the guest rooms where Almorthanos had tried to bend me to his will. 'No, thanks. I'm going home. I'll call you as soon as I have anything. In the meantime, you need to start working on a list of who might have it in for you, other than the Grim Reaper and all of the Tr'lirians who fought for Almorthanos.'

He gave a terse nod. 'Very well. You may leave. But I expect a full report in two hours.'

I choked out an incredulous laugh. 'I don't work for you. I'm not one of your soldiers. I'll be in touch when I have something. If you don't like that, feel free to find someone else to contact the Grim Reaper for you.'

I didn't give him a chance to respond, spinning around and

heading for the door. With each step I stared down the brawny Tr'lirian standing in the middle of the doorway. Unlike his winged brethren, he wore a loose fitting top, probably to hide the scars left behind after the loss of his wings. He did have a sword though, sheathed on his back, making him a dangerous adversary.

I was not going to let that deter me.

Sam matched his steps to mine and with the two of us bearing down on him the Tr'lirian moved aside. Whether that was because of an unseen command from Killian or because he sensed my determination to walk right through him if necessary, I didn't really care. I wanted to set the ground rules for any future dealings with Killian.

I hadn't come to him as a supplicant or subordinate. I wasn't looking to him for protection or guidance. I was the reaper for Easton and I would not let him get in the way of me doing my job. And for me, a huge part of my self-designed job description was to protect souls, dead or alive.

I pushed open the large double doors and marched down the long hall to the front door. Sam didn't say a word as we stepped out into late afternoon sunshine and headed to where his car was parked beside mine. Not that the silence wasn't filled with plenty of unanswered questions.

Still, I was grateful for the short reprieve I would gain during the drive home in separate cars. That would give me a chance to come up with a better reason for not going to him when I'd first discovered the body of Killian's man.

Try as I might, all I could think about as I navigated my way through peak hour traffic was what it would be like to come face to face with the Grim Reaper once more.

Which persona would I find? The one I had freed from Almorthanos's taint, or the one that devoured the souls of those who died violently in order to increase his power?

CHAPTER 7

I would get no answers unless I managed to free my astral body from my physical body.

Lips pursed, I pulled into the driveway and parked beside Sam's unmarked police car in the double garage attached to our house. The second I got out of my car he wrapped his arms around me, hugging me tight.

'Christ, Tyler. When I saw your car at the compound I thought the worst.'

I pushed against his chest, getting him to release me a little so I could see his face. 'The worst?'

'I've known all along that some kind of deal was made between Bradbury and Killian to get your body back, I just didn't know the details. Hoped it would never be an issue. But when I walked in and saw Bradbury standing there, when I know he hasn't been back in Easton in the last six months, not even for the opening of Riverside Plaza, I thought the time had come when the deal was going to bite all of us in the arse.'

He shook his head, a stunned look in his hazel eyes. 'Not once did I even consider it was something as far-fetched as an arranged marriage. I feel bad for Bradbury, I really do, especially as his deal brought you back to me.'

His expression turned serious. 'Did you know he was going to be there, when you headed out to the compound?'

'I was just as surprised as you were, by all of it.' I shook my head. 'I still can't believe he agreed to an arranged marriage, or to accept Cade as his father.'

'You do not owe him, or Killian and his daughter, anything. Certainly not a trip to the Underworld to confront the Grim Reaper. Let them sort out their own mess.'

I gave him a rueful smile. 'Does that mean you're going to stop investigating the deaths of Killian's business associates?'

'That's different. I'm a homicide detective.'

'And I'm a reaper. I have to do this.'

His arms tightened around me. 'Tyler, sweetheart. I've held you in my arms when you've woken up shaking, soaked in sweat and choking down screams. Coaxed you back when the night-mares threatened to drag you under. The last place you want to be is in the Underworld. The last person you want to face is the Grim Reaper.'

'Technically, he's not a person,' I said, attempting levity despite his words bringing back the horror of nights when my dreams were filled with Jonathon Grimm, the tainted version of the Grim Reaper. They'd happened more frequently in the beginning, interspersed with ones where I hadn't been able to escape Almorthanos's thrall, where I became his willing slave and used my talent with aether and skills as a reaper to hurt those I loved.

But it was the dreams where Sam had been in love with Malia, in which he turned away from me to be with Almorthanos's twisted sister, that scared me the most. Not that I'd ever told him about those dreams. I never would.

Time to change the subject. 'So, you're not mad at me for going to Killian about the dead Tr'lirian?'

'Of course I'm pissed,' he said with a grimace, 'and a little disappointed. But I understand why you did it.'

I cocked my head to the side. 'And that would be…what?'

'You were protecting me. Unnecessarily, but I guess it's the thought that counts.' He gave me a gentle squeeze. 'Yes, it sucks when I know things and can't share them with my colleagues because it will expose your secrets or make them think I'm crazy. It also doesn't sit well with me when I have to hide evidence or look the other way during an investigation. But I'm a big boy. I can handle it. You have to stop trying to shield me from that part of your life. We're a team.'

I smiled up at him, sure my eyes were shining with tears I was determined not to shed. 'In that case, partner, how about you help me get out of this body and into the Underworld?'

Within minutes Sam had called the police station to log off for the rest of the day and I stretched out on our king size bed. I fought to relax tense muscles as Sam lounged beside me, eyes closed as I tried to figure out how to shed my physical body.

After half an hour with nothing happening other than my nerves stretching even thinner Sam said, 'Close your eyes and listen to my voice. You're on a tropical island, wearing the skimpiest bikini known to man and sipping on an exotic fruit cocktail.'

I huffed out a laugh. 'That is not helping.'

'Sure it is,' he said, voice low and husky, and I realised he was right. The ridiculous image he'd created in my mind had helped ease some of the tension thrumming inside me.

'Okay, back to the beach. You're surrounded by the sound of waves, soft and gentle in the background. Now, put your hands on your chest and feel for the cold spot, the part of you that connects to the Underworld.'

I followed his instructions, focusing on the cold spot that warned me when someone was about to die. There, elusive and insubstantial, it lay dormant beneath my hands, waiting for the right trigger. The longer I concentrated on it, the harder it became to hear Sam. The sound of waves he'd generated with his words becoming a heartbeat, matching its beat to mine. Cold blossomed beneath my hands and I gasped as I slipped out of my body and saw my astral form in the mirrored doors of our built in wardrobe.

That couldn't be me, that beautiful vision with silvery wings and long dark hair flowing around my face in ethereal strands. My entire body glowed with a luminescence only slightly dimmer than my wings.

Is this how I appeared to my clients when I came to reap their souls? Like an angel?

I wished Sam could see me, but had to settle with running a hand lightly down his cheek and leaning in to kiss him goodbye.

'I'll be back as soon as I can,' I said, concentrating on making sure he could both feel my touch and hear my voice.

'Be careful.' Concern lit his eyes as he scanned the air in front of him.

'Of course,' I said, putting as much confidence as I could manage into my voice. The wind created by my wings stirred his hair and he ran a hand through it as I lifted up, losing sight of him once I passed through the ceiling.

It was all a lie, of course. I had never felt less confident in my life as I searched for the entrance to the Underworld. I focused on the memory of the black expanse dotted with the light from the thousands of twinkling souls of Easton's citizens, hoping it would guide me to the boundary between the Underworld and the physical world.

The last time I passed through it had been in the other direction, coming from the Underworld, and I had no idea how to do that in reverse. The souls I'd reaped had been sent on their way towards rebirth and I couldn't afford to hang around in the astral plane waiting for someone to die.

Perhaps if I focused on the Grim Reaper instead, picturing the version of him I'd encountered six months ago.

I placed my hands over the hollow below my neck, closed my eyes, and thought about the terrifying vision that was the Grim Reaper in his natural form. Neutral harbinger of death, and Lord of the Underworld. A chill swept over my astral form seconds before a strong wind buffeted me about. I opened my eyes to reorient myself, disappointed to find I was still hovering in the air over Easton.

The wind still pushed at me. I tried to slip below it, to find a calmer spot of air in which to think, but it did not relent. It pushed me sideways, and I dropped even lower, wings struggling to keep me upright. Soon I was only metres off the ground, still moving sideways.

Mango trees barred my path and I instinctively shielded my face as my astral form slipped through the branches. Once I reached the other side the wind abruptly dropped away and my momentum slowed.

I sucked in an uneasy breath as I took in my surroundings.

I was on the edge of the hockey field that had been the scene of some of my worst nightmares six months ago.

It was here I found the body of one of the victims of my serial killer brother, Andrew. That same night I'd also discovered Chris Bradbury was the missing reaper Jonathon Grimm had resurrected me to find. A week later I'd been called back here when wraiths attacked partygoers at an eighteenth birthday celebration in the hockey club's hall.

My ex-boyfriend, Logan, had been murdered here by Talaom, Almorthanos's right hand man, and he'd tried to frame me for the crime. A few nights later I had been killed for the third time, by Talaom, when I'd bargained for the freedom of Sam and my younger brother, Connor. Grimm had come for me, ripping my body out of the physical world and taking me back to the Underworld to use me to free Almorthanos from Demania.

Worst of all was the last time I'd been called here, when I'd had to reap Emily's soul. Thanks to Chris, I'd been given the chance to return to my own body. But I'd then had to stand by as Emily's grieving parents collected her body, pretending I didn't know what had happened to her, that it wasn't my fault she was dead.

I shook my head, ethereal hair flowing in the air around me as I tried to ward off such gloomy thoughts. It appeared I would have to wait for someone else to die to find my way to the Underworld after all

I turned to fly home, and stopped. A ball of light, dimmed by dark smudging around the edges, hovered in the air in front of me.

A lost soul.

From the dull glow it was emitting I guessed it had been floating around the astral plane for some time. Perhaps it was one of the souls who had paid the price for Grimm's voracious appetite for those who'd died violent deaths. Many of the people who had died in more mundane ways had been left behind, unreaped, serving no purpose in his evil scheme to take corporeal form on the physical plane to be at his master's side.

That was one of the best things to have come out of my destroying the Grim Reaper's alter ego. No souls were left behind. Not on my watch. I would do for this soul what I had done for all the other lost ones I encountered, not wanting to prolong its suffering any longer.

I stretched out a hand to touch it, intending to send it on its way to rebirth. The soul darted out of reach. It bounced in the air, darting in towards me and then away again. It didn't take long for me to understand the message.

'Thank you,' I said, waiting for the soul to lead the way.

I don't know what I expected; a hidden pathway to reveal itself or a tear in the fabric that comprised the astral plane perhaps. I certainly wasn't ready for the soul to zip away at a pace I would be hard pressed to match. But I unfurled my wings and prepared to give it my best shot. Surely the lost soul would soon realise I was being left behind and come back to lead me the rest of the way at a more manageable speed.

I never got a chance to move before the soul reappeared in the distance, travelling so fast it was a blur of light. Making straight for me.

I dodged.

Too late.

The lost soul slammed into my chest, spinning me head over heels, wings flapping uselessly. I screamed, the sound echoing in the air around me as I was sucked into a vortex. I tucked my wings against my body, sure they were about to be ripped off my back, closing my eyes. I was tossed this way and that, never still, the constant movement testing the insubstantial nature of my stomach while in astral form.

Suddenly it was over. I was still screaming when the bone-leaching cold hit me, followed by a complete absence of sound. I didn't need to open my eyes to know I was in the Underworld. Or more accurately, the void where I had first encountered Jonathon Grimm.

CHAPTER 8

J opened my eyes and found total darkness. All I could hear was my ragged breathing, the harsh sound deadened the moment it left my mouth. I strained my eyes and ears, dreading the moment when Grimm would appear and confirm all my worst fears. Yet, conversely, I wanted him to hurry up and get it over with, to end the torturous build-up of terror inside me.

There was no sign of the lost soul that had brought me here or of Jonathon Grimm, but my surroundings slowly began to change. The darkness fencing me in softened, while wisps of mist wound their way through the air toward me. Wispy fingers of nether, they swirled around me, tasting, testing, but never touching. Yet I swear I could feel their clammy fingers on my soul.

They withdrew a short distance, forming an aisle for their master to glide down.

I could see him now; black cloak billowing around his abnormally tall skeletal frame, dark light shining from the blade on his scythe, face shadowed by his hood.

I stopped breathing as he drew closer.

The bones of his jaw creaked as he opened his mouth. 'Reaper.

Why have you come here?' He lifted a skeletal hand and pushed his hood back far enough that I could see his eyes. Fire lit up his skull from within, shooting out of the empty eye sockets, just as it had after I'd freed him from Almorthanos's taint.

The relief I felt at knowing this was not the Grim Reaper who had been subverted by an alter ego died when he moved closer, looming over me, scythe ready to strike.

His voice boomed all around me. 'Your kind is an abomination. A living reaper should not, cannot, be allowed to exist.'

I sank to my knees, trembling as he unleashed the full glory of his dark guise upon me, far more terrifying than any version I had encountered before.

I bowed my head, struggling to force words to my lips, desperate to plead for my life.

What could I say? What hope could I have of convincing such a majestic and horrifying being to let me live?

'Please, I didn't know.' My words were barely intelligible, even to me, my astral body shaking so hard I felt sure I was going to fly apart at the seams. He wouldn't need to kill me. The violent shudders racking my astral frame would do it for him. No soul could endure the torment his displeasure was forcing upon me.

Nothing happened in the Underworld without his say so. If I had any hope of getting him to relent, of sparing my life, I had to find it fast.

'A dark reaper is in Easton. I need your help to stop it.'

The torture ended so abruptly I fell headfirst onto the invisible floor of the void. I quivered all over as my astral body reformed around me. I sucked in a deep breath, grateful to still be alive, even if I didn't know how long I would remain that way.

'Tell me.'

It was an effort to lift my head. The last thing I wanted to do was to meet his gaze, but I forced myself to do it. As I told him what I knew, voice still somewhat shaky, I dragged myself to my feet, determined to face whatever happened next with as much dignity as I could muster considering I felt as though I'd just been flayed alive.

The silence after I finished speaking threatened to drive me to my knees again and it took every ounce of strength I had to remain standing. The mist of nether coiled and roiled around him, seething with the agitation of its master, blocking him from view.

After an eternity the mist settled and the Grim Reaper once again stood unobscured in front of me; a silent omen of death.

Finally he said, 'He is another abomination. Like you, he is a symptom of the disease that once infected me and should not exist.'

'So you didn't send him to Easton, to reap souls?'

He roared, the sound dropping me to the ground, head bowed, ears covered.

When the roar died away I uncovered my ears and dared look up at him, dreading the need to ask another question, but determined to find the answers I sought.

'He's targeting Tr'lirians who fought against Almorthanos. If you didn't let him loose on Easton, who did?'

'The machinations of the living are of no concern to me.'

'What about the souls he's taking? Do you care about them? Please, help me stop more innocent people dying before their time.'

'Very well, as payment for the debt I owe you for clearing me of the taint that afflicted me I will tell you what I know. All Jonathon Grimm's foul creations were pulled back to the Underworld with me and were destroyed, bar one. That one eluded my wrath by resurrecting one of his fallen brethren. Once he was in a living body I could no longer sense him. He is the one you seek.'

'I'm also looking for a woman. She may have been taken or killed by the dark reaper. Her name is Rebecca Killian. Do you know where she is, or what might have happened to her?'

'I already told you; the actions of the living do not concern me.'

'So she's still alive? Is that what you–?'

'Leave now. Never return or the next time you will not be allowed to cheat death. You, even more than the other, are an abomination that should be destroyed. No human should have dominion over aether and none of the living should ever have the ability to reap souls.' He pointed his scythe at me. 'Leave this place before I change my mind.'

I didn't have a chance to say anything more. The wind that had pushed me here now pulled me away, the force of it stinging my eyes and lashing my astral body. I cried out, huddled in a ball as I was swept up and thrown.

I had a sense of immense speed as I streaked through the air. I didn't dare open my eyes until my movement stopped. When I did I found myself hovering above the field where Logan's body had been displayed for me to find.

I heaved a shaky sigh and headed for home, struggling to process what had happened. One thing I was sure of was that this Grim Reaper was far more terrifying than Grimm had ever been. No force in the world would make me set foot in the Underworld ever again.

I pushed that fear aside as I entered my house and found Sam sitting on the bed beside my body. After I reconnected with my physical self, he helped me sit up and, from the look of sheer relief on his face and the stiff way he moved, I guessed he hadn't moved the entire time I'd been gone.

'The dark reaper is one of Jonathon Grimm's sadistic pets. It avoided the Grim Reaper's cull by slipping into a dead body and bringing it back to life,' I said when my vocal cords were working again.

Sam grimaced. 'Grimm couldn't find Bradbury once he was inside a living body, so I'm guessing this latest version of him won't be much help in tracking this reaper guy down.'

I shuddered at the mere thought of another encounter with the Grim Reaper. Even if he'd been able to help, I'd never survive asking for it.

Sam's eyes narrowed. 'What is it? What's wrong? My God, Tyler, you're shaking.'

I allowed him to hold me, snuggling in as he stroked my back, the reaction to my Underworld visit setting in. It had been worse than any of my nightmares, more so because it was real.

I'd survived, just.

I'd faced down the Grim Reaper and come out of the Underworld scared stiff but otherwise unscathed. When the shakes subsided I moved out of Sam's arms.

'We need to go back to Killian's. The reaper had to have Tr'lirian heritage and be related to the body it took or the resurrection would never have worked. It must have happened during the battle, as the Grim Reaper was aware one of Grimm's people escaped. That means the reaper is either in the body of one of Almorthanos's men or Cade's. As I hardly think they'd be attacking their own people, they have to be Davilian.'

Sam's lips twisted at the thought of returning to the compound, but he didn't argue.

It was dark when we started to make our way back there, and I struggled to keep my eyes open. I didn't know if that was because of the emotional upheaval I'd been subjected to or because I'd been out of my body for over three hours. Whatever the cause, I didn't have time to rest so I pushed my fatigue down and brainstormed different scenarios with Sam while he drove.

We were ushered through the gates without ceremony and Killian was waiting at the front door of the main building, Chris at his side, when we got out of the car.

'Did you go to the Underworld? Did you find her? Did you find my daughter?'

'I'm sorry, I don't know where she is. But I'm sure she is still alive. When I asked the Grim Reaper about her he said he doesn't concern himself with the actions of the living. He wouldn't have said that if she was dead, I'm sure of it.'

'If all you have is a feeling and false hope, why bother driving all the way out here to deliver your news?' Killian stiffened; eyes narrowed.

'We need to question the Davilians you captured after the battle. The dark reaper took over a dead body and brought it back to life, hiding them from the Grim Reaper's sight. It has to be a Davilian, unless you think one of your own men would turn against you.'

Storms entered his dark blue eyes. 'My men would never betray me or Clan Godden.'

'Okay then. A Davilian it is.'

'Impossible. I already told you, all those taken prisoner after the battle are under constant surveillance. If one of them was the dark reaper they would have been discovered long before now.'

'We'd like to question them anyway, to see if they know who might be the dark reaper or if they know of any Davilians who disappeared after the battle,' said Sam.

Killian drew himself up, glaring at me. 'The Davilians are not your concern. You need to focus on finding my daughter before she becomes the next soul you are called to reap.' He turned around and marched inside, beckoning imperiously for Chris to join him.

Chris ignored the command and moved to stand in front of me. 'Don't take it personally. He's been in a bad mood ever since Rebecca took off, and mention of the Davilians makes him short-tempered at the best of times.'

I shook my head, angry with Killian for his abrupt dismissal. 'We need to talk to them, Chris. They may be the only ones who can help us find the dark reaper, and maybe Rebecca too.'

'I'll talk to him. Tomorrow, when he's calmed down. See if I can convince him to let you speak to some of them. But enough about him. How are you holding up? I'm guessing a trip to the

Underworld was not the highlight of your day.' He moved closer, sympathy in his vivid blue eyes.

I shrugged. 'I survived, but the new and improved Grim Reaper made it clear my visit was a one-time deal. He considers a living reaper to be an abomination even worse than Grimm's dark reapers.'

'Let's make sure you never have to go back there, then.'

'Don't worry, I have no intention of returning and giving him the chance to make good on his threat to destroy any and all abominations.' I shuddered, remembering the terrifying nature of this aspect of the Grim Reaper. 'But at least we can rule him out for being involved with the deaths of Killian's men. He'd never deal with a dark reaper and seemed pretty pissed off when I mentioned the missing souls.'

'If neither he nor Killian will help us, how are we supposed to find and stop this dark reaper killing more people?' Sam said. 'Four have been murdered in as many days, and I'm thinking this guy is just getting started.'

'We go see Rhonda,' I said. 'She's the only Davilian we know who isn't being hidden away by Killian.'

CHAPTER 9

'Do you mind if I come with you?' Chris asked.

'Of course not,' I said, forcing a smile, not at all sure this was a good idea. I mean, seriously, what could be more awkward than to have a man who professed to love me six months earlier sitting in the back seat of my boyfriend's car. Then again, the three of us were seeking to discover the identity of a dark reaper on a killing spree. Not to mention the whereabouts of Chris's missing fiancée.

We were barely out of the main gate when I twisted around so I could see his face. 'Are you really going to go through with it? The engagement, I mean?'

'I knew what you meant.' He sent a cool smile my way. 'A deal is a deal. If we find Rebecca, and if she's willing, I'll hold up my end of the bargain.'

'That's crazy. You don't even know her. How could you contemplate marrying a complete stranger?'

'I gave my word.'

I shook my head, trying to shake off his words as much as the guilt from knowing why he'd given his promise. 'Because of me.'

He leaned forward and stared intently at me. 'No, Tyler,

because of my selfishness in not wanting to lose you. That's on my head, not yours.'

I wanted to protest, point out the flaws in his logic, but Sam reached over and took my hand in his, taking his eyes off the road long enough to give me a considering look. 'You sacrificed yourself to save those you care about. You can't turn around and blame Bradbury for doing the same thing.'

'It's not the same.' I tugged my hand free.

'Yeah, it is. Anyway, from everything I've heard so far, Killian's daughter isn't keen on the idea so he may not even have to make good on his promise.'

'Lockwood's right. She was pissed when she found out why he'd summonsed her to the compound. She tore into him, and me, said there was no way in hell she was marrying a guy hand-picked by a father who'd been absent most of her life. Refused to even discuss it and demanded to be allowed to leave. Would not back down until he agreed to let her stay in town.' A thread of admiration coloured his words.

I crossed my arms in front of my chest. 'I don't blame her for being pissed. Why would Killian think she would agree to an arranged marriage?'

Chris shrugged. 'Guess he thought being told it was her duty to her family and her clan to go through with it would be enough. Might have been, if she'd been raised by him. But her parents had a falling out when she was a child, so she was raised by her human mother. It wasn't until a year ago, when the mother died, that Rebecca reached out to find her father again.'

'Bet she's regretting that now,' said Sam in a dry tone.

'You think getting told your father wants to marry you off is bad. You should have seen the look on her face when he told her about her Tr'lirian heritage.' Chris's eyebrows lifted. 'Poor girl, she didn't know what to do, where to look. At one stage I thought she was going to cry. Then she lifted her chin, looked him square in the eyes and told him he was no longer her father.' Admiration once again filled his voice.

I couldn't help feeling the same. I vividly remembered how it felt to discover I'd been lied to my entire life, and to find out I wasn't completely human. No wonder Rebecca had run off. I only hoped her lack of contact since then was her choice and not because of foul play.

We pulled up outside the flat where I used to live, which now bore little resemblance to what it looked like when I called it home. The building had been completely renovated, inside and out, turning the two flats into one house. The exterior had been rendered in a pale cream and the front lawns were now a landscaper's paradise of greenery and colour.

'Rhonda told me what you did,' I said to Chris as we got out of the car. 'She was so happy the day the title deed was signed over to her she actually cried. Of course, she did the same thing when the quickie divorce your lawyer negotiated for her came through too. Thank you for everything you've done to help my family.'

He dipped his head, looking embarrassed. 'It was nothing. What's the point of being resurrected in the body of a rich and handsome playboy if you can't help your friends out?'

His dismissal of my thanks made me regret not doing it sooner. Chris had been a huge part of my life during the battle to stop Grimm and Almorthanos. I should have made more of an effort to keep in touch after it was all over, but had been worried he'd be hurt by seeing how happy I was with Sam.

He wasn't even friends with my stepmother, Rhonda, yet he had paid for an architect and a designer to work with her on the changes to the flat, and for all the renovations, furniture and furnishings. He'd also given Connor a brand-new Commodore to replace the one blown to bits by Almorthanos, courtesy of a grant from the Bradbury Corporation. His comment about being a playboy was also no longer true. According to the few articles I'd read about him, the only reason he'd been making news was because of his humanitarian activities, not which starlet he was dating.

The events of six months ago had produced changes in all of us, and it pleased me that something good had come out of so much death and destruction. Not least of these was the change in Connor. No longer a younger version of my chauvinistic father, he'd matured a lot. I now considered him one of my best friends, something I could never have imagined happening, not in a million years.

I smiled, just thinking about how much we had both changed as I knocked on Rhonda's front door.

Her welcoming smile faded when she opened the door and saw us. 'If you three are together again, whatever you're here to say can't be good. Should I be packing my bags and getting out of Dodge?' She moved back to allow us entry.

It always surprised me how young she looked now she was away from Dad. Gone were the immaculately groomed hair and impeccable outfits. Now she was more inclined to lounge around in jeans and a T-shirt, barefoot and with her long brown hair loose. I'd been to her house a number of times with Connor and while I wouldn't say we had become friends, at least we no longer actively hated each other.

'We have a problem,' I said.

'Obviously, or you wouldn't all be here. Just tell me straight, is Connor in trouble?' Her attractive features hardened as she prepared for bad news.

'He's fine. Connor's fine. But a dark reaper has been targeting Killian's men, and we need to know if you have been in touch with any of the Davilians who have been exiled to the physical plane in the last six months.'

'Ha.' Her laugh was bitter. 'Any one of them would kill me the second they saw me. I betrayed them; betrayed my clan.'

'So you have no idea where any of them might be.'

Her eyes widened. 'You think one of them is controlling the

dark reaper? I thought they were all pulled back to the Underworld, after you worked your magic on Grimm.'

'One of them got away, and is in a new body.'

'Talaom?'

I blanched, thinking of the man who had killed me so I could free Almorthanos from Demania. He'd then sacrificed his own life so his master could have a full Tr'lirian body as host. Time stood still in the plane known as Hell, but once Almorthanos stepped outside of it he'd started to age rapidly as the centuries of captivity caught up to him. After he'd sacrificed himself, Talaom had become a dark reaper and tried to reap my soul during the final battle.

'If it was him, why would he wait six months to get his revenge?'

Sam's question was valid, and eased some of the panic I felt at the possibility of facing Talaom in a stranger's body.

'With Killian and Cade rounding up every Davilian they could find he might have been lying low, waiting for the right time to strike back,' said Chris.

'If Talaom was going to go after anyone, it would be Tyler. She's the one who ruined his life,' Rhonda said as we moved into the spacious kitchen. She indicated for us to take a seat at the dining table as she switched on her coffee machine.

I screwed up my mouth. 'I'm not the one who killed Almorthanos and Malia. That was Cade.' Even as I said it, I knew that didn't matter. None of it would have happened if I hadn't been able to defy Almorthanos's will and side with his enemy.

Rhonda's next words echoed my thoughts and sent shivers skittering over my body.

'If it is Talaom, I'd be watching your back.' Rhonda frowned as she got down four coffee mugs and filled them with a rich smelling brew. She carried them over to the table, and set them down in front of us.

'Perhaps it's time I spent some of the money I got from your father in the divorce settlement, and Connor and I took a long overdue holiday. And if any of you tell my son why we're leaving town I will save Talaom the trouble of killing you. I'll never be able to persuade Connor to leave if he thinks you are in danger,' she said as she stirred two spoons of sugar into one of the mugs before handing it to me.

I took a fortifying sip, needing the caffeine and sugar to jolt my brain into gear.

'Let's not get ahead of ourselves,' said Sam. 'We don't know for sure that it is Talaom we're dealing with. Killian was adamant none of the Davilians on this plane could be involved because he has them all under surveillance. But what about the ones who are still in Angellin?'

It was my turn to frown. 'I didn't think there were any left up there. Cade's terms of surrender were for them to give up their wings and submit to exile on the physical plane.'

'I hope they are all down here,' said Rhonda. 'Even if that means they'll eventually grow old and die. They're better off down here than living as second-class citizens under Cade's rule, especially now he's won the war and no longer needs to keep up the pretence of being a fair and just leader.'

I put down my mug and stared across the table at her. 'What do you mean?'

'Before Cade and Almorthanos declared war, Angellin was a beautiful city, full of light. God, there is nothing on this plane that compares to what she once was. Formed by aether by the first of our kind, our home was a shining palace where all the different clans lived in harmony. Sure, there were tensions, disagreements between clans or people, but these were minor issues and didn't affect the city's energy.'

'Then Malia organised for her worshippers to attack Cade's sister, Liren,' I said, remembering what Chris had told me when I'd first discovered my Tr'lirian heritage. Malia's actions had been the spark that started the war between Clan Davila and Clan Godden.

Rhonda gave a sigh. 'After Almorthanos was defeated and trapped in Demania, Cade declared himself leader. He forced all those who supported my clan to move to the lower levels, where the light had begun to fade. So if Cade did force my people to leave, at least they will no longer have to live in virtual darkness.'

I thought about what it must have been like for the Davilians, to be banished from the light. 'Is that why you agreed to marry Dad, to leave the darkness behind?'

'I would never have willingly sacrificed my immortality, but I wasn't given a choice. They tore the wings from my back, and once they were sufficiently healed I was brought to Easton to befriend your mother.' Her face screwed up. 'I hated her on sight, blaming her for what had happened to me. Then when she died, and I was forced to marry your father to keep an eye on you, well, we all know how well that turned out.'

I winced, not needing a reminder of the way she'd treated me. 'That was in the past. What matters now is making sure we all get to enjoy the future. And to do that we need to find whoever is targeting Killian's men and stop them, because we do not want to start another war.'

Mention of Killian and war in the same sentence prompted another thought. 'Unless that's what Cade wants? An excuse to wipe out the Davilians for good?'

'What do you mean?' Sam asked.

'You saw what was happening at the compound. Killian said it was just a precaution, but what if it's more? He hasn't exactly been forthcoming. He won't tell us what his dealings were with the men who were killed. He won't tell us where the Davilians are, and yet he is one hundred percent certain they are not behind the attacks. But if he is so sure the Davilians are not a threat, why take the precaution of turning the compound into a fortress? Who does he think might attack them?'

CHAPTER 10

The thought that there might be an unknown force out there just waiting to take a shot at Killian and Cade's men did not sit well with any of us.

I heaved a deep sigh and looked over at Chris. 'I'm starting to wish you'd never involved Killian, when we were looking for a way to defeat Grimm. That way he would never have come to Easton and set up his compound here.'

Rhonda gave a bitter laugh. 'Killian was involved long before Chris contacted him, and that compound of his isn't recent. The location might change, but Cade has had an outpost in this area ever since Tr'lirians started coming to this plane.'

'Why here?' I frowned. Surely there were far more interesting places to set up an outpost. What was so important about Easton?

'Geography. It is directly below Angellin.'

My first instinct was to look up, even knowing all I would see was the ceiling of Rhonda's kitchen. Instead I asked, 'How can that be? If this was some kind of gateway between Angellin and Earth, there would have been clues, artefacts, something to show Tr'lirians existed.'

'We were careful to hide our tracks as much as possible, once mankind became more technologically aware, allowing the myth we were angels to spread. A small number of Tr'lirians have chosen to live here over the centuries, mainly due to injuries that stripped them of their wings and their immortality. But they have all pretended to be human, shunning our winged brethren whenever they visit the physical plane.'

'Do you ever wish you could return to Angellin?' Sam asked.

Rhonda shook her head. 'It has been almost thirty years since I was there last. Even if I could return, with no one to challenge Cade the word of Clan Godden would be law. Besides, without wings I would need to be carried to even gain access to the city.'

Chris raised an eyebrow. 'As interesting as all this is, it doesn't help us with our current problem. We need to find Rebecca before whoever is targeting Killian's men gets to her, if they haven't already.'

'Chris is right, and if Killian won't help us find the Davilians then it is up to us.' I turned to Sam. 'Is it possible to check police reports in other towns or states to see if any of them mention victims with similar scarring on their backs, or unexplained deaths in abandoned houses?'

'I'll head into the station in the morning, and see what I can come up with.'

I looked over at Chris. 'I need you to go back to Killian's compound. Find out where he's hiding the Davilians, what his dealings were with the men who were murdered, and why he's fortifying the compound.'

Chris grimaced. 'The guy may want me to marry his daughter, but he's close-mouthed at any time other than when he's telling me what is expected of a son of Godden.'

'What expectations would those be?' Sam asked, eyes narrowed.

'Keep a level head, avoid scandal, and be the best in the business.'

'So that's why your name hasn't been coming up in the

tabloids recently. You're keeping your nose clean, on Daddy's orders.'

'Why, Lockwood, have you been keeping tabs on me?' Chris screwed up his mouth. 'If you have, you'd realise my lack of enthusiasm for playing the field has nothing to do with Daddy's orders. After everything that happened last time I was in Easton, the party scene seemed rather tame by comparison.'

Sam gave a grim nod. 'Yeah, nothing like almost getting killed to set your priorities straight.'

'Exactly. I left Easton determined to make a change, to see if I could make a real go of being Chris Bradbury rather than using the name as an excuse to get away with all the things I didn't get a chance to do in my first life.'

'Speaking of changes,' said Rhonda, a wry twist to her smile, 'if you're the one who gives out orders now, Tyler, what is it you want me to do?'

I pulled my gaze away from Chris, still amazed at the new maturity he displayed, and focused on my stepmother. The changes in her had been just as marked as those in Chris. A short time ago she'd said she was going to skip town, and now she was offering to help.

'You said Easton is where some of the Tr'lirians came after losing their immortality. Are any of them still here, who might have been missed by Killian and Cade when they were rounding up those who sided with Almorthanos? Surely not all of them were involved in the battle. We need every little scrap of information we can get, so if you could find even one of them it would be a huge help.'

Rhonda set her coffee mug down on the table, spinning it around in her hands. 'Those who have fled Angellin due to disability don't usually want to be found and someone like me, who was sent here for a purpose, would be the last person they would want to associate with. Even though I didn't willingly relinquish my wings, they would still see me as someone who gave up what they would give anything to have back.'

'What about the ones who were here to work with Talaom? Would they all have been involved in the battle or is there a chance one of them might have got away?'

'I'm sorry, Tyler. I might as well be the last Tr'lirian on Earth for all the good it does me. I'm a pariah. Traitor. I chose family over clan, and I'd do it again if it came down to it. No one is more important to me than my son.'

I gave her a reassuring smile. 'It's okay. We'll figure out another way to find what we need. Cade and Killian can't have rounded up every single Davilian on the physical plane.' The trouble was I didn't believe what I was saying. A cold ball of dread sat in the pit of my stomach, and it was getting bigger with each passing minute.

Giving out orders and acting as though I knew what I was doing didn't change the fact I was missing something. None of it added up, least of all why Killian would want Chris to marry his daughter.

The compound was being fortified. Men he had business dealings with were being murdered. He refused to tell Sam and me where any of the exiled Davilians were.

Visions of hundreds of people crammed into concentration style camps, backs still bleeding from where their wings had been torn away, filled my head each time I closed my eyes. And there was a possibility Talaom had taken a new body and was getting revenge on those who killed his master.

I rubbed my temples, trying to soothe away the tightness starting to build inside my head. The last thing I needed was a migraine.

Strong hands covered mine. 'Enough. You've done enough for tonight. It's time to get some rest.'

I looked into Sam's steady gaze. 'There's no time. We have to figure out what Killian is up to, and find Rebecca.'

'We've got no leads, so there's nothing we can do about any of that now. First thing tomorrow I'll go to the station and log into the national database, check for any signs our guy has been active anywhere besides Easton. Bradbury here can put his Sherlock Holmes hat on and go sleuthing. In the meantime, you need to take care of yourself. Chances are you'll be called to reap through the night. You're going to be no good to your clients if you're in the grip of a massive migraine.'

I knew he was right, and from the looks on the faces of Chris and Rhonda so did they. But that didn't mean I had to like it. 'What if the next client I get called for is Rebecca Killian?'

'Then we deal with it, just as we'll deal with everything else; in the morning, after you've taken your medication and got rid of the headache I can see building up.'

'Go home, Tyler. All your problems will still be here in the morning,' said Rhonda with a sympathetic smile, 'but maybe a good night's sleep will help you look at them with more clarity.' She plucked the empty coffee mug out of my hands and stood up.

'I can't say it was wonderful to have you drop in, considering the circumstances, and right now I'm regretting not installing a wine cellar. Although, with how long it's been since I had a drink I'm pretty sure one glass, let alone a bottle, would send me to oblivion. Might not even sober up in time to see you save the world, again.'

Her comment forced a laugh out of me. 'I didn't exactly save the world.'

'You saved Connor, and for me he is the world.'

I gave a nod, recognising the truth in her words. I had saved Connor, but so many other people had been lost in the process, on both sides of the battle. I only hoped the coming conflict I sensed was just around the corner would have a better outcome.

I'd been pulled back into a world I thought I'd left behind six months ago and the death count was already rising.

How many more would lose their lives before I figured out what was going on and how to stop it?

How many innocent souls would I have to reap before it was over?

'Can you drop me at the Plaza?' Chris asked as we walked to Sam's car. 'I'll stay in one of the suites and head back to the compound in the morning.' He yawned and rubbed his face with one hand. 'Don't think I'm up to playing Sherlock tonight.'

'Fair enough,' said Sam, looking as though he was trying to stifle a yawn of his own.

I didn't even try, eyes watering as weariness hit me. I gave Sam a smile as he opened the passenger door for me, then slipped into the seat and buckled up. I leaned back, eyes closed, and let my body relax. The only tension came from my temples, where the thud-thud-thud of my pulse throbbed through my head.

I felt the engine start, keeping my eyes closed as Sam pulled away from the kerb and drove off down the street. Unlike earlier, the silence did not feel uncomfortable. I guess bonding over a potential threat had worked out all the awkwardness.

'Anybody want to grab a bite to eat before heading home?' Sam asked.

My stomach immediately grumbled, loudly.

He laughed and said, 'I guess I have my answer.'

I opened my eyes and gave him a sheepish smile. 'It's not my fault. We skipped dinner, and I didn't even know I was hungry until you mentioned food.'

'Any preferences?'

I twisted around to look in the back seat. 'What do you feel like eating, Chris?'

He opened his mouth to speak but never got a word out.

Headlights gleamed in the window beside him a split second before a car rammed into the side of Sam's unmarked police car. The sound was intense, explosive in such a confined space. The concussion flung me sideways, head slamming into the window beside me.

The seatbelt pulled tight, securing me in my seat.

A loud bang sounded, white powder filling the car as the front airbags deployed. Metal screeched, the car skidding out of control. Sam shouted out, calling my name.

Then came silence.

CHAPTER 11

*E*ars ringing, chest hurting, I struggled to focus. I pushed at the airbag in front of me, trying to see around it. 'Sam? Chris?'

A faint groan was the only answer I received.

Hand fumbling for the seat belt, I fought down the rising panic threatening to engulf me. My hands found the seat belt buckle and I depressed it, sighing in relief as the pressure around my middle eased.

Relief fled when the hollow below my neck went cold.

Someone was dying, and I had no urge to travel to get to my client. That meant whoever was dying had to be close by.

No. Not Sam. It couldn't be Sam.

I choked back a sob as I pushed and pulled until I could see past the airbag. Sam was slumped in the driver's seat, partially hidden by the driver's side airbag. I couldn't see his face. I thrust out a hand and grabbed his arm, pushing down the reaper within me, feeling my way until I found his wrist.

I latched on, feeling for his pulse, crying out in relief when I felt it strong and unmistakable.

But the call to reap was undeniable.

I tried to twist around and reach into the back seat, but I couldn't see Chris. I heard nothing but my own harsh breathing.

'Chris. Can you hear me? Chris. Are you okay?'

A faint groan sounded from somewhere in the back. He was alive, for now.

I pushed aside my fear and focused on the call to reap. The pull of it was to my right, not the back seat, presumably coming from the car that hit us. I sagged into my seat and allowed my astral form to rise out of my body. I slipped out of the car, gasping as I caught my first glimpse of the mangled wreck it had become. A white sedan was wedged into the side of it, bonnet crumpled, windscreen smashed.

No airbag obscured my view of the other driver as I flew to the sedan's window.

Blood drenched his short blond hair and streamed down his face where he leaned back in his seat, eyes closed, breathing shallow. His eyes opened as if he sensed my presence, a pain-filled blue gaze meeting mine.

'I'm sorry,' he said, voice little more than a whisper. 'He made me do it. I didn't want to hurt you or your friends.'

A shiver swept through my astral form. 'The crash? It wasn't an accident?'

He shook his head, groaning, teeth clenched. 'He said he'd kill Rebecca if I didn't do what he said.'

I froze. 'Rebecca Killian? Do you know where she is? Who has her? Please, you have to tell me.' I wanted to reach out and touch him, reassure him, shake him so he would answer me, but couldn't risk accidentally releasing his soul.

He opened his mouth to reply, but his eyes rolled back in their sockets and he slumped in the seat.

The need to reap intensified. I called his soul out of his body but did not attempt to touch it.

'I'm sorry,' I said. 'I can't release you, not yet. I need you to show me where Rebecca is. Can you do that?'

The soul's light brightened. It darted off to the left, stopping after a moment to see if I was following.

I looked back at Sam's car. He and Chris were still inside, unconscious. I didn't want to leave them, but this might be the only chance I had to find Rebecca. I had to take it.

Sirens could be heard coming closer. Ambulance. Police. They would soon be here to take care of them, and my physical body. I had no idea how badly any of us had been injured. I had to act now, while I was still capable of doing something.

Decision made, not wanting to leave Sam and yet knowing I had to, I turned and followed the soul as it led me towards where Rebecca was being held captive.

The soul led me across the river, and over South Easton. I frowned as we soon left the town behind, heading along the western highway. There were a number of small towns out this way. Was Rebecca being held in one of them?

Half an hour out of Easton, the soul I was following veered off the highway to the right, towards an old abandoned service station. The concrete driveway was cracked and choked with weeds, the windows in the front of the service station broken and boarded up. The soul ignored the dilapidated building and passed over the top, heading to a large shed behind it.

I slowed my pace as the soul slipped through the door of the shed with no sign of hesitation.

What if all of this, the accident, the mention of Rebecca, was a trap? Whoever was targeting Killian's men could have created the accident as a way to lure me out here, disconnected from my body. Had I left Sam and Chris, and my physical body, in even more danger?

Then again, what if Rebecca Killian really was inside the shed, in danger, and I was the only person who could help her? I had to go inside, to be sure.

I sucked in a deep breath, silencing the clamour of questions in my head. I spread my wings to their fullest extent, and slipped through the wall of the Colorbond shed, alert for any sign of the dark reaper. A dim light on the far wall illuminated the interior of the shed, allowing me to see it was virtually empty, except for a battered black van.

The soul of the man who'd hit Sam's car appeared at the side of the van, spinning in slow circles. Eyes darting throughout the empty shed, still not convinced this wasn't a trap, I slowly flew over to him. When I drew close, he slipped through the side of the van and I forced myself to follow.

A young woman lay on a thin mattress on the floor of the van, wrists and ankles tied together with rope, with what looked like a patterned scarf acting as a gag. Her eyes were closed, sleek blonde hair covering most of her face, the slow rise and fall of her chest letting me know she was alive.

She was alone.

I moved forward, concentrating on giving my astral form substance as I kneeled beside her.

'Rebecca,' I said, keeping my words low so as not to startle her. 'Rebecca Killian. Wake up.' I gently touched her shoulder, giving her a slight shake.

Her eyes flung open, and she shrank away from my touch. Her dark blue gaze searched the interior of the van, darting here and there, body trembling.

'Rebecca. It's okay, I'm here to help you.' I reached out and gently pulled the gag out of her mouth.

She jerked away from my touch. 'Who's there? Why can't I see you?' Her eyes widened. 'Are you dead?'

'My name is Tyler, and I'm not dead.' Not yet anyway. I had no idea what condition my body was in. 'I don't know how much time we have. We need to get you out of here.' And I needed to get back to make sure Sam was okay, and Chris as well.

I tugged on the ropes tied around Rebecca's ankles, talking all the while to stop her from freaking out. 'I know your dad. He asked me to help find you.'

She pulled her hands away from me, expression hardening. 'Are you one of them? A Tr'lirian?'

'Not really. It's complicated.'

'Then un-complicate it.'

'I will, I promise, just as soon as we get you out of here.' The rope was stiff, hard to manipulate, and I had to keep focused on maintaining solidity so I could work at it. Minutes passed before I was able to unravel the first knot. From there it was easier going, and I soon had her hands free.

She bit her lip, grimacing as blood returned to her hands, rubbing them together to restore circulation while I went to work on the rope binding her ankles. Once she was free and able to move she made for the van's rear door and struggled to open it. She wiggled the handle.

'It's locked.'

'Shift to the back of the van,' I said, moving in front of her.

'Why? What are you going to do?' Rebecca asked as she sidled backwards on her knees.

'This,' I said as I sent out a concentrated blast of aether, aiming for the lock. The door burst off its hinges, flying several metres through the air before crashing to the shed floor.

'Holy shit. How did you do that? Can you teach me?'

I smiled and shook my head, forgetting for a moment that she couldn't see me.

'Sorry, it's not the kind of thing you can be taught.'

She scrambled out of the van, holding on to the side of the opening to steady herself as she looked around. The soul that led me to her buzzed around her head and then came over to me.

I reached out and tapped it once, sending it on its way to rebirth. Its light blossomed until it filled the shed before it disappeared, leaving Rebecca and me alone.

'Okay, time to get you out of here,' I said as I looked for the switch for the roller door. 'Rebecca, can you see if the keys are in the van? It's a long walk back to Easton.'

While she climbed into the front of the van I floated over to the panel beside the roller door and studied the buttons, trying to figure out which one to push.

I reached out to tap the button I thought would open the roller door, snatching my hand back when it started to open before I could do so.

I zoomed backwards, using my wings to increase my speed as the door cranked open to reveal a black sedan with tinted windows. I couldn't see who was in the driver's seat and didn't waste time trying. Instead I reached the van and slipped inside, shouting at Rebecca.

'Get out of here.'

'It's a manual,' she shouted back at me. 'I only know how to drive an automatic.'

'Are you serious?' I asked, even as I moved closer to the driver's seat, thankful it was a bench seat. I put my hands on the gear stick, concentrating on making my astral form as solid as possible, stretching until I could get a foot on the clutch. 'You handle the accelerator and the brakes. I'll take care of the gears.'

It must have been such a crazy time for her, having to rely on someone she couldn't see, but she lifted her chin and gave a quick nod. 'Okay, let's do this,' she said.

The black sedan drove slowly into the shed, stopping beside the van, and I heard a clank as the roller door began to close.

'Time to go,' I said. 'Start her up.'

I put the van in reverse as the engine roared to life. The tyres screeched as it took off, backwards. A tall young man with dark brown hair bounded out of the black sedan, features obscured by a dark haze as he ran after the van. I didn't need to see his face to recognise him.

Talaom.

A dark reaper, brought back to life in a stolen body.

An abomination, like me.

CHAPTER 12

A loud bang at the back of the van shook me out of my horror induced daze as we shuddered to a halt.

'What the hell was that?'

I tore my eyes away from Talaom to look in the side mirror. 'The roller door. We hit it.' The bottom of the door had slammed into the roof of the van. 'Hit the accelerator. Keep going.'

'It's not working.'

'I'll fix this,' I said, looking out the front window to where Talaom was smirking as he stalked towards the van. 'You need to get out of here. Don't stop, for anything, until you're safe.'

'What about you?'

'I'll be fine. Just be ready to get out of here the second I blast the door out of the way.'

I slipped out of the van and faced Talaom, calling on the aether surrounding us and wrapping it around me like a cloak. Then I did something I thought I would never do. I turned my back on him, sending a wide blast of aether into the roller door that whipped it off the van and tore it away from the shed completely.

Rebecca and the van hurtled out of the shed. I spun around to face Talaom, ready to blast him. It was disconcerting, to have him standing there, in the body of a young man around my own age when I knew he was far older. His new body was a leaner version of the original, swarthy and handsome but with an intensity that made him look more like a bad boy than the boy next door.

He wore a satisfied smile as he performed a series of slow claps. 'Well done, Tyler. You've saved the day. Again.' He stepped forward.

'Don't come any closer.' I readied myself to blast him, confused by his actions. Why hadn't he attacked me when I'd had my back turned? Perhaps he'd been able to see the barrier of aether I'd formed around me and had known it would be useless to try.

He stopped walking and held his hands palm out. 'Relax, I have no intention of hurting you.'

'You expect me to believe that? You shot me, and you tried to reap my soul.'

'That was during battle. This is different. I'm different. I would never harm another member of Clan Davila.'

'Bullshit. You just forced a man to ram the car I was in, to kill me, and Sam and Chris.'

His brown eyes went wide. 'You were in the car with Chris Bradbury.' He shook his head. 'I'm so sorry, I didn't realise you would be with him. I just wanted to kill the Godden scum, to send a message. I never meant for him to hurt you. Are you okay? Is your physical body damaged?'

Arms crossed, hovering just off the ground, I glared at him. 'Is that why you've been killing Killian's people, and kidnapped his daughter? To send a message?'

He recoiled, vehemently shaking his head. 'Do you think I wanted to torture and kill those men? They've left me no choice.'

'Murder and kidnapping are not choices. They're crimes.'

'If you just let me explain, you'll understand why I had to do what I did.'

'What makes you think I would believe anything you say?' I shifted my hands to my hips, wings stretching as I prepared to propel myself out of the shed.

Talaom took a step towards me, entreaty on his face. 'I know you must hate me, and I understand why, but if you just listen I can explain everything.'

After everything he had said and done to hurt me and those I cared about I was in no way convinced by his statement of contrition. But the longer I stayed the more time it gave Rebecca to get away. 'Start talking.'

He took a deep breath, straightened his shoulders and said, 'You're fighting on the wrong side.'

'What are you talking about?'

'You can't trust anyone from Clan Godden. Cade will kill every Davilian, including you, if we don't stop him.'

'There is no "we", and if–'

I didn't get a chance to say anything more. My astral form was yanked backwards. I twisted around; sure this was an attack organised by Talaom. No one was behind me, yet the tugging increased, pulling me farther away from the shed.

I fought the pull but it was so strong, hurtling me along, I was at the outskirts of Easton within seconds. Before I knew it, I was nearing the Easton Base Hospital. I flitted through walls and rooms so fast it was all a blur, until I stopped suddenly, hovering in a room where hospital staff were leaning over my body.

'Clear,' said one of them as another placed two paddles on my chest. A machine whirred, and electricity zapped my body, the force of it zinging through my astral frame. I gasped as I was pulled the last few feet to my body, slamming into it.

I opened my eyes, wincing at the bright lights shining down on me.

'She's back.' A male voice rattled off a series of medical mumbo jumbo terms and I tuned out as my eyes searched the room.

A woman's face loomed in front of me, the bottom half covered by a surgical mask. 'It's all right, Tyler. You're in the hospital. You were in a car accident but you're going to be fine.'

I tried to sit up but she pushed me back down. 'Take it easy. You need to lie still while we check you over.' Her face disappeared and an oxygen mask was placed over my mouth and nose.

My head immediately started spinning. I blacked out, and when I opened my eyes the mask was gone and I was looking into Sam's worried eyes.

'Hey there,' he said, voice husky. 'You gave us quite a scare.'

'Us?' My voice cracked, and I swallowed, trying to create moisture to soothe the raspy dryness in the back of my throat.

'Bradbury's here, too. They're doing a check-up on him in the next room,' said Sam as he handed me a cup and a straw. I took slow sips, letting the cold water slip down my throat, disappointed when it was all gone.

I struggled to sit up, only to find I had electrodes with wires attached stuck to my chest and temples. My clothes were gone. In their place was a hospital issue gown.

'Take it easy,' said Sam, putting his free hand on my shoulder to pin me down. 'The nurse said you need to keep still, or you'll dislodge all their fancy gadgets.'

'What's wrong with Chris?' I flopped back against the pillows, surprised by how exhausted the effort to move made me.

'Don't panic. He's fine. Just a nasty bump on the head. Can't be too bad or they would never have let him go home last night.'

'What about you?' Bruising covered the right side of his face and his movements were stiff.

'A couple of bruised ribs. Nothing major.' He grimaced. 'The poor guy who hit us wasn't so lucky. Unlike us, he wasn't wearing a seatbelt and didn't have airbags. He didn't make it.'

I scanned the room. Mine was the only bed, giving us some privacy, but I could hear voices and see hospital staff hurrying past the open door. I'd wait until Chris had finished his check-up, and the door was closed, before telling them what I'd discovered.

Hang on.

Eyes wide, I stared at Sam. 'You said they let Chris go home last night. How long have I been out?'

'Fourteen hours, give or take a minute or two.'

Fourteen hours. Rebecca could be anywhere by now. And so could Talaom.

I struggled to sit up. 'I have to get out of here. We have to find Rebecca.'

'Take it easy.' Sam gently pushed me back down. 'You've just woken up, after surviving a pretty nasty car accident. You can save the world after the doctors have checked you out and given the all clear.'

'It wasn't an accident. Talaom was trying to kill Chris.'

His grip on my shoulders firmed and his eyes narrowed. 'Talaom was driving the other car?'

I shook my head, wincing when the movement made it ache. 'No. It was the Tr'lirian Killian had sent to look after Rebecca.' As quietly as I could, I told him what had happened from the moment I'd gone to reap the driver's soul, until I'd been forcibly returned to my body.

'You were in the astral plane. That's why the doctors couldn't revive you.' He sagged against me, hugging me tight. 'Thank God. They thought there was something seriously wrong with you, a head injury, something they couldn't see. You barely had a pulse, your vital signs were next to nothing, and the heart monitor was going crazy. That's when they decided to use the defibrillator.'

I grimaced, rubbing my chest, the cannula in my left hand pulling with the movement. 'Remind me to never take astral form when my body is going to be poked and prodded by doctors.'

'How about we avoid car accidents as well,' said Chris as he poked his head through the doorway, a white bandage on his left temple and bruising evident around his eyes.

'You look like shit, Bradbury,' said Sam as he helped me to sit up.

'You're not exactly the picture of health yourself, Lockwood.' The two of them grinned at each other, and I shook my head.

'Can one of you find a nurse so I can get unstrapped?' I waved a hand over the wires and tubes connecting me to the machines monitoring my vital signs. 'We need to go find Rebecca before Talaom gets hold of her again.'

'You found her?' Chris stiffened.

'Yes, but that was hours ago. I told her to keep driving until she found help. Who knows where she ended up?' I swung my legs over the side of the bed, while Sam hit the button that signalled for a nurse.

'Where are my clothes?' I asked as I peeled off the sticky pads connecting the electrodes to my chest.

'Ah, they had to cut them off when they were working on you,' said Sam, giving me a rueful shrug. 'I called Rhonda first thing this morning. She's going to swing by our place on the way here and pick some stuff up for us.'

I looked at him closely, noting the shadows in his eyes, the unshaven chin and rumpled shirt. It was the same shirt he'd been wearing yesterday. 'You stayed here all night?'

He gave me a wry smile. 'You were here. Where else would I be?'

I leaned into him. We stayed like that for ages, uncaring of Chris's presence, until a nurse with grey hair twisted up into a bun bustled into the room.

'Young lady, you should not be on your feet. You were supposed to be taking care of her, detective. Shame on you.'

I smiled at the nurse, not wanting to get her off-side and make this more difficult than I feared it would be. 'I'm feeling much better, and I'd like to go home now. Are there papers I need to sign so I can be released?'

'You're not going anywhere. You were in a car accident. You

have possible head trauma. You need to lie back down in that bed, right now, and wait for the doctor to come and see you.' Her pale blue eyes narrowed as she glared at me, hands on her hips.

'I'm afraid I can't do that. If you could please take care of those papers, I'd really appreciate it.' I held out the hand with the cannula in it. 'I'd take this out myself, but it's probably better if you do it.'

The nurse's eyebrows formed an arch. 'Detective Lockwood, can you talk some sense into Miss Morgan? Surely you won't condone such reckless behaviour?'

'I'd do as she asked, if I were you. One way or the other, she's leaving this hospital.'

The nurse's face went red, eyebrows raised almost to the hairline. Chris stepped in front of her and blocked her view of me. He started to murmur to her in a quiet voice, leading her out of the room with a firm grip on her arm.

I scanned the room, looking for my handbag. 'I need to call Anne, let her know I won't be at work today.' Anne Porteous was my boss at the *Chronicle*.

Sam reached down and lifted my bag onto the bed. 'Already done that. Considering you were in a car accident, and unconscious, you're now on indefinite sick leave.'

I smiled, relieved he'd taken care of it. Anne was not the type of person to take it kindly when I called in sick. As long as she didn't find out too soon that I was awake and relatively uninjured, I would be fine.

'What about you? Is your boss okay with you taking off more time to be with me?' I asked.

'It's all good. She understands how important you are to me, and that you come first.'

I was glad he wouldn't be getting into trouble on my account. Besides, he had been in the same accident. He deserved some time off, time we would need to figure out what Talaom was up to.

A knock at the door sounded a moment before Rhonda bustled in, holding two bags of clothes.

'You go first,' I said to Sam. 'I need to get this stuff taken care of before I get cleaned up.' I waved the hand with the cannula in it.

I don't know what Chris said, but by the time Sam emerged from the adjourning bathroom, the nurse had returned with a doctor and the paperwork to have me released from the hospital's care.

I stole a few moments for a quick shower before dressing in the clothes Rhonda had selected for me, the hot water doing wonders for the aches and pains all over my body. A long purplish bruise indicated where the seatbelt had locked me in place, and my neck twinged each time I twisted it, but otherwise I considered myself lucky. It could have been a far worse outcome, for all three of us.

I pushed those thoughts aside as I stepped back into the room and found Connor had joined the others. He hugged me to him, and I stifled a wince as he connected with the bruise from the seatbelt.

'I can't believe you're walking around,' he said, hugging me even tighter. 'When Mum said you'd been in a car accident, I was picturing broken bones and blood everywhere.'

'Sorry to disappoint you,' I managed to wheeze out.

'Connor, let your sister breathe.'

Thankful for Rhonda's intervention, I took a step back when he released me. I searched for something to say that wouldn't cue Connor in on what was really going on. Rhonda hadn't wanted him involved in the latest Tr'lirian drama, and I didn't blame her.

'I think it's time we–'

'Here's your medica–'

'We need to go out to the com–'

Sam, Chris and I all spoke at once, stopping mid-sentence when we realised we were talking over each other.

'Relax. He already knows the basics,' said Rhonda, giving me a rueful smile.

'I thought you didn't want him involved?'

'I don't. But after Sam called me and said you'd all been in a car accident; I knew your brother would never forgive me if anything happened to you because of your investigation and he'd been kept in the dark.'

I blew out a soft breath, half wishing he'd still been in the dark. The reappearance of Talaom in Easton was unsettling enough. His assertion I was fighting on the wrong side, and the Davilians were in danger, coupled with Killian's evasiveness, made for troubling thoughts. I had to find out what Killian was hiding, and see if there was any truth to what Talaom had said.

I turned to Chris and completed the sentence he had been half way through. 'We need to go to the compound and speak with Killian. He may have heard from Rebecca. At the very least, we need to let him know it is Talaom who is going after his people. It's time we found out why.'

CHAPTER 13

Despite his objections, I refused to let Connor accompany us to the compound.

'I need you to go out to the old service station on the highway heading to Westmere, see if there is any sign of Talaom or Rebecca there.'

'Connor is not going anywhere near Talaom. It's too dangerous,' said Rhonda.

'That's why I want you to go with him. You can see into the astral plane. Besides, if Talaom was telling the truth about wanting to protect all the remaining Davilians then you won't be in any danger.'

When it looked as if she would protest some more, Connor stepped forward. 'I'm doing this whether you come with me or not, Mum.'

With that settled, I described what Talaom now looked like, as well as Rebecca. 'The van will have a big dent in the roof from when the roller door smashed into it.'

I turned to Sam and Chris. 'Let's go and see Killian.'

The five of us walked out of the hospital together, separating at the car park. Sam led Chris and me to a gold BMW. 'You've been visiting the impound yard again.'

He shrugged. 'Got to drive something while they see if they can fix my car. This is as good as any, and I'll be putting it to a far better use than the drug dealer who had it before me.'

I slid inside, exhausted by the short walk, grateful for the plush interior of the BMW as I relaxed in the front passenger seat. During the twenty-minute drive to Killian's compound I thought about what Talaom had said; that I was on the wrong side.

Almorthanos had planned on enslaving mankind, and was ready to kill anyone who got in his way. That could never be the right side.

Still, with what was happening at the compound now, and Killian's secrecy, the niggle of unease in the pit of my stomach was getting bigger. I couldn't wait to get to the compound and find out once and for all what was going on.

But first we had to get through the front gate.

When we reached the compound and stopped the car, Sam wound his window down and spoke into the intercom. 'This is Detective Sam Lockwood. I need to speak with Michael Killian.'

A buzz was soon followed with, 'I'm sorry, Detective Lockwood, but the professor is not receiving visitors today.'

'This isn't a social visit. I need to speak with him now.'

'I'm afraid that won't be possible. If you call his office, his secretary can arrange a time for you to interview him.' The buzz sounded again and the light on the intercom box went out.

Sam turned to look at me. 'Looks like we're not welcome anymore.'

'Let me try,' said Chris, getting out of the car and heading over to the gate. He peered through the bars for a moment, scanning the grounds. No one came near him, though I could see a number of people patrolling. He pushed the buzzer on the intercom, but no one responded to his hail.

Chris returned to the car and leaned down to look through my open window. 'Guess I'm not welcome either.'

'That's it.' I unbuckled, motioning for Chris to step back so I could exit the car. I marched over to the gate, narrowing my eyes as I looked into the astral plane. Four winged Tr'lirians stood in a line across the driveway on the other side of the gate. I depressed the button on the intercom and called on aether as I stared down the Tr'lirians who stood silently watching me.

'You have five seconds to get this gate open or I will do it for you, and you'll be picking up pieces of it for the next month.'

The words had barely left my mouth when the gate swung open. Still holding as much aether as I could, I strode back to Sam's car and got in. 'Let's go get our answers,' I said as I buckled up.

Sam didn't hesitate, driving smoothly into the compound, with the gates clanging shut behind us seconds later. As he drove down the winding driveway, dozens of Tr'lirians popped out of the astral plane to watch us. The boom gates at each of the guard posts were raised as we approached, giving us uninterrupted access.

'Guess Killian doesn't want you blasting his compound to smithereens,' said Chris as Sam pulled up in front of the house.

'I still might, if I don't like the answers I get.' I climbed out of the car and waited for Sam and Chris to join me before marching to the open front door.

There was no sign of anyone as we made our way down the long hallway, and I kept my guard up as we approached the closed double doors leading into Killian's main room. Seeing as he knew we were coming, and had made it clear we weren't welcome, I didn't bother knocking. Instead, I used a thread of aether to push the doors open. The slam as they hit the walls on either side reverberated throughout the hall.

'Way to announce your presence,' said Chris.

I grinned at him as I stepped through the doorway. The grin faded when I found an empty room.

'That's it. I've had it with being stuffed around.' I faced the hall and let loose with the aether I still had hold of, sending it flying through the house, flinging open doors and knocking over furniture. I felt a grim satisfaction at the many cries of alarm that sounded in the immediate aftermath.

It didn't take long for Killian to come storming into the room, fury in his eyes as he strode towards me. 'What is the meaning of this?'

'You tell me. You're the one hiding in your room while we're out there risking our lives to find your daughter.'

'You didn't find her. She found her own way home, five minutes ago.'

'She's here? Is she okay?'

'That is what I was trying to ascertain before you barged your way in and scared the hell out of her.'

'Where is she? I want to see her.'

His nostrils flared, but I refused to back down. Eventually Killian stepped over to his desk and pressed a button on his phone. 'Could you ask my daughter to join me in the main room?' He took a seat behind his desk, still glaring at me, while we waited for Rebecca.

She walked into the room five minutes later and froze, a frown marring her pretty features. 'What's he doing here?' She pointed at Chris. 'I already told you there is no way in hell I'm marrying him.'

'Relax, sweetheart, I'm no longer in the market for a fiancée,' said Chris, a smirk curving his lips.

Killian shifted his glare to Chris. 'We had a deal.'

'Well, maybe you should have checked with your daughter before you decided to run her life.'

'Rebecca will do as she's told. The wedding will go ahead as planned.'

The stormy look on Rebecca's face warned me World War Three was about to erupt. I decided it was time to interrupt. 'Rebecca, I'm so glad you're okay. You obviously worked out how to drive a manual,' I said with a smile.

She stopped glaring at Killian to turn wide eyes on me. 'Tyler? You're Tyler?'

I gave a nod. 'In the flesh.'

She squealed and ran across the room, throwing her arms around me. 'Thank you. Thank you. Thank you. I don't know what I would have done if you hadn't come along and rescued me.'

'Rescued you?' Killian sprang to his feet and marched over to us. 'What are you talking about? I thought you'd just decided to come home.'

Rebecca tossed him a glare. 'This is not my home. My home is in Sydney, where I will be going back to as soon as I finish packing the rest of my things. I would never have come back here at all if I hadn't left half my stuff behind.'

'You are not leaving. You are going to stay here and marry Chris Bradbury.'

'Like hell I am.'

'I'm not going to marry a woman who is clearly against it.' The glare Chris shot at Killian was just as fiery as the one Rebecca wore.

'You will both do what you're told.'

'Can we forget about who is marrying who for a minute? I need to talk to Rebecca about Talaom,' I said.

Killian's face went pale. 'Talaom had her?'

'Yes, and he's also the one who has been torturing and killing your men. So be quiet while I talk to your daughter.'

He fell silent, fortunately, and I faced Rebecca. 'Did he come after you?'

She nodded; eyes shadowed. 'I couldn't figure out how to get the van out of reverse so I kept going backwards, until I hit a tree.

I jumped out and started running down the road, trying to put as much distance between us as possible. Next thing I know he was behind me in his car. I would have taken off into the bush, but it was so dark I would have got lost for sure. I turned around, intending to fight him. Take the car. Get away. I don't really know what I was thinking or planning to do. I wasn't exactly thinking straight at that point.'

She shrugged. 'Turns out he was no longer interested in me. All he wanted to do was talk about you. Now that I can actually see you, I understand why. You're gorgeous.'

I flushed, shaking my head. 'He didn't try to tie you up again?'

'He did the complete opposite. Apologised for kidnapping me, and offered me a lift back into town. When I asked him why I should get in the car with him, he said he needed me to deliver a message to you.'

'What message?' Killian's voice was gruff, insistent.

Her gaze slid to him and then back to me. 'He said to make sure you were alone when I delivered it.' She smiled. 'Give me a lift to my hotel and I'll fill you in when we get there.'

Killian strode forward. 'Don't be ridiculous. You are not going to a hotel, and you can tell us the message right now.'

She spun around, hands on her hips, and glared at him. 'When are you going to get it through your thick head that you do not get to tell me what I can and cannot do? Just because you supplied the sperm does not make you my father. I've had it with your overbearing, autocratic ways. I am leaving with Tyler and there is nothing you can do to stop me. Try it, and I'll get her to blow this place up. I've seen what she can do, and I'm guessing you have too, so don't piss either of us off. Right, Tyler?'

I couldn't stop a grin forming as I stared at Killian. 'Absolutely.'

'In that case, I'll go and get my bags and be right back.' She marched out of the room, sleek ponytail swinging, without saying another word.

I faced Killian. 'While we're waiting for Rebecca, you can tell me what's really going on around here. I'm not leaving until I get answers, even if I do have to start blowing holes in the walls. You will tell me what I need to know. Got it?'

Killian visibly controlled his temper, taking deep breaths before answering me. 'I've seen firsthand what your kind is capable of. Can you blame me for wanting to protect my people?'

'My kind?' I asked. Did he mean Davilians?

'Humans. You distrust anyone who is different. How do you think the people of Easton would react knowing we were living nearby? You know they'd hate us, fear us. There might be a few more enlightened ones who would welcome us because of our differences, but mob mentality would fire up the rest. That's why I'm fortifying this place, to make sure any of my people who are stranded on the physical plane have a safe haven in case our existence is ever discovered.'

It sounded plausible, in theory. 'What about the men who died? Why wouldn't you tell Sam what your business dealings were with them?'

'Because it was none of his business. If you must know, I had them scouting out possible locations in other states in which to build similar compounds in case any of my people chose not to settle in Easton. I don't want them to feel they are imprisoned here. When they are ready to leave the compound and enter the human world, I want them to know they are never far from safety.'

He moved over to his desk and sat down. 'Now then, if you don't mind, I have a lot of work to do. You can wait for my daughter out front.'

His answer seemed reasonable, though I still had that niggling sense of doubt. But it was clear I had pushed enough for one day. I followed Sam and Chris into the hall and found Rebecca waiting for us.

'Ready to leave?'

'Past ready to leave. I am not going to be sorry to see the back of this place. These guys give me the creeps, the way they disappear and reappear somewhere else. I always feel as if one of them is watching me.'

Knowing Killian, I guessed Rebecca was right but didn't want to go into it here. What I wanted was to hear Talaom's message and to understand why he would let her go after kidnapping her and forcing her bodyguard to attempt to kill Chris. Why go to all that trouble when he could have approached me with the message himself?

CHAPTER 14

The drive back to Easton started with an awkward silence, with Chris and Rebecca doing their best to ignore each other in the back seat. When I turned around to look at them they were facing away from each other. Rebecca had even placed her overnight bag on the seat between them to act as a barrier. It felt like being back in high school, and I wanted to laugh about how silly they were both being. Refusing to talk to or even look at each other would not make the situation any easier.

'Where are you staying?' I asked Rebecca, to break the ice.

She darted a look at Chris, lifting her chin as she said, 'Riverside Plaza. I have a room booked under my mother's name.'

'Great. We can drop Chris off at the same time,' I said with a huge smile. 'The two of you will be neighbours; give you a chance to get to know each other better.'

They both glared at me and I stifled a sigh, deciding it was time to get to the real issue.

'What is Talaom's message for me?'

Rebecca frowned. 'Ah, he said I had to wait until you were alone to tell you.'

'I would tell Sam and Chris the message immediately after I heard it, so you might as well tell me now.'

'He was most insistent, about you being alone.'

'I trust them with my life. I don't trust Talaom at all. Tell me what he said.'

Rebecca cast a sideways glance at Chris and said, 'Fine. He wants you to meet with him at midnight. He said to go to the place where he killed you, which doesn't make sense seeing as you are obviously still alive. But that's what he said. Oh, and he wants you to go alone.'

'You are not meeting him alone,' said Sam.

'You got that right. I'm coming too,' said Chris.

I stayed silent, rubbing my chest where the bullet had penetrated my flesh, killing me instantly. The physical wounds inflicted by Talaom, and then Grimm, had been repaired when I was resurrected, but the mental scars remained. The thought of returning to the hall at the hockey grounds terrified me almost as much as the thought of going to the Underworld had. But I'd survived that visit. I would survive this one too.

'Talaom might not appear if I've got company,' I said, dropping my hand as I looked over at Sam.

His jaw tensed. 'Do not ask me to stay behind. I lost you once. I am not going through that again.'

I gave a nod, not ashamed to show my relief. 'If Talaom doesn't like the fact I have an escort then that is his problem. We go together, or we don't go at all.'

'You better be including me in that, because there is no way in hell I'm going to let you walk into that hall without me to back you up,' said Chris.

'Then it's settled. The three of us go,' I said.

'Four,' said Rebecca. 'I'm part of this too. After all, I'm the one he kidnapped and then released to deliver his message.'

'I don't think that's wise,' said Chris. 'You're much better off getting as far away from Easton as possible.'

'If I won't let my father tell me what to do, what makes you think I'd listen to you?'

'You can do whatever you want. I'm just suggesting you take a step back before you get so deep in this mess that you'll look on getting kidnapped with fond memories.'

'Do you think I wanted to be kidnapped? To be tied up and tossed in the back of a van? Forced to listen to the screams of the man who was supposed to protect me with no idea what was happening to him or if I was going to be next? Only to then find out it was all part of a sick plan to get back at my father and his boss.' She gave a snort. 'But then, seeing as you're one of my father's lackeys, I guess I shouldn't be surprised you're spouting off about doing what's best for me.'

Rebecca leaned across her overnight bag and poked Chris's arm repeatedly. 'I'm telling you right now, buddy, you are not what is best for me. I don't care if my father thinks you and I make a perfect match. It is never going to happen. So you can get that idea out of your head. I wouldn't even date you let alone marry you.'

Chris grabbed her hand, stopping her from poking him again, a cool smile on his lips. 'Relax, sweetheart, I wouldn't date you either. You're not my type.' He flung her hand away.

'Hey, do you two mind sorting your love life out later?' I said to forestall another tirade from Rebecca. 'We have more important things to worry about. I don't believe a word Killian said back there, and I don't trust Talaom either, but we do need to figure out what is going on.'

I took a deep breath to calm my irritation at their squabbling. 'Rebecca, apart from giving you the message, did Talaom say anything else that might explain what he's up to? Your father, too, for that matter. I know you weren't at the compound long, but maybe you overheard something that can help us figure out this mess before anyone else dies.'

'Dies? Somebody died?' Rebecca's eyes went wide.

Chris threw his hands up in the air. 'My God, woman, haven't you been paying attention to anything?'

'Chris,' I said. 'That is not helpful. Rebecca only found out she was part Tr'lirian a couple of days ago. She's been thrust into this world of ours with no warning and no one to help her understand it. How about you explain it instead of criticising her for something she could not be expected to know.'

Chris grimaced. 'I'm sure you'd do a much better job of explaining it than me.'

I gave him a sweet smile. 'But Chris, you did such a wonderful job when you were filling me in on the nightmare my life was about to come. I'm sure you'll do just as good a job for Rebecca. Besides, I need to check in with Rhonda and Connor, to see what they found out.' I held up my phone and twisted around to face the front again, catching the hint of a grin on Sam's lips when I sneaked a look his way.

Not giving Chris or Rebecca any more time to object, I dialled Connor's number and held the phone up to my ear. As I listened to it ring, I could hear a low murmur coming from the back seat.

Connor answered the phone and I focused on his words. 'Hey, Ty, there's nothing at the shed except for one smashed up van. We checked out the service station too, and found nothing to indicate where this Talaom guy might be now.'

'Thanks for checking it out. He's been in touch to set up a meet tonight. We're on the way to Riverside Plaza now. Chris has a suite booked.' I gave him the room number. 'Meet us there as soon as you can and we'll fill you in.'

'Righto.'

I hung up the phone, and closed my eyes. I did my best not to listen as Chris explained to Rebecca about Grimm and Almorthanos and the part I'd played in defeating them both. I'd lived through it. Mostly. I didn't need to relive it all over again.

When we got out of the car in the car park allocated to Chris's suite, Rebecca dumped her bag on the ground and hugged me.

'You poor thing. I can't imagine what is has been like for you, being murdered so many times, and then to get sucked into someone else's body. No wonder you don't trust Talaom or my father. I'm surprised you can trust anyone.' She cast a sideways glance at Chris.

'Ah, thanks, but I'm doing okay.' I extricated myself from her hug. 'You'll be okay too, once you get your head around the whole picture. Although, it's not too late to back out. You could walk away now and forget everything you know about Tr'lirians, reapers, and Killian's crazy plan to marry you off to Chris. You could catch the first flight back to Sydney and get on with your life, as far away from this mess as possible.'

'Are you kidding? You don't even know me and yet you risked your life so I could get away. I'm not leaving. I'm here to help, any way I can.'

'Okay then, let's go up to the suite and wait for Connor and Rhonda to arrive.'

We squeezed into the elevator and were silent on the ride to the top. Sam wrapped his arm around my waist. Grateful for his quiet strength and complete confidence in me, I breathed in the fresh scent of him, soaking it up to fortify myself for what was to come.

The suite was an elegant and modern set of rooms, with an expansive open-plan living space that faced a large balcony with views over Easton. None of us paid any attention to the view as Chris took over, ordering room service and supplying drinks. Connor and Rhonda arrived minutes later and were introduced to Rebecca.

It made me smile to see the sour look on Rhonda's face when Connor immediately started flirting with Killian's daughter. What amused me even more was the jealous look in Chris's eyes because of my brother's flirting. For her part, Rebecca seemed oblivious to it all. Instead, she wanted to hear more about what had happened six months ago, and what all of our reactions were when it happened.

She was particularly interested in Rhonda's experience. 'Wow, I can't believe they made you marry a man you hated. That must have been so awful for you.' Rebecca paused to look over to where Chris was setting out plates on the dining table. 'Sure, you have a son who you clearly adore, but to have to pretend to be in love with a guy who sounds truly hateful, staying with him for nearly twenty-five years, that would have taken a lot of guts. How did you manage to stay sane?'

'Wine. Lots and lots of wine. Connor and Tyler's father would drive a saint to drink.' Rhonda held up her glass of lemonade. 'Of course, ever since my divorce I've been sticking to the soft stuff.'

Rebecca twisted around to where Connor and I sat side by side on the couch. 'Are either of you still in contact with your father? He sounds just as bad as mine, and I'm pretty sure I never want to see him again.'

I grimaced. 'I haven't seen my dad since he told me I was no longer his daughter. But that's his loss, not mine.'

Connor shifted uncomfortably when Rebecca turned her enquiring eyes on him. 'Yeah, I've seen him once or twice. No big deal.'

'Even though he disowned your sister?'

He shrugged. 'He's still my dad, and I keep hoping he'll wake up one day and realise he's being an arsehole and apologise to Mum and Tyler for how he treated them.'

Rhonda snorted. 'Never happen. I've never met anyone who was more convinced they are right and everyone else wrong than Robert Morgan.'

'What about you, Tyler? Would you like him to change his ways, and be a real father to you?'

I was silent for a moment, thinking about how to explain what my feelings were for my father. Finally, I shook my head. 'No. I'm done with hoping he'll change or accept me for who I am. I moved on from my old life six months ago and he is not a part of it. This is all the family I need.' I waved a hand over the people in the room.

'Even me?' Rhonda asked; a wry twist to her lips.

'Even you.'

And I meant it.

Now I just had to make sure my family was kept safe from whatever scheme Killian was hatching with Cade, as well as the revenge Talaom was clearly still after.

Come midnight I was going to get some of my questions answered and what happened next would depend on what I learned.

Rebecca's enthusiasm for learning everything there was to know about the dark world she had stumbled into paled when I announced I was being called to reap a soul.

She sat heavily beside Connor on the couch. 'You don't want company, do you? Not sure if I could handle seeing a dead body.'

I shook my head. 'You couldn't come with me anyway, unless you are able to take astral form.'

'Oh, okay. Good to know.' She gave me a sheepish look. 'I don't know if I should be saying good luck, or have fun. My formal education never covered what to do when someone is called to reap a dead person's soul.'

'Good luck is fine. Not that you have to say anything,' I said, as I looked over at Chris. 'Is there a guest room I can use?'

He gave a nod. 'Second room on the left, as you head down the hall.'

I quickly found the guest room and positioned myself on my back on a large bed covered with a plush velvet quilt. Considering everything that had happened lately, Rebecca's blessing of good luck could come in handy. In the last couple of days, none of my reaps had been of the ordinary kind. It would be nice to be called and not find yet another drama to add to the list.

When the call took me to one of Easton's largest nursing homes my first reaction was relief. I flitted through the halls in search of my client, thankful I was not about to reap the soul of yet another murdered Tr'lirian. I slipped inside the room of an elderly gentleman for whom every breath was a wheeze and shifted my focus to easing his suffering. Reaping the souls of the elderly had become almost a daily occurrence since the Grim Reaper had been freed from Almorthanos's taint.

Not that more of them were dying. Now I was no longer only called for those who died violent deaths, I got to experience the more peaceful ones too. I treated it as a privilege to be able to usher those souls on to the next part of their journey.

The walls of my latest client's room were covered with photos. A black and white wedding picture was the largest, showing a beaming young man with eyes only for his bride. Smaller colour photos showcased children and grandchildren, dozens of happy smiling faces to keep him company and remind him of a life well lived.

I stretched out my hand and placed it on his frail chest, calling forth his soul. Its light was bright and vibrant, a stark contrast to the body he was leaving behind, and it spread to fill the room, saying a final farewell before I sent it on its way.

I rose through the roof of the nursing home, intending to return to Riverside Plaza to wait until it was time to meet with Talaom. The moment I was in the open I froze, a shudder rippling through my astral form.

Something was wrong. I could sense it even though all that met my eyes was blue skies and the familiar cityscape of Easton. I drifted in a circle, wings flapping slowly to stop me straying too far. Everywhere I looked I found nothing amiss and couldn't pinpoint the source of my unease.

I closed my eyes, using my wings to keep me in place as I opened myself up to the aether surrounding me, tasting it, sifting through it, hunting for clues as to what was wrong. My shudders intensified and I spread my wings, letting them support me as I stretched my head back until I was facing the sky above me. I opened my eyes and winced at the sense of wrongness that poured into me from above.

Angellin.

Rhonda had said it was directly above Easton.

If what I sensed was coming from Angellin, then there was something terribly wrong within the city where the Tr'lirians dwelled.

I tore my eyes away from the seemingly innocent patch of sky above me, debating what to do next. Should I return to the penthouse or try to reach Angellin? Before I could second guess myself, I lifted higher into the sky.

Up I went, strong sweeps of my wings taking me through clouds and into clear air. But Angellin did not appear. I could probably fly right up into space and still not find it. I needed a Tr'lirian to show me the way.

I returned to lower skies and made my way back to the suite, questions crowding into my brain. How could Angellin be directly above Easton, with Tr'lirians using the astral plane to travel to and fro, but I could not see it even when I was in astral form? There was so much I didn't know about Tr'lirians and their abilities. But at least I had one of them who would be willing to answer all my questions, I hoped.

After I reconnected with my body I went in search of Rhonda, finding her sitting on the balcony that overlooked the river sipping a black coffee.

'How was it?' Rhonda asked as I sat down in the chair beside her.

'It was okay.' I said. 'Just a normal everyday reaping.'

She shook her head. 'I don't know how you do it, facing the

dead and the dying every single day. I'd go crazy if that was my life.'

'Somebody has to do it. It might as well be me.'

She peered at me. 'You've changed so much in such a short space of time. I almost don't recognise you. From a scared little girl desperate for her daddy's love to a capable and confident young woman in six months. That's quite an accomplishment.'

'I'm not the only one who changed,' I said. 'I could never have imagined us having a civil conversation over coffee six months ago. Now look at us.'

She shrugged, looking vaguely embarrassed. 'I should never have blamed you, or your mother, for what was done to me. Neither of you had any idea what was going on, or that Tr'lirians existed.'

'Finding out you were a Tr'lirian finally explained how you always seemed to know when I had done something wrong.' I shook my head. 'All those times I thought I was on my own when I broke something or did something I wasn't supposed to… you were watching me from the astral plane. Talk about having eyes in the back of your head.'

She gave me a tight smile. 'Being able to slip into the astral plane did have its advantages during my marriage, not least of which was hiding from your father when I couldn't face him or slipping away to refill my wine glass without anyone being aware of it. Even if I didn't enter the astral plane, I could distract myself from what was going on around me by watching what was happening there. It sure beat sitting through all those endlessly boring football games.'

I leaned back in my chair. 'What's it like, to be able to see into the astral plane all the time? It must be so distracting.'

'I'm not always aware of what is going on. Yes, I can see into it, but I have to concentrate to do so, otherwise it would be hard to differentiate between what is happening there and what is happening in the physical plane.'

That made sense, and it was similar to my own experience. Ever since I had been brought back to life, my soul in Emily's body, I'd been able to see into the astral plane. In the days immediately afterward, with so much going on, I hadn't realised the ability to "see" came and went according to my needs. In tense situations instinct kicked in and I was able to see what was happening in the astral plane. Then, after I was returned to my own body and life calmed down I had to think about the astral plane to be able to look into it.

Chris had the same ability but Connor didn't, leading us to assume it was the dying and being brought back to life issue that allowed us to see into the astral plane, and not just being part Tr'lirian. For all I knew, anyone who'd died would have the same ability, Tr'lirian or not.

I shook my head. There was so much I didn't know about being part Tr'lirian, and how that differed from Rhonda's life.

I looked over at her. 'How does it work for you, when you enter the astral plane? You don't leave your body behind, like me.' Any time I encountered a Tr'lirian in the astral plane their form had a haze to it, a smudging around the edges.

Rhonda shrugged. 'For us it is simply another mode of travel, one where we can shift through any landscape or obstacle without interference. We could fly where and when we wanted, regardless of weather or fear of being seen by humans. Angellin is a city apart, surrounded by clouds, our food grown on the physical plane. Being able to harvest our crops without being seen became even more important after we withdrew from human contact.'

'How did you get to and from Angellin? I'm sure it is more than a case of just flying through the astral plane from there to Easton and back again, or souls and reapers would be able to do it. Is it like when I went to the Underworld, to speak to the Grim Reaper?' I shivered at the reminder of that particular journey. 'When the lost souls came to help me fight Grimm, they found their way through a tear in the barrier surrounding the Underworld.'

'It isn't a barrier, as such, that separates this world from Angellin, and when I said my home is above Easton that is only true in a certain sense. I mean, obviously you can't look up into the sky and see Angellin. All you see is sky, and if you were to fly through the astral plane it would be exactly the same. It is our wings that make the difference.'

'What do you mean?'

'Here on Earth, wings are used for transportation. Birds, aeroplanes; without their wings they can't take flight. For us, our wings are even more important. They are the source of our immortality, and they also act as the bridge between our world and this one. Angellin and Demania are like two spheres, one above and one below the physical world, anchored to the same point.'

'Easton.' I screwed up my mouth, memory taking me back to my brush with Demania. The sense of wrongness coming from Angellin was nothing compared to the foul stench put out by the plane commonly referred to by humans as Hell.

'Exactly. A tunnel of aether connects Angellin to the astral plane above Easton, while a similar tunnel of nether connects Demania to the Underworld. Our wings are the key that opens the portals at the end of the Angellin tunnel.'

'So the only way for you to re-enter Angellin would be if you were carried by a Tr'lirian who still had their wings,' I said, pushing aside thoughts of Demania to dredge up something Rhonda had said in an earlier conversation.

'Of course, seeing as Cade has exiled all of my clan to the physical plane, I'm sure none of his people would be keen to give me a lift, even if I wanted to return home.'

'Is it the same with Demania?' I asked, frowning. 'It can't be, or one of you would have been able to carry Almorthanos out of there after he lost his wings.'

'Demania is a fixed plane, and the only way to get in or out of it is to have wings.'

My frown deepened. With the debilitating stench that emanated from the portal between the Underworld and Demania, I was unable to understand why anyone would want to go there in the first place. The memory of being trapped in the chasm near the portal to Demania, and how it had eroded my spirit, reminded me of the feeling of wrongness I'd experienced after I'd left the nursing home.

'Can you sense Angellin, from here?'

It was Rhonda's turn to frown. 'Sense it? As in feel where it is?'

'Would you be able to tell if something was wrong in Angellin, without having to go there?'

She stiffened. 'Tyler, why are you asking me this?'

'I'm not really sure, but I think something is wrong up there.' I told her about the shudder that had swept through me, followed by the notion it was resonating through the aether. 'It felt out of balance, twisted, distorted. I can't exactly describe it, but I'm sure the feeling came from Angellin.'

'Do you still sense that wrongness?'

'No. As soon as I moved away the feeling disappeared.'

Rhonda put down her empty coffee mug and rubbed her arms. 'Normally I would say you were sensing a disturbance in the aether tunnel that leads to Angellin, but the opening is nowhere near a nursing home.'

'Where is it then?'

Rhonda gave a slight shake of her head, lips pursed. 'It is forbidden to tell outsiders where the tunnel is.'

I let out a laugh, shaking my head slightly. 'Seriously? After everything else I know, you think telling me where the tunnel opening is will make a difference? I'm not full Tr'lirian, and I don't have wings, so I couldn't use it anyway.'

'You have wings when you're in astral form.'

'Yeah, and they didn't help me get into the Underworld. I doubt they'd be any help in getting me to Angellin.' I thought it better not to tell her I had recently tried, and failed, to do just that.

She heaved a sigh. 'The tunnel opening is on the outskirts of Easton, heading north. The area used to be uninhabited, perfect for hiding our crops, but with the way this town is booming, more and more housing estates are popping up all around it.'

A bitter taste flooded my mouth. 'Estates like Greenlakes.'

Rhonda pursed her lips. 'Not even Cade would be so blatant as to build his compound directly under the tunnel. But it is close by. I'm sure they've done their best to buy up as much of the land in that area to avoid prying eyes seeing what they don't want them to see.'

I thought about Kilian's claim that his dealings with the real estate men Talaom murdered were on account of the need to provide safe havens for his people in other states. 'When Sam gets back from the station, it might be worthwhile seeing if he can find out more about the estates positioned where the tunnel opening is.'

'In the meantime, what are the chances of me getting a refill?' Rhonda held up her coffee mug. 'Seems to me it's going to be a long night.'

I headed into the kitchen and found Rebecca and Chris already there. I stifled a laugh at the way they were purposefully not looking at each other as one made coffee and the other arranged a selection of sandwiches on a platter.

'Lunch will not be a fancy affair,' said Chris when he looked up at my arrival. 'The restaurant is booked solid, as are the conference rooms, so the kitchen staff are flat out.'

'Hmmm,' said Rebecca. 'Sad when you can't get a decent meal in your own hotel. Surely they could make more of an effort for their boss.'

'I'm sure they could, but it would be a poor boss who expected them to cater to his every whim when they were already working to capacity,' said Chris, sounding as if he was grinding his teeth.

'Sandwiches are fine,' I said before Rebecca could respond. I placed Rhonda's empty mug on the bench beside the coffee machine and grabbed down another cup for me.

'Want a hand?' I asked Rebecca with a smile.

The smile she gave me back was strained, and she shot a sideways look at Chris before answering. 'That would be great, thanks. My coffee machine has one button, not a gazillion like this thing.'

'Once you get the hang of it, it's easy,' I said as I smoothly inserted the coffee pod and got the next coffee brewing.

'I'll leave you ladies to it and take these out to the table,' said Chris, picking up the platter of sandwiches and suiting his actions to his words.

I filled one mug with steaming fresh coffee and set the next one going.

'Let me guess, you have one just like this at home?' Rebecca's smile was genuine this time.

'Ah, not exactly. Chris taught me how to use it months ago.'

Rebecca's brow creased. 'Oh, I didn't realise you were that close. But I guess you must be, with knowing how to operate his coffee machine. I guess you know all there is to know about the guy.'

'Hardly,' I said with a laugh. 'We were just caught up in the same mess six months ago. When things got real bad, I ended up staying with him for a few days and pretty much lived on coffee.'

'How did your boyfriend feel about that? Sam seems like a secure kind of guy, but surely he wouldn't have appreciated his girlfriend spending so much time with another man.'

'Sam and I weren't together then. We were all caught up in a murder investigation. That's how we met.'

She shook her head, long blonde hair falling over her face. She flicked it back and tucked it behind her ears. 'From what I've seen, I'm guessing there is a lot more to that particular story than you're letting on.'

'It was a difficult time, for all of us.' And from what had been happening lately, another difficult time was ahead. But I didn't mention that as I placed an empty mug beneath the coffee spout, and piled the ones I'd already filled onto a serving tray along with a jug of milk and a container of sugar. I handed the tray to Rebecca.

'Can you take these out to the table, please? I'll bring the last one with me.'

Alone in the kitchen, I listened to the faint murmur of voices coming from the dining room. I could discern Chris's deep baritone and Connor's voice as they talked about his new car. I smiled when Sam's voice chimed in, glad to have him back. With everything that had been going on lately, it would be a good idea for all of us to stick together. Safety in numbers.

If anywhere was safe when we were unsure who to trust and what was really going on…

My smile dipped. It was an effort to force it to reform before I left the kitchen and went in search of my family and friends.

Sam greeted me with a kiss after I placed the last coffee on the dining table.

'Did you find anything?' I asked.

He smiled. 'Let's eat first. Then we can go over it.'

'Why not tell us now?' Chris asked.

'Because the last time any of us had a decent meal was this time yesterday. If we want to stay sharp we need to take care of ourselves or we'll be no use to anyone.'

'Fair enough,' said Chris, a faint smile on his face as he used Sam's favourite phrase and took a seat.

I sat beside Sam, surprised by how hungry I was. I demolished a plate full of sandwiches and went back for seconds. I wasn't the only one who seemed to have a healthy appetite. We all tucked in to the simple but tasty lunch, washing it down with coffee.

I waited until there was nothing left on anyone's plates but crumbs before I said, 'All right then, Sam. Time to spill. What did you find out at the station?'

Sam stretched his arms above his head, wincing a little as he did so. He then eyed each of us in turn, leaving me for last. 'You were right. Three others have been murdered in similar circumstances to Killian's real estate guys over the last month, and only one of them has scars that suggest he might have once had wings.'

'Were they tortured, before they died?' I asked, sure I already knew the answer from the grave expression on his face.

'None of them died easy, that's for sure.'

'Are the deaths related?' Rebecca asked. 'I don't mean as in were they members of the same family. Did they work for real estate companies as well?'

'One did. The other two worked for a law firm based in Melbourne. But according to the detective handling their case, they specialised in property law.'

I shook my head. 'Why would Talaom be torturing and killing Killian's people over property deals? He wouldn't have anything to gain by stopping Cade from creating safe havens for Tr'lirians stuck on the physical plane. That would benefit Davilians too, in the long run.'

'He would have everything to gain if one of those property deals revealed where my father has stashed the Davilian clan members you said he and Cade took captive after the battle,' said Rebecca. 'Maybe that's why this Talaom guy is doing it.'

'Is it that simple?' I turned to Rhonda. 'Would Talaom go so far just to find out where Killian and Cade have hidden the exiled members of your clan?'

Rhonda gave a grim smile. 'Clan loyalty means everything to Talaom. He would do whatever it took to ensure their safety. If he thought for one second that any of them were in danger, he would not hesitate to kill to save them.'

My eyes went wide. 'Do you think that's why he wants to meet with me tonight? To see if I know where they are?'

Rhonda nodded. 'It makes sense. I can't see him seeking you out for any other reason unless it was for revenge, and he's had plenty of opportunity to do that.'

I swivelled in my chair to face Sam. 'We need to find the Davilians, and not just for Talaom. I'm willing to bet the reason Killian is fortifying his compound has something to do with them being missing.'

'If they're even alive,' said Chris.

'Why do you have to be so negative?' Rebecca rounded on him. 'It almost sounds as though you want them to be dead.'

Chris raised his eyebrows and gave her a cool look. 'I'm just saying what everyone at this table is thinking. Cade and your father despise the Davilians. In fact, despise is too mild a word to explain their ancient enmity. Frankly, I was surprised Cade didn't wipe them out completely, six months ago, rather than give them the choice of exile and loss of immortality.'

'Bradbury has a point,' said Sam. 'How sure are we that any of Rhonda's clan members are still alive?'

I blanched, not wanting to contemplate the idea, forcing myself to face it regardless. 'Why lie about it, if that's the case? Why go to all the trouble of getting them to vow to never take up arms against Clan Godden again, and to make them give up their wings? And I don't buy Killian's line he is fortifying the compound to protect his people from the possible threat of exposure to the general populace. None of this adds up, which is why we need to find the Davilians. We need to find out what's really going on.'

'I don't suppose there's any point in going out to the compound and asking Killian one last time?' Connor shrugged as he said it.

I shook my head. 'He's Cade's man to the core. He'd never go against him.'

Beside me, Rebecca let out a soft sigh. 'I'll do it.'

I turned to look at her. 'What are you talking about?'

'I'll return to the compound and talk to my father. It can't hurt to see if he'll tell me what he's done with the Davilians. At the very least I could do some snooping; try to discover why he's really buying up property and turning his compound into Fort Knox. I'll be your inside man...woman,' she said, her attempt at a smile looking more like a grimace.

'You don't have to do that,' I said, though the idea of having someone on the inside was tantalising. I knew firsthand what it was like to be around a father you had mixed feelings about.

'Actually, it's not a bad idea,' said Chris, rubbing his chin. 'As long as she had a good enough reason for going back, Killian might drop his guard enough to let something slip. It's worth a try, at the very least.'

Sam tapped his fingers on the table. 'Rebecca made it pretty clear she didn't want anything to do with Killian. What possible reason would be convincing enough to get him to let his guard down?'

I choked on my coffee when Rebecca said, 'I could tell him I've changed my mind, about not wanting to marry him.' She pointed across the table at Chris. 'I could say I'm considering the idea, anyway, as I'm sure he wouldn't believe me if I told him I'd changed my mind completely.'

Sam patted me on the back as I coughed down the bitter taste left in my mouth by coffee going down the wrong way. 'There is no way he'd believe that.'

'He might, if I went with her,' said Chris.

CHAPTER 17

I stared at Chris, mouth open but no words coming out.

'You go back there with Rebecca, and Killian's going to have the two of you hitched before you know it,' said Sam. 'He seems awfully keen for a wedding to take place.'

Chris shrugged. 'It shouldn't be hard to stall him, not if we play it right.'

I finally found my voice. 'How on Earth are you going to convince him you've changed your minds when the two of you can barely say two words to each other without starting a fight?' I looked from Rebecca to Chris. 'This is the craziest plan I've ever heard.'

'I can assure you; I am perfectly capable of playing the part. The real question is whether Rebecca can do the same.' Chris quirked an eyebrow and looked over at her. 'What do you say? Think you can manage to act as if I am the love of your life?'

Rebecca scowled at him. 'I'll have you know, in my senior year I played Hamlet in my high school's production and garnered rave reviews for my performance. I'll bet I can act rings around you any day.'

'Undoubtedly.' Chris sent her a smirk before smoothing his

expression when he turned to me. 'We wouldn't rock up to the front door and say we were madly in love and wanted to get hitched. All we have to do is say we are considering the idea, and have chosen to get to know each other a little better before making our final decision.'

'And what would you tell Killian was behind your sudden change of heart?'

Chris shrugged. 'Forced proximity during recent events made us realise how much we have in common, as well as having the two of you to show us just what we're missing out on.' He waved a hand between Sam and me.

'Seriously, that's the best you can come up with?' I huffed out a laugh, almost wanting to say yes just to get the opportunity to see Chris and Rebecca forced to pretend they were developing feelings for each other. 'Let's keep that as Plan B. Now we need to come up with Plan A. Any suggestions?'

When no one offered anything I said, 'There can't be that many places to hide half the population of Angellin.' I turned to Rhonda. 'He'd practically need a city just as big to hide them all in, right?'

Rhonda grimaced. 'That may have been true before the war between Clan Godden and Clan Davila started and our people filled every inch of Angellin. Now, thanks to our penchant for killing each other, and a less than stellar birth-rate among our kind, I would say less than a tenth of us remains. Maybe three thousand Davilians, with close to five thousand in Clan Godden.'

'What about the smaller clans who you said chose sides?'

'They no longer exist. They were either killed off completely or absorbed into Davila or Godden when their numbers declined to such an extent that calling themselves a clan became laughable.'

I shook my head at the chilling picture her words were painting for me. The chill intensified as the hollow below my throat signalled a soul to be reaped. I sighed. It was times like this, when I was in the middle of something important, that I wished there was another reaper in Easton to help take some of the load. Technically, Talaom was a reaper and would be able to help out, but as I still wasn't sure what he was up to, and considering the situation we were in the middle of, asking him to share the load with me would not be a good idea.

I pushed my chair back and stood up. 'Duty calls. While I'm gone you guys can figure out where Cade and Killian might have stashed three thousand Davilians.'

I left them to it and headed back to the guest room. Moments later I was winging my way across Easton in astral form, pondering the problem of the missing Davilians as I went. Perhaps Talaom would have the answer. He wasn't going to be happy when he realised I had no intention of meeting him alone, as requested, but he would have to deal with that. None of our past encounters had been the type to foster trust on my side.

I pushed thoughts of Talaom aside when the call to reap drew me to the hospital. I flitted in through the emergency doors and down gleaming white hallways. I passed into an area marked "Theatre", stomach clenching as I slipped through one last set of doors.

Surgical staff, gowned, gloved and masked, bustled around an operating table, their manner rushed and yet calm as the surgeon in charge called commands to his staff. A man lay on the table, tubes and wires connecting him to an array of machines monitoring his vitals.

Most of the patient was covered by a sheet, except for an open section in the shape of a square that allowed the surgeon to access the internal organs. Right now, the surgeon's gloved hands, covered in blood, were inside the chest cavity, deftly massaging the man's heart, while surgical nurses calmly read out the patient's stats.

I sucked in a breath. With so many members of the surgical team crowded around my client, there was no way I'd be able to reach him without having to pass through someone. Not an enticing experience. Unless I could call his soul to me from where I was, watching the futile effort to save his life…

I focused on the call, the draw that had carried me halfway across town to release his soul. To my relief, the soul answered, floating out of the man's body and over to me. I reached out and tapped it with one finger, sending it on its way. With all my attention on the soul, I sensed rather than saw the activity around the operating table cease.

I looked up, tears filling my eyes at the solemn process taking place in front of me as the surgical team spent a moment of stillness and silence. I waited with them, head bowed, until they once again began to move around the operating theatre, voices and movements brisk as they dealt with the loss of their patient. With my duty done, I headed back the way I had come.

From the moment I'd been called, the man's fate had been sealed, no matter what the surgical team had done to try and save him. Now the surgeon would have to face the dead man's family and deliver the bad news.

As a reaper, I had to be present for the deaths of my clients, but for the most part I didn't have to experience the lead up if someone were sick or injured. I was also spared the aftermath, not having to witness the outpouring of grief at a loved one's loss. My admiration for the emergency services personnel and medical staff who faced possible tragedy every working day, and yet continued to care and fight for their patients, buoyed me up as I neared the Plaza.

I was almost there when a familiar sense of wrongness enveloped me, coming from above. I shuddered, the weight of the bad feeling taking some of the buoyancy out of my flight. My stomach churned, and if I was in physical form I was sure bile would be rising in my throat. What the hell was going on in Angellin?

That had to be where this sense of wrongness was coming

from, though I was nowhere near the tunnel Rhonda said was the only way to get to the city. Perhaps after we'd found the Davilians there would be time to uncover what was happening in the birth place of the Tr'lirians. If I could find one of them willing to carry me there.

I slipped inside the suite and reconnected with my body, taking a moment to reorient myself before going in search of my family and friends. They were all still grouped around the dining table, the remains of our lunch in front of them. None of them had noticed me and I hoped their intense concentration meant they'd miraculously found a cure-all for our problems while I'd been gone. Loud knocking on the front door sounded before I could announce my return and voice this faint hope.

'Expecting company?' Sam looked over at Chris.

Chris shook his head as he stood up. 'Not without someone at the reception desk letting me know first.' A frown creased his brow as he strode over to the front door.

He opened it and then swiftly backed up, hands out in front of him as Cade and Killian, swords drawn, entered the suite.

CHAPTER 18

Six Tr'lirians, wings furled and weapons bared, entered the room behind Cade and Killian.

'To what do I owe the pleasure of this unexpected visit?' Chris's back was straight, gaze fixed on Cade. 'Although, I suppose I should be grateful you knocked this time.'

Cade, an older, winged, version of Chris, narrowed his eyes at the mention of the time he'd barged into the penthouse to throw his weight around six months ago. That was the night I'd sacrificed myself in return for Cade's promise to protect those I cared about. I winced at the memory, hoping tonight did not have a similar outcome.

'You know why I'm here,' said Cade. 'It is time for you to fulfil your duty to your clan.' He looked over at the dining table where everyone else was now standing. 'Rebecca, you and my son are to return to the compound immediately. We need to begin preparations for your wedding. It is past time for your family to be joined with mine.'

I stepped out of the hallway and moved to confront Cade before either Chris or Rebecca could respond. 'They're not going anywhere with you.'

Cade's lips curled into a sneer as he looked over at me. 'This does not concern you, girl.'

'Are you kidding me?' I edged closer to Cade, positioning myself between the two groups. He and his goons weren't carrying swords for the fun of it. It wouldn't be long before his demands became threats. I called on aether, drawing in as much as I could hold, taking slow steady breaths as I prepared myself for whatever happened next.

In my peripheral vision, I saw Sam step up beside me. Seconds later Chris appeared on my other side. It felt good to know they were both there, supporting me, but I didn't like the idea of them putting themselves in the firing line.

Cade bristled, wings shifting as he tightened his grip on his sword. 'Do not push me, Davilian. You will not like the consequences.'

I raised my eyebrows. 'You don't scare me.'

It wasn't false bravado. The leader of Clan Godden wasn't half as intimidating as the Grim Reaper, and I'd managed to face him down and survive.

Confident in my ability to manipulate aether, I considered myself more than a match for eight Tr'lirians. I could create an aether barrier that none of them could penetrate. For a time, at least. Things might get tricky if they decided to wait me out.

Cade stepped forward, shoulders tensing. I reacted instinctively, throwing up my aether wall a second before he tried to skewer me with his sword. The sword point hit the barrier and bounced back, the force of the blow rocking him backwards.

Expression livid, Cade shook off the steadying hand provided by one of his men. 'You will come to regret crossing me.'

I shrugged. 'Possibly, but right now it looks as if I'm in charge here. You want to have another go at skewering me, go ahead. You'll get the same result. So I suggest you turn around and walk out the door, because no one here is going with you.'

My defiance appeared to rob Cade of words, leaving it to his right hand man to come up with the next move. Killian put a restraining hand on Cade's arm as he faced me.

'Perhaps our approach to date has been somewhat lacking, but I can assure you this,' he waved a hand at the barrier between us, 'will not affect the outcome. The wedding will take place and our two families will be joined.'

He looked over my shoulder to where Rebecca had remained at the table with Rhonda and Connor. 'It is your duty as a daughter of Clan Godden to submit to the will of your clan leader. You should be honoured he wishes you to marry his son.'

'Honoured?' Rebecca shot to her feet. 'To be told who I'm supposed to marry? To be given no choice, whether I like the guy or not?'

'Whether you like each other is immaterial. You will both do as you are told, for the good of Clan Godden,' said Cade, his voice almost a roar. 'Furthermore, I forbid you to have further contact with these Davilian scum. It is galling to see you prefer their company to that of your own kind.'

I winced, surprised when Rebecca didn't retaliate with a tirade of abuse sure to sizzle Cade and Killian's ears. Her expression said she was thinking about it, but Rhonda had a hand on her arm and was whispering in her ear. Whatever she said took the fire out of Rebecca's stance. She huffed out a sigh and looked over at Killian.

'I realise you think you know what is best for me, and for Clan Godden, but you need to accept that I have my own opinions and plans. I wasn't raised in the midst of all this Tr'lirian stuff. You sprang it on me a few days ago, and haven't given me any time to process it. All you've given me is demands and expected me to fall in with your plans. If you want me to be a part of your life, to be your daughter, you need to give me time to absorb everything you've dumped on me.'

She brushed her hair back from her face, shaking her head slightly. 'I'm not saying time is going to make me agree to marry

Chris Bradbury. I'm just asking you to let us get to know each other, outside of your compound, without any expectations or prejudice against who we want to be friends with.'

She took a deep breath before continuing. 'You and your boss need to back off, give us space. When we're ready to discuss our futures, we'll come to you. Deal?'

I shut my mouth; sure it had been hanging open for the entirety of her speech. It took my brain a while to connect this more compliant Rebecca to the one who had earlier offered to return to the compound to spy for us. Perhaps this was her way of leaving the option open, by pretending she was willing to consider an arranged marriage rather than rejecting it out of hand. Whether that was the case or not, I was sure I wasn't the only person in the room stunned by what she'd just said. I turned around to see what Cade and Killian's reactions to her offer were.

Predictably, they acted as if she had never spoken.

Cade stepped to one side and ushered the six Tr'lirians at his back forward. Swords raised, they came at me, trying to force their way through my barrier. It pulled and stretched with the wildness of their swings but I was able to hold them off, even doing a little pushing of my own to force them back towards the front door. A wave of dizziness hit me and I fought to keep my face impassive and my back straight, not wanting them to realise manipulating aether took a toll on my energy levels.

I forced a grin to my lips and aimed it at Cade, wanting him to think I was still confident in my ability to hold him at bay. 'In case you hadn't noticed, barging in here and throwing your weight around isn't working. If you don't want Chris and Rebecca hating you for the rest of your miserable immortal life, you need to back off and let them make their own minds up.'

His answering grin sent shivers down my spine.

'You will rot in Demania, girl, when I'm finished with you.'

I didn't have a chance to come up with a retort. A shout from behind had me swinging around, to find the source of Cade's bravado. Six more winged Tr'lirians had landed on the balcony, still in the astral plane, taking physical form once they'd passed through the sliding glass doors. Three of them made straight for Rebecca while the others sought out Chris. The ones targeting Rebecca roughly shoved Connor and Rhonda aside in their haste to get to her.

I readied a blast of aether, but held it back as Chris launched himself at the Tr'lirians, dodging the three who were intent on nabbing him, to grab hold of Rebecca. He pulled her towards me, an intent expression on his face, with Connor and Rhonda on his heels.

With them in the midst of the Tr'lirians I couldn't risk blasting anyone. I stretched my barrier as far as I could. Shakes racked my body but I gritted my teeth against the weakness invading my limbs. I had to make the barrier large enough to encircle all of us; could not let up for a second. My breath came in pained gasps as I put my all into maintaining as strong a barrier as I could, for as long as I could.

Two Tr'lirians were caught inside the circle with us. I fought the urge to help Sam, Chris and Connor subdue them, risking the integrity of the barrier if I moved. The Tr'lirians who had entered the suite with Cade continued to slash away at the aether with their swords, causing ripples through it that echoed the shudders in my limbs.

At a barked command from Cade they sheathed their swords and started throwing furniture. I instinctively flinched each time a chair was flung at my head, fighting to maintain control. Beads of sweat dripped down my face as I sought to keep them out. At the same time, I struggled to manipulate the rear of the circle so Sam and the others could toss out the two Tr'lirians caught on the inside.

With so much happening, the drain it was making on my energy levels, something had to give. I called for the others to get closer, waiting until they were huddled around me before reducing the size of the barrier. Sam wrapped his arms around my waist, while Rhonda and Connor crowded in at my back. Chris, with his arm around Rebecca's shoulder, squeezed in on my free side.

Once I was sure the structural integrity of my barrier was intact, I faced Cade once more, forcing myself to ignore the chairs being tossed at us and the urge to collapse to the floor in a puddle of sweat and exhaustion.

'Give it up, Cade. I'm not going to let you take them.' My voice was strong, despite everything, giving me hope I could endure and save my family and friends.

Fury filled his eyes as he glared back at me until Killian stepped in front of him, blocking my view. Killian looked to my left, at Chris and Rebecca. 'You are just delaying the inevitable. You must submit to clan law, or die. Those are your only choices.'

I held up a hand to forestall any comment from either Chris or Rebecca, realising that risking them in an attempt to spy on the compound from the inside was no longer an option. 'You need to leave, before it's your life on the line.'

The rest of them were immortal, but Killian's soul would respond to my call. I didn't want to kill anyone, but he had to know I would not stand by and let him hurt those I cared about. I closed my eyes and stretched my senses beyond the aether barrier, searching for his soul. I wasn't going to call it. I just wanted to let him know I didn't need to touch him to take it.

Killian's soul responded immediately, and I heard him gasp as I gave it a tug. I slowly released my hold on his soul, sure my warning had been received loud and clear, waiting to see what he and Cade would do next. As I concentrated, the draw of more souls called to me. This didn't concern me at first, sure these were the souls of those I was protecting. Yet, the draw of these souls felt different, sluggish, as if they were only just becoming aware of my purpose, my strength.

And there were too many of them. As I concentrated, I felt the strands of thirteen different souls.

They were souls that could only belong to Cade and his men.

But that was impossible. Tr'lirians with their wings intact were immortal. Not even the Grim Reaper could reap their souls. He'd said so himself, when he'd been infected by Almorthanos's taint.

Had he been lying? Was it possible I could actually reap the soul of an immortal?

Before I could test my theory, and see if I could call one of the Tr'lirian's souls, I felt a pull on the strand connecting me to Killian's soul. I opened my eyes and watched as he faded away, two of Cade's men gripping his arms as they stepped into the astral plane before launching themselves up and through the ceiling of the suite.

CHAPTER 19

'Well, that was bracing,' said Sam, once it was clear Cade and his Tr'lirians were well and truly gone.

'That's one way to put it,' I said, legs shaking as I surveyed the mess in Chris's open-plan living and dining room, looking for a safe place to sit before I fell down.

Broken chairs and other furnishings were scattered all over the floor. The only clear space was the circle within my aether barricade. I let it fall and sighed in relief as the strain on my body lessened. I wasn't ready to run a marathon, but the urge to collapse in a puddle on the floor eased as I watched Sam stride over to the front door to slam it closed.

'Not that a locked door will stop them getting in, but it makes me feel better,' he said with a wry grin when he turned around to find me watching him.

'Me too,' said Rebecca.

I managed a smile for her, too tired to ask why she was still standing within the shelter of Chris's arms when the threat had seemingly passed. Chris didn't look inclined to move away from her any time soon as he scanned the mess.

'Might be time to relocate to a new hideout, before they come back and try again,' said Connor. 'I'd offer up my place, but it's not exactly visitor friendly or big on space. Not exactly a secret either.'

'It's clear we can't stay here anymore, not if we want to avoid any more sneak attacks.' Sam frowned, rubbing his chin. 'Don't suppose you have shares in any of the other hotels in town, Bradbury?'

'Unfortunately, no. Though I might be able to get us booked into the old penthouse,' he said, referring to the one he had been staying in when I'd first met him.

The thought of returning to the penthouse, where I had learned the truth about being a reaper and my Tr'lirian heritage, did not appeal.

'We could go to the old service station, where Talaom was holding Rebecca. I'm sure Cade and Killian wouldn't think to look for us there,' I said.

Rebecca shuddered. 'I'm not sure if I can cope with that. Not yet, anyway. Isn't there somewhere else we can go?'

'We'll figure something out,' said Chris, pulling her closer towards him. 'You don't have to go back there.'

'I guess it's the penthouse, then,' I said, hiding a wince.

Minutes later, we trooped down to the car park and squeezed into Sam's borrowed BMW. I let Chris have the passenger seat, to accommodate his longer legs, while Connor, Rhonda, Rebecca and I crammed into the back seat. Connor's offer to let Rebecca sit on his lap was met with a black look from Chris and a quiet refusal from her.

'If we get pulled over by the cops and they get picky about overloading, think you can talk your way out of a ticket, Lockwood?'

Sam shot Chris a quick grin. 'You want to drive, Bradbury?'

'No, it's all good. You got this.'

'Yes, I have,' said Sam, as he drove out into late afternoon traffic. Within minutes he pulled into the underground car park of

Chris's old stomping ground and we piled out of the car. It felt good to stretch after being crammed in between Rhonda and Rebecca. Connor seeming to take up half the back seat all by himself.

As I stretched, I couldn't contain a yawn.

'That's it,' said Sam. 'Soon as we get up to the penthouse, it's rest time for you.'

'I don't have time to rest.' My protest was automatic, as the thought of lying down for a few minutes sounded heavenly. 'What if Cade has some of his goons follow us, and they try to kidnap Chris and Rebecca again? If I'm asleep, I won't be able to save them.'

'I'm armed and dangerous,' he said with a wink. 'I'll just shoot them. They might be immortal, but firing a bullet at one of them is guaranteed to make them pause long enough for you to wake up and save the day.'

I smiled, shaking my head. 'I love you.'

He pulled me into his arms, kissing me on the top of my head. 'Because you love me, you're going to have a rest. I might even be persuaded to join you.'

I lifted my head and pretended to frown. 'You join me and I'm not sure how much resting will be going on. Is that going to be a problem for you?'

'Nope. No problem at all.' He leaned down and captured my lips in a kiss that made my body forget all about how tired it was. Now all it wanted to do was get as close as humanly possible to his.

The sound of slow clapping recalled my attention to our surroundings and audience.

I took my time moving away from Sam, the stolen moment reminding me why I'd fallen in love with him in the first place. Steadfast, honest and always ready to back me up without getting all macho, he was the one constant in my life. No matter what happened, I knew he would be there supporting me, whatever decision I made. And I would do the same for him, which is why I didn't protest when he ushered me to the guest room I'd previously stayed in, moments after we set foot in the penthouse.

I stretched out on the bed, on my side, facing Sam, and while a huge part of me wanted to continue what we'd started in the car park I knew this was not the time. If I was going to steer all of us through the coming days, I needed to stay sharp. I couldn't do that if I was fighting to keep my eyes open.

Secure in the knowledge Sam was watching over me, I closed my eyes, a faint smile curving my lips as I imagined him shooting any intruders who dared to interrupt my nap. That wouldn't work if the interruption was a call to reap a soul, but any sleep was better than none.

Not that it felt as if I'd slept at all when Sam gently shook me several hours later.

I blinked sleepily at him. 'What time is it?'

'Just after eleven. Thought you might need some time to refresh before we head out to meet Talaom.' His eyes glittered despite his even tone. 'I'm looking forward to getting up close and personal with the bastard who killed you right in front of me. We're going to have some words, he and I.'

The last vestige of sleepiness vanished. I narrowed my eyes. 'Words? Is that all you're planning or should I be checking you for concealed weapons before the meeting?'

'There'll be no concealing going on. I want him to see me and know the only reason he's still alive and breathing is because this meeting is important to you. His status as one of the living depends entirely on your goodwill and continued health and safety. He so much as twitches wrong, I will end him. I'm not taking any chance on losing you again.'

I put a hand on his cheek, his bristles rough against my palm. 'While I'd much rather never being face to face with Talaom again, threatening to kill him might make dealing with him even more difficult. Don't get me wrong, there were times when I'd have happily put a bullet in him myself, as payback for what he did to me. But it wouldn't solve anything. He was doing what he thought was right, on his master's orders. I had agreed to be killed, and I did get brought back to life eventually.'

'I didn't agree to anything, so I'll reserve the right to carve out whatever payback I feel necessary, after we see what he has to say.'

'Fair enough,' I said as I leaned forward and pressed my lips to his. He pulled me against his body and deepened the kiss, making me forget about Talaom, Cade, everything other than the feel of his body pressed against mine and the glorious taste of him.

A long moment later we broke apart, breathing heavily as we got off the bed and rearranged our clothes. I didn't want to leave the room. I wanted to dive back onto the bed and spend the next lifetime loving and being loved by this man, but that would have to wait. When my breathing steadied I headed for the door, smoothing out the tangles in my hair.

It was time to face the man who had killed me in cold blood.

CHAPTER 20

I climbed into the passenger seat of Sam's BMW. Rhonda and Connor had elected to remain at the penthouse, leaving plenty of room for Chris and Rebecca to spread out in the back seat. Not that there appeared to be much distance between them since the attempted kidnapping. The only good thing to have come out of the situation, Chris's willingness to protect Rebecca had seemingly soothed the antagonism between them.

Not entirely happy to have our group split up, I couldn't deny Rhonda had a point when she'd said Talaom would not be happy to see the woman who had betrayed their clan for her son. With luck, the meeting wouldn't take long and we'd all be back together soon enough.

It was fifteen minutes to midnight when we pulled up at the hockey hall and exited the car. There was no sign of Talaom as we scouted around, careful to remain together in case this was a trap. With nothing jumping out at me as a threat, I led the way into the hall, footsteps echoing in the large empty space, purposely not looking at the spot where Talaom had shot me. I couldn't help thinking about it though, or how I'd returned here in astral form to find Emily dying and Cade's plan to stop Almorthanos once and for all in tatters.

Despite everything that had gone wrong that night we had emerged the victors, and I let that buoy up my confidence as I waited for Talaom to arrive.

'You were told to come alone.'

I turned slowly, not wanting him to think I was jumpy or afraid, even though I'd inwardly shuddered at the sound of his voice. This was the first time I'd been in physical form in his presence since he'd killed me. Despite his new body, I recognised his soul and the dark stain upon it from his time as a dark reaper. But I forced down my unease at being around the second person to murder me. I had to take charge of this meeting.

'You don't get to make the rules, not anymore.'

'While we're on the subject of rules,' said Sam, stepping forward, gun in hand, 'you don't take one step further until I can assure myself you are unarmed.'

Talaom immediately stopped walking towards us, hands raised in the air in front of him. 'Detective, there's no need for guns. I came in good faith. I'm no threat to you, or to Tyler.'

'Yeah, well, you let me be the judge of that. Bradbury. Frisk him.'

With Sam covering him, Chris strode forward and patted Talaom down.

'He's clean.' Chris wasted no time returning to stand between Rebecca and me.

I lifted my chin and glared at Talaom. 'So, talk.'

'Would you mind getting your boyfriend to lower his weapon first? Kind of hard to concentrate with him waving a gun in my face.'

'Not going to happen.' I hadn't needed to check with Sam before replying. 'I don't like you and I sure as hell don't trust you. If you've got something to say to me this is the time to do it. Otherwise we are out of here.'

He shifted his feet, broad shoulders rolling backwards. 'I need your help.'

'What makes you think I would do anything to help you?'

'Because they are your people too. Regardless of what happened six months ago, you are part of Clan Davila. You probably don't think you owe them anything, after what Almorthanos did to you. What I did to you. But not all of them were involved in the battle or any of that other stuff. They're innocent. Cade and Killian are punishing them just the same.'

I narrowed my eyes. 'Do you know where they're being held?'

'No, and I've looked everywhere I can think of.' Frustration filled his words and he ran a hand through his hair. 'Ever since I woke up and found myself in my neph—' His voice broke and he sucked in several deep breaths before continuing.

'When I came back to life in this...body...I went into hiding. I was so out of it, I'm not even sure how I got away. By the time I returned to the compound to see what had happened to the rest of our clan they were gone, spirited away by Killian's people. I spent the next five months tracking down every lead, every hint I could find in my search for them, and came up with nothing. That's when I resorted to more drastic measures.'

'Kidnapping, torturing and killing Killian's real estate men,' I said, realising where his tale was heading, curious about the reluctance I heard in his voice when he mentioned his new body.

He grimaced. 'I was desperate, getting nowhere, losing hope I would ever find them. Not that I got much out of them. All they could tell me was that Killian was buying up land in all the states, as well as every property on the market in and around Easton. None of it got me any closer to finding our people.'

'Your people. Not mine.'

'No matter how many times you deny it, it doesn't change the fact you would not exist without Clan Davila. It is your heritage, and will be your legacy to your own children should you choose to have any.'

Instead of arguing about it, I went on the attack. 'Whose body did you steal?'

He blanched, taking a step back before straightening up and blanking his expression. 'That's not relevant.'

'It is to me. You want me to help you, I need to know how you ended up in that body.'

He remained silent, staring at me, dark eyes shadowed.

I turned to Sam. 'We're out of here.'

He nodded, holstering his gun and also turning his back on Talaom.

'No. Wait.'

I turned back to face Talaom. He didn't speak for a long moment. Finally, he heaved out a deep sigh and said, 'This is my nephew's body.'

'You killed your nephew just so you could live again?' Horrified, I took a step back.

He put up his hand, palms facing out. 'No. That's not what happened. I would never hurt Blane. It was an accident; I did not mean for this to happen.' Tears shimmered in his eyes, his words echoing the pain and confusion I'd felt when I'd discovered I'd taken over Emily's body.

I thrust the rush of empathy threatening to overwhelm me aside, voice harsh as I said, 'Tell me.'

'I didn't want him to come, wanted him to return to Angellin to be with his mother, my sister. But he went behind my back and approached Malia.' His lips twisted into a grimace. 'I didn't find out he was still down here until just before we launched our attack on Godden's people. I ordered him to remain on the outskirts of the compound, with a handful of others who were to remain in reserve, in case things went wrong.'

He rubbed his eyes with both hands, before letting his arms fall to his sides. 'When I saw what you were doing to the Grim Reaper, cleansing him, I realised we'd lost. I left the battlefield and went to find Blane, to send him away.'

His large body shuddered, horror and guilt meshed in his tortured gaze, and for a moment I thought his legs were going to buckle. But he steadied himself and met my eyes once more. 'I was too late. A group of Godden's men had found them before they entered the compound. Their wings had been torn from their backs. The other five were already dead. I don't know how Blane had managed to hold on so long. When he saw me, he reached out a hand and asked me to tell his mother he was sorry. I didn't think. Wasn't capable of thinking. I took his hand. The next thing I know I was being ripped apart. I thought it was you, attacking me, and I spun around to defend myself, and that's when I realised I was in Blane's body. That I had stolen his life.'

His legs did buckle then. He fell to his knees, shoulders heaving, head bowed as he gave in to his sorrow. I stifled the urge to comfort him, to wrap my arms around him and tell him it was going to be okay. I would have been lying if I did. He'd taken over the body of someone he cared about. It didn't matter that it was an accident. It had happened, and only time would tell if he would be able to live with what he had done. While I had no comfort to offer him, I could do nothing about the tears streaming down my cheeks.

I stepped closer. 'What makes you think I can help you find the Davilians?'

Talaom stiffened, head lifting. He stared at me, showing no shame as he wiped away his tears. 'You're Godden's pet reaper.' He got to his feet, frowning. 'You're a prized member of his inner council. You must know where they are.'

I grimaced. 'You're not the only one who believes I can never leave my Davilian heritage behind. Cade despises me.'

'How can that be? You're here with his son, and the daughter of his right hand man.'

'Not by his choice or Killian's. They hate me just as much as they hate you.'

Talaom's shoulders slumped and he turned away. 'I'm never going to find them.'

I frowned, not liking his defeatist attitude. 'I didn't say that. We've been looking for them too. Maybe if we share information we can figure out where Cade has stashed them.'

Talaom twisted back around, surprise on his face. 'You've been looking for them? Even though you don't consider them to be your people?'

'Just because I don't consider myself a member of Clan Davila doesn't mean I don't care about what happens to them. You're right, many of them are innocent. They have been punished enough. I want to make sure Cade and Killian don't make them suffer even worse than they already have.'

I paused, thinking back to the night I'd discovered he was the living reaper. 'Last time I saw you, you said something about me being on the wrong side. That I would come to regret siding with Clan Godden. You were about to tell me something when I was pulled back to my body. What were you going to say?'

He straightened up, a sneer on his lips. 'Thought you would have figured that out by now. Cade and Almorthanos ultimately had the same goal, to be God. Now he's rid himself of his ancient enemy, Cade's eyes will be focused on the physical plane; a plane filled with mortals just crying out for something, someone, to believe in.' He shrugged. 'It won't be long before humans will all be worshipping Cade.'

I stared at Talaom, shaking my head. 'That will never happen. He doesn't have the numbers to take over the world.' But he might have enough to take over Easton, if he hadn't already. Was that what Killian's real estate men were doing? Buying Cade a town ready to be converted to the worship of a false god?

A pained cry sounded behind me and I spun around.

I gasped, scrambling to call on aether as hundreds of winged Tr'lirians appeared inside the hockey hall. The cry had come from Rebecca, who was being wrestled into submission by two of the Tr'lirians. Chris was fighting off another two, while two more held Sam at bay. They'd appeared so quickly, without any warning, and immediately separated us. It would be useless to create a barricade until I could get everyone free and close to me.

I sent a concentrated blast of aether at one of the Tr'lirians holding Rebecca, pushing him away from her. As the aether touched him I felt the draw of his soul. But I had no time to wonder about that. The other one had wrapped his arms around Rebecca and lifted in the air with powerful strokes of his wings, body shimmering as he prepared to take her into the astral plane.

I had to stop him.

Pain ripped through my body as something latched onto my soul. I dropped to my knees, hands on my chest as I fought against the pull. I held on to my soul, just, needing all my strength to stop it being ripped out of my body. The pull abruptly ceased and I toppled sideways, head banging into the concrete floor. I rolled onto my back, dazed and disorientated, head aching. Eyes stinging, I looked up at Talaom.

He leaned over me, despair on his face. 'I'm sorry, Tyler,' he said as he swung his fist at my head.

I opened my eyes, wincing at the pain the movement caused in my right temple.

What the hell happened? Why was I lying on a cold, hard surface?

I struggled into a sitting position, groaning and shutting my eyes as a fresh wave of pain roared through my head. Nausea bubbled in my stomach and I swallowed it down as I once again opened my eyes.

'Sam.' I forgot my pain, forgot everything as I got to my feet and ran to where he was spread out on his back on the floor of the hockey hall. He was motionless, silent. Tears sprang to my eyes when I saw the livid bruise on his right temple; a match for the one sure to be blossoming on my head.

I kneeled next to him, careful not to touch him, as I looked to see if he was breathing.

His chest rose in a steady rhythm, and now the initial panic had subsided I could feel his soul, hear its song, strong and vibrant. There was no pull for me to reap it. Confident he was going to be okay, that I wouldn't inadvertently kill him by touching him, I stroked his cheek.

'Sam? Can you hear me? I need you to open your eyes.'

He moaned, eyelashes fluttering, as he sought to respond to my request. I kept talking to him, tears running down my cheeks to fall on his shirt as I coaxed him back to consciousness.

I choked back a sob when he finally opened his eyes and looked at me, a crooked smile curving his lips. 'Hey, beautiful, don't cry,' he said as he lifted one hand and wiped away my tears. 'It's all good. I'm good.'

'Yeah, you're good,' I said, smiling in relief as I helped him to sit up. He leaned into my touch as I looked around the hall. We were the only occupants.

'Talaom betrayed us,' I said, thinking back to the last glimpse I had of him. 'But I don't think he was happy about it.'

'He's not going to be happy once I catch up with him, either.' Sam's hand brushed aside my fringe and gently probed the tender spot on my temple. 'I saw him hit you.' His arms shook. 'You went so still, I thought he'd killed you, again, and taken your soul.' His voice was rough, and it broke on the last word.

I hugged him as tightly as I could, to reassure him I was okay. 'I don't think he was trying to kill me. It was more about neutral-ising a threat. Cade knows full well what I can do with aether. He had Talaom make sure I was unable to stop his men taking Rebecca and Chris.'

'What I don't get is why Talaom would do anything for him. He hates Cade.'

'But he loves his people, and Cade is the one holding them. I'm willing to bet Cade promised to tell him where they are, or take him to them, if he double-crossed us. And it's not as though Talaom and I were allies.' Still, he had looked conflicted, and apologised before knocking me out. 'I'd probably do the same, if Cade was holding you and everyone else I cared about hostage.'

'No, you wouldn't. You'd find some other way to free us that didn't involve betraying a potential ally, which is why I'm still going to kick Talaom's arse when we find him.'

'First, we need to rescue Chris and Rebecca.'

'My head is killing me.'

'Mine too,' I said as I struggled to my feet. 'I have some painkillers in my bag. We can take care of our heads while on our way to the compound.'

I marched outside, Sam beside me, head pounding with each step. But I didn't slow my pace. With each passing second, my anger was building. I'd known Cade and Killian wouldn't give up, and were determined to make Chris and Rebecca bend to their will. But if they thought I was going to let them get away with it they were very wrong. Chris had only agreed to an arranged marriage with Rebecca to give me the chance to return to my own body. He and Sam might say it was his choice to make but that didn't stop me feeling responsible.

I clenched my fists, jaw tensing. 'I am not going to let Cade bully Chris and Rebecca into getting married. It's not right.'

'He's not going to hand them over to you just because you ask nicely,' said Sam.

'I wasn't planning on asking.'

Sam unlocked the car and as soon as we were seated I grabbed the painkillers out of my handbag and we both swallowed a couple of them dry.

Sam gave me a grin as he started the engine. 'Can't wait to see the look on Killian's face when you pull his compound down around his ears.'

While that was exactly what I felt like doing, razing the compound to the ground, I would have to hold off my wrecking ball instincts until after we'd freed our friends.

It didn't feel weird at all to consider Rebecca and Chris as friends.

Chris had been there at the start, when my world started to unravel, and having him back in my life felt natural. After not seeing him for so long, it was a relief to find out there was none of the awkwardness usually associated with running into someone who'd been potential boyfriend material.

As for Rebecca, even though I'd only known her such a short time, I admired her resilience and courage. She'd been thrown in the deep end when she'd learned about her Tr'lirian heritage and everything that went with it, and yet she was still determined to help. She could have taken the first plane to Sydney and forgotten all about us, but she stuck around, putting herself right in the firing line. I would make sure she didn't regret choosing to help us.

The drive out to the compound seemed to take forever, and I tapped my fingers on the passenger door's armrest all the way, willing the car to go faster, a hard knot of anxiety forming in my belly. What if I couldn't free them? Or find the Davilians?

Talaom may have been aiding the enemy, but his fear for his clan had been real, and I had a feeling everything he'd told me had been true. His pain at having taken over his nephew's body had been all too familiar. That wasn't to say I was in the mood to forgive and forget what he'd done, but I could understand why. I wasn't after revenge. I just wanted an end to all the fighting. I wanted everyone; human, Tr'lirian or a mixture of both, to be able to live their lives according to their own desires and not be forced to bow down to a dictator.

Talaom had said Cade was looking to set himself up as God. Almorthanos had had the same grandiose plan, and I'd stopped that from coming to fruition. I would stop Cade.

If I could.

I'd had to side with Clan Godden to be able to defeat Almorthanos. How was I supposed to defeat Cade on my own? I would have to pitch my ability to manipulate aether against an entire clan of Tr'lirians hell-bent on carrying out their leader's every order.

Rhonda had estimated Clan Godden had around five thousand people, many of them still in Angellin, wings and immortality intact. Five thousand people Cade could call on. Some of them were bound to get hurt, especially those who no longer had their wings. Could I take their souls, knowing they were only following orders? And the ones with wings; could I strip them of their immortality just so I could then kill them?

I grimaced, no closer to getting answers for any of the questions circling in my brain when we finally pulled up in front of the gates of Killian's compound.

'You ready for this?' Sam asked.

I nodded slowly, taking deep breaths to steady my nerves as I called on the aether contained in my surroundings, drinking it in.

I opened the passenger door and got out of the car, getting a faint sense of dozens of souls on the other side of the gate. It was as if I was hearing the song they broadcast into the astral plane through earmuffs, making it sound muffled and difficult to concentrate on. From earlier, when Cade and Killian had appeared at the compound, I knew what that meant. I was facing a large number of winged Tr'lirians, immortal and impervious to harm unless they lost their wings.

But that wasn't what I had in mind. I focused on the gate in front of me, straightened my shoulders and thrust my hands towards it, palms facing the ground. Beams of silver lightning shot out of my fingers, spearing into the gate.

It exploded with a huge whoosh, fragments of it raining down and bouncing off the barrier I had erected around Sam's car and me.

Tr'lirians rushed through the gap, roaring in fury, swords held high. I sent out more lightning, waving my hands from side to side, shooting it into them. It wouldn't kill them, but the impact sent them tumbling head over heels, unable to control their flight as they were flung back into the compound, landing with concussive thuds hundreds of metres away. They might be immortal, but not one of them bounced straight back up.

I didn't let my success so far go to my head. I'd only bowled over a few dozen soldiers. Cade had thousands more. I had to get to the main house while I had the upper hand. I dived into the car and Sam accelerated the second I was in the seat.

I gripped the door and slammed it shut as he roared down the driveway.

'You planning on blasting your way through the guard posts too, or is it my turn to have some fun?' Sam asked.

'They're all yours. I need to conserve my energy for the main event,' I said with a tight smile as I buckled my seatbelt and braced myself as best I could for the coming impact.

I hadn't felt a drain on my abilities yet, but manipulating so much aether would inevitably take its toll on me. While the amount of aether I could draw on was infinite, my ability to control it was not. I had to concentrate, using everything I had to direct it where and how I wanted. It was my spirit, my body's own form of aether, that gave me control over the energy existing in all living things. Far from being an infinite source, my body's spirit would need time to replenish itself once I had used it all up.

Sam didn't hesitate as we approached the first guard post, the BMW hurtling forward, ramming into the lowered barricade and ripping it off its supports. The car's momentum slowed as it jolted from the impact. I gripped the dash with one hand and the armrest with the other, body rocking with each shudder of the big vehicle. When the shudders ceased we picked up speed as Sam prepared to ram the second barricade.

It fared no better than the first and soon Sam had the car screeching to a halt in front of the main house. We'd barely scrambled from the car before we were surrounded by hundreds of Tr'lirians. Many of this lot didn't have wings and I could clearly hear the songs of their individual souls. I could reap them, but I wasn't a murderer.

I formed a barrier around Sam and me as we marched towards the front door, using it to push anyone who got in our way aside. They pressed against the barrier, trying to force their way in or at least to stop us from going any farther. The crush of bodies made it hard to see where we were headed, and it was getting difficult to make them shuffle back. At this rate I'd be exhausted before we made it to the top step, let alone got inside the building.

I pulled on Sam's arm, getting him to stop as I closed my eyes and concentrated on sending out a continuous wave of aether. Instead of pushing at the Tr'lirians blocking our way, it ebbed and receded, picking up momentum as it went, until finally I sent it out in one huge whoosh that knocked everyone in the immediate vicinity to the ground. Sam and I swept through the fallen bodies and into the hall, coming face to face with Killian.

'Stand down.' Killian's calm order sent a whirl of confusion through the Tr'lirians surrounding us, but they quickly obeyed and lowered their weapons.

I lifted my chin and glared at Killian, noting the empty hallway behind him. 'Where are Chris and Rebecca?'

His top lip curled into a sneer. 'They are no longer your concern. You and your detective need to leave, while you still can. Walk away now, and Cade will show you mercy. Remain, and your lives will be forfeit.'

The icy gleam in his eyes chilled me, but I refused to let it show. 'I'm not going anywhere until my friends are free, and I will do whatever it takes to ensure that happens.'

'No, you won't. I know you. Davilian though you might be, you would never deliberately harm another to get your way, unless they were trying to kill you.' He turned to the Tr'lirians who stood watching us. 'You may leave. The reaper is no threat to me.'

A number of grumbles and dark looks were sent my way, but his people did as ordered and left the building via the front door.

Once they were gone Killian gave me a cool smile. I narrowed my eyes, trying to figure out what he was up to.

'You have already proved your willingness to sacrifice yourself to save others, but you no longer have anything Cade or I need. You have nothing to bargain with. As I am unarmed, and pose no immediate threat to you, I know you will not harm me.'

I wanted to prove him wrong, to reach out and grab his soul, yanking it from his body and dangling it in front of him until he gave me what I wanted, as I'd once done to Almorthanos. But he was right. I hadn't been able to bring myself to kill Almorthanos when he was helpless in front of me. I couldn't carry through on a threat to kill Killian, not unless he attacked me or Sam. Even then, I wasn't sure I could do it. But that did not mean I was backing down without a fight. I'd just have to come up with another way to free the others.

'I'm not leaving until I've seen Chris and Rebecca. And I want to know where the Davilians are. You've got them stashed somewhere. That's how you got Talaom on side, by threatening their safety or agreeing to tell him where they are.'

His expression gave nothing away, but I knew I was right. I moved closer to Killian, bringing Sam and the barrier I had created with me.

'You're right. I'm not a killer. I won't hurt you to get you to free my friends or tell me what I want to know. But what I can do is bring this compound down around all of our ears. It's important to you, to whatever schemes you and Cade have been cooking up ever since you were made mortal, and I'm going to take it all away.' I crouched, placing my hands on the floor, searching for the aether that existed in the ground below the compound's foundations.

The building shook as the aether responded to my will, forming cracks in the foundation of the main house, spreading fast to include every building. The shaking became more violent as I pushed the cracks farther, extending out into the surrounding estate.

I looked up at Killian, a fierce grin on my face. 'I hear you've been buying up the properties in Greenlakes, and are all set to create a haven on Earth for your people. Well, looks as though you might need to get back in touch with your real estate guys. Once I'm done here this estate will be nothing but rubble.'

He moved towards me, anger twisting his handsome features into an ugly mask. I sent out a ripple of aether in his direction, making the floor undulate beneath his feet. He lost his balance, tumbling to the ground. He tried to rise several times, and each time I dropped him back down.

Cracks appeared in the walls as the house shook with each movement and I heard cries of alarm from all around me. Dust and bits of plaster fell from the ceiling. Thanks to the barrier, Sam and I were protected from falling debris. Killian and his men were not so lucky. As the tremors grew more violent and the entire house shook, people rushed down stairs and out of doors, making for the front door.

Killian slipped into the astral plane, his form going hazy, narrowly avoiding getting squashed by a large section of ceiling. Even blurred, there was no mistaking the fury in his icy blue gaze.

'Enough.' The shout came from behind Killian.

I looked past him to where Cade stood in the entrance to the main room of the compound. Chris and Rebecca were on either side of him, arms held by winged Tr'lirians. They were all in the astral plane and the worry I'd had about hurting Chris and Rebecca by creating a mini earthquake subsided. But while they were uninjured, they were far from free.

'Let them go, Cade, or I will make sure everything you have built on this plane is destroyed.' I no longer needed to touch the ground to control the aether. I stood and faced him straight on.

'You don't scare me, girl, and I would rather see it all gone than give in to the threats of a Davilian.' He waved his hand and the men holding Chris and Rebecca stepped out of the astral plane, pushing their captives in front of them. They forced my friends to their knees and drew swords, glaring balefully at me while they placed their weapons against Chris and Rebecca's necks.

'You have three seconds,' said Cade. 'Stop whatever it is you're doing, or they die.'

I let the rumble of the ground beneath us subside, the merciless look in his eyes telling me this was no bluff. But even though I had let go of the aether, Cade did not order his men to stand down.

'You got what you wanted. Let them go,' I said, a tingle of apprehension sweeping over me.

Cade gave a nod and the Tr'lirian holding Chris moved his sword, but did not release him. The one with his sword pressed into the back of Rebecca's neck did not move at all. He tightened his grip, preparing to strike.

Killian got to his feet. 'Cade, what are you doing?'

Cade focused on him. 'Those that defy me must die.'

'She's my daughter. You can't–'

'Silence.' Cade's wings unfurled, filling the hallway. 'I am your clan leader. It will be as I command. If the girl does not submit to my rule she will die, along with anyone else who refuses to obey me.' His fierce expression did not soften as he looked at Killian. 'You can make more daughters, full Tr'lirian ones, who will be raised to know their place. This one is not worthy to marry my son. He, at least, has agreed to fulfil his duty, to uphold the deal he made in return for us retrieving the reaper's body. Yet your daughter still refuses to submit to my will.'

'She will do as she is told, I promise. My daughter will marry your son.'

The look on Rebecca's face said she wanted to say something, but I was glad when she remained silent. With the mood Cade was in, all it would take was one wrong word for him to order her execution.

I tested the aether around me, tested my control of it to see if I could slide a barrier between Rebecca and the sword at her neck as well as cover Chris. It was hopeless. I couldn't find a gap, and bludgeoning my way through was a sure-fire way to get Rebecca killed, and maybe Chris too. Even if I used aether to wrench them both out of their captors' grasps, I couldn't guarantee being able to do it quickly enough, get them far enough away, to stop them from being hurt.

I'd lost, defeated by Cade's willingness to kill to maintain control.

Sam's hand gripped mine. I shot him a reassuring smile and straightened my shoulders. Just because Cade had won this round did not mean I was ready to give up completely. I would find a way to get Chris and Rebecca out of here.

Cade indicated for the man holding his sword ready to execute Rebecca to step back. Chris instantly moved forward to help her to her feet. He put an arm around her waist and guided her to a short distance away from the Tr'lirians surrounding Cade and Killian. Meanwhile, dozens more of them crowded into the hallway. I didn't need to look behind me to know they had blocked off any chance Sam and I had of retreating.

Chris shot me a look of warning, before addressing Cade. 'Father, you've got what you wanted. Let Tyler and the detective go.'

Cade took his eyes off me to glare at Chris. 'Do not presume to tell me what to do. You are not my only son. I can easily adjust my plans to make use of one of them instead.'

Chris's eyes widened at the mention of potential brothers. He quickly smoothed his expression and gave Cade a slight bow. 'Of course, I would never tell you what to do. I just wanted to avoid any potential scrutiny. Lockwood is a police detective, one with strong ties within the local community. If he were to disappear, it could bring unwanted attention to us.'

Cade stared at Chris for a long moment. 'Very well, the detective may leave. But not the reaper.'

Sam stepped forward; fists clenched. 'If you think I'm leaving here without Tyler, you need to think again.'

'Relax, detective. Despite everything she has done to annoy me, I have no intention of harming her.' Cade wore a smile probably meant to be reassuring, but it fell far from the mark.

Sam obviously thought so too. 'You really expect me to believe that? To trust you? She stays, I stay.'

'You do not get to make demands. Besides, I'm sure Tyler will be the first to urge you to leave. After all, once you are gone I'm going to give her what she wants.'

I narrowed my eyes. 'What are you talking about?'

'Killian tells me you want proof your fellow Davilians are alive and being cared for. Once your detective leaves I'll take you to see them. You can judge their wellbeing for yourself.'

'Tyler's not going anywhere with you, not without me.' Sam bristled, taking hold of my hand and gripping it tightly.

'I'm afraid, Detective Lockwood, that even if I wished you to join us, it would be impossible. You need to be able to access the astral plane, to travel to where the Davilians are being housed. As you have no Tr'lirian blood in you whatsoever you are incapable of accompanying us.'

'I'll go with her,' said Chris, letting go of Rebecca and stepping forward.

'Your place is here, with your fiancée.' Cade gave Chris a cool smile. 'But as I understand your reluctance to leave Tyler in my care, I hereby vow she will come to no harm while we make this journey. This is my vow to you, father to son, I will carry her myself and neither I nor any of my clan will attempt to harm her in any way as she ascertains the wellbeing of her people.'

'A vow to a son you threatened to kill just minutes ago, or to replace if he doesn't obey your every whim?' I made no attempt to hide my scepticism. I could see from the looks on Sam and Chris's faces that they felt the same way.

'Do you want to see your people or not? I will not make this offer again.'

I hesitated, aware of the danger in trusting Cade's vow. But what if Talaom was right and the rest of the Davilians were in danger? I had to take this chance. There was just one thing I had to take care of first.

'Sam leaves, before I go anywhere with you.'

'Very well.' Cade turned to his men. 'Escort the detective to his vehicle and see to it he leaves the compound and does not return.'

Before Sam had a chance to protest, four of the Tr'lirians grabbed hold of his arms and dragged him away from me. No matter how much he kicked and cursed, he couldn't break their grip as they steadily carried him out the front door.

Though it hurt to have to block out Sam's voice as he called my name, I turned to face Cade, conscious of the concern in Chris's eyes as he watched on.

'Let's do this.'

ade strode forward and took hold of my arm. With rough movements, he turned me around so my back rested against his chest. His arms shifted to my waist, wrapping around my torso as he pulled me even closer.

Uncomfortable being held so intimately by anyone other than Sam, I attempted to put some space between us. His grip tightened even more, and I could feel the rise and fall of his naked chest against my back.

'Killian, make sure neither my son or the detective does anything stupid while I'm gone,' said Cade, the rumble of his deep voice vibrating through my body.

Before I could say anything, he launched himself into the air.

I let out a startled squeak, sure we were going to ram into the ceiling. But he seamlessly slipped into the astral plane. I shuddered as I was pulled physically into a landscape usually reserved for souls. I'd travelled extensively in the astral plane in my astral form. This was nothing like that. Then I flew with ease. Now, it felt as if I was being pulled through a swimming pool, my skin rippling as a dry wave passed over me. I had no time to process this strange sensation before being hit by another. We had reached the ceiling.

My head passed through the layers of timber and carpet as we emerged into the room above the hall, the drag so strong I thought it would pluck me out of Cade's arms and leave me stuck halfway between floors. When the rest of my body made it through without incident I sucked in a breath, relieved to be back in open space.

My reprieve was short-lived as we continued up and through the next two floors. I didn't breathe easily until we reached the construction area. Not that I was feeling comfortable.

I was in Cade's arms, the arms of a man who had shown no compunction in getting rid of anyone who stood in his way. It was not the safest place to be at any time, let alone when he was flying and I was in my physical body.

Once we cleared the building, Cade stopped, hovering in mid-air about ten metres above the metal framework for the extension.

'Why have we stopped?' I asked, craning my neck in a useless effort to see his face.

Cade didn't respond to my question, but I got my answer when a dozen Tr'lirians appeared in the air around us. Once the escort had arranged themselves he set off again, the powerful sweeps of his wings carrying us high into the sky. The forms of the Tr'lirians flying in formation around us grew hazy as they also entered the astral plane.

I didn't want to look down, to see how far from the ground I was, but I couldn't help myself. It was dizzying, seeing the compound so far below me. I closed my eyes until my head stopped spinning. This was nothing like the times I'd flown over Easton previously.

Cade may have vowed to Chris that I would be unharmed by this little excursion but I had little trust in that. Cade's sudden urge to curry favour with the man he considered his son, regardless of whose soul inhabited the body, was no comfort as he took me even higher, angling slightly to the north.

I frowned, searching for landmarks. When he'd said he would have to carry me to where the Davilians were being held, in order to ensure I was in my physical body when we arrived at our destination, I had imagined a horizontal journey, not a vertical one.

'Where are we going?' I asked, the wind of our passing whipping the words out of my mouth.

Once again Cade ignored my question, though his arms tightened around me to the verge of being painful.

I squirmed and banged on his forearms. His response was to tighten his grip around my middle. I gasped as the air was forced from my lungs by the pressure. I tried to suck in more air, but he didn't let up. The dizziness I'd experienced before came back tenfold. I scratched his arms with my nails, digging in as hard as I could, desperate to get him to let go, forgetting all about being hundreds of metres above the Earth. I kicked backwards, finding nothing but empty air.

My vision blurred, darkening around the edges as my lungs screamed for oxygen.

My eyes rolled back. I went limp in Cade's arms as unconsciousness took me.

I OPENED my eyes to darkness, head aching, body shaking. Nausea flooded me in constant waves and I fought not to retch. I made an effort to rise, but my body didn't move. Something heavy pressed me down. I was lying on my back, arms at my sides. I stretched out my fingers, finding a cold, hard lumpy surface beneath me.

I groaned, the nausea worsening as I moved my hands to my chest, seeking to remove whatever was weighing me down. I needed to get up; had to find painkillers to take care of the vice squeezing my head. With luck that would dispel the sick feeling bubbling away in my stomach. All I felt was the material of my shirt, groaning again as my fingers pressed against my body. It felt as if bruising covered half my torso, a denser, deeper pain than the one caused by the seatbelt when Sam's car had been hit.

'She's awake,' said a gruff voice that showed little compassion.

'Get her up and moving.'

I recognised the second voice.

Cade.

Memory returned with the recognition. He'd tried to kill me, squeeze me to death. Chris was not going to be happy. My doubt at relying on a father's vow to the man he considered his son was vindicated. Not that being proved right gave me any sense of satisfaction in my current situation.

Rough hands grabbed my arms. I held back a pained cry when they pulled me upright. I bent over, only their tight grip keeping me on my feet as I retched uncontrollably, emptying the contents of my stomach on the floor where I'd lain. Grim satisfaction filled me when my efforts were rewarded by cries of disgust and curses.

Served them right for hauling me to my feet with no consideration for my physical state.

Satisfaction fled when they wrenched my limp body along, fingers digging painfully into my arms. Faint light appeared up ahead as they dragged me out of wherever I'd been held. I struggled to get my feet under me, determined to meet my fate with as much dignity as I could muster. The man holding me abruptly let go. I stumbled, falling sideways, putting out my hands to stop me tumbling to the ground.

My hands found purchase on a cool rock wall. I took a second to steady my breathing, fighting to keep myself from vomiting again. A hard shove in the middle of my back almost sent me to my knees. Sheer willpower kept me standing. I shuffled forward, the light up ahead getting brighter with every step. My nausea worsened, roiling in my belly and making it difficult to think about anything else other than not throwing up.

It didn't dawn on me that the sick feeling enveloping me was familiar or that it was coming from outside my body until I reached the source of the light, stepping onto a stone balcony to look out over a blackened and bleak landscape.

A multi-levelled city was spread out below me. A dark mist concealed the lowest levels and only a few sporadic lights lit up the level immediately below the balcony on which I stood. This was the only sign the city was inhabited, at least below me. Forgetting my nausea, the pain, everything, I stepped out and twisted my neck to look above me.

Instead of more black rock, the levels above me gradually became lighter in turn, until the very top where a gleaming tower shone with a silvery-grey light as it reached high into the sky. The tower was wreathed in aether, pure and beautiful, and it was this that made it shine. I felt a tug deep inside, a desire to go to it, and obviously I wasn't the only one. I could see people with white wings flying in air untainted by the dark mist, sticking close to the silver tower as they flew.

I gulped in air, realising what this meant.

I was in Angellin.

CHAPTER 24

The sense of wrongness I'd previously felt while in the astral plane above Easton hit me with staggering force. This was the source, the reason for my nausea. Angellin was diseased, dying, only the upper levels closest to the tower giving off a familiar sense of aether. It was the pale remnant of the aether Rhonda said had been used to create the Tr'lirians' home many centuries ago.

I looked below me once more, the reek emanating from the lowest levels bringing tears to my eyes. It was similar to the debilitating stench that suffused the chasm marking the border between the Underworld and Demania. Uncontrolled nether; it poisoned everything it touched. Soon it would devour the remaining scraps of aether clinging to the tower high above me and this place would become another Hell.

A violent swirl in the dark mist coating the lowest level caught my eye. The sense of wrongness was so strong, I couldn't stifle a cry of disgust. My cry turned to one of alarm when the stone beneath my feet shifted. I stumbled backwards, seeking safety as a loud rumble came from far below me. This was swiftly followed by the crash and boom as what sounded like huge cracks of lightning came from within the mist, accompanied by large stone chunks tumbling down the side of the city.

'You are safe enough up here, for the moment.'

I spun around at Cade's cold words.

He glared down at me. 'But with the earthquakes becoming more frequent and the damage to the lower levels more severe, I fear my city has little time left.'

I stared at him; sure my horror was reflected in my eyes. 'What have you done?'

He stiffened. 'You think I did this? That I would destroy my home? Render my people homeless?'

I shook my head, struggling to understand what the scraps of aether were telling me and translate it into words. 'You and Almorthanos, with your hatred and your anger, you poisoned Angellin. All the killing, the need to destroy each other no matter the cost. Your home is dying because of you.'

'How dare you.' Cade loomed over me, jaw clenched, gaze furious. 'It is the taint of your kind that has destroyed my city. Davilians, with their filth and their lies, corrupted the heart of Angellin and they shall reap a just reward for their treachery.'

I gasped at his use of the word "reap". 'You're going to kill them all.' If he hadn't already.

'I am no murderer,' he said, appearing oblivious to the lie he was spouting, as if threatening to execute Rebecca if she continued to defy him didn't count. 'No, the city itself will decide their fate.'

He gave me a cool smile. 'Come, it is time for you to join your brethren.'

Before I could question him further he strode forward and grabbed me around the middle, lifting me off my feet. His tight grip squeezed the breath from my lungs as he kept walking.

I had no air left to scream when he launched us both off the balcony, the snap of his wings unfurling giving me little comfort as we dropped in the darkened sky, heading straight for the dark mist obscuring the lower levels.

The nether mist in the void, controlled by the Grim Reaper, was cold and deadly. This mist, formed of uncontrolled nether, slid across my skin like sludge, ripping a shudder from my body. I closed my eyes and shut my mouth, racked with an overwhelming nausea. Sweat broke out all over my body and my shudders grew in intensity until I was sure I was going to shake right out of Cade's arms.

I was too far away from the tower to use the remnants of aether wreathing it to create a barricade to keep the nether away from me. The stench was so strong it forced me to the edge of consciousness, my body shutting down as a defence mechanism against what assailed it.

In desperation, I called on the aether existing inside me, draining as much of my energy as I dared to form a thin blanket to cloak myself. Immediately the emanations from the wild nether were reduced, though I still had a foul taste at the back of my throat which made me long for a glass of cool water to wash it down. I felt wrung out, drenched in sweat that made my skin cold and clammy even with the wind of flight pressing against me.

I didn't open my eyes until we landed and Cade released me. Even then I was reluctant to look at where we were now, considering we had to be surrounded by the mist coating the lower levels. I knew from experience that pretending the bad stuff wasn't there didn't make it go away.

I moved away from Cade and lifted my head to take my first look at my surroundings. A number of Cade's men stood in a semi-circle in front of me, holding lanterns that did little to push back the darkness. Shadows covered every surface I could see, giving off a disturbing gleam. I didn't need to touch anything to know the dark mist had coated everything in a thick, black sludge. I was grateful I was wearing closed in shoes. Bad enough to know it was on my skin, let alone squelching around in it while wearing sandals or in bare feet.

I pushed thoughts of the residue left by the dark mist aside, more interested in what stood behind the Tr'lirians. An enormous building made up of thousands of gleaming black bricks stood before me. Each brick was at least one metre high and two across, with elaborate patterns carved into them. A silvery metallic substance had been poured into the carvings, and not even the nether could obscure the glittering array of fanciful creatures that flickered in the light of the lanterns.

'Before the city began to fail, the temple shone brighter than the sun.'

I jumped, and tried to cover it by smoothing my clothes, having not realised Cade was standing right behind me.

'Temple?' I frowned. The carvings and the gleaming black bricks were certainly striking, but not what I expected a temple to be made of. Then again, I'd never imagined that a race of winged beings, reportedly Earth's first inhabitants, lived in the sky above Easton. But other than the carvings, the building was plain, rectangular in shape with a wide row of stone steps leading to a large opening.

'Initially constructed to house those who were tasked with building the city, it was abandoned once my ancestors created more comfortable lodgings for themselves in the higher levels. After lying vacant for centuries, during my childhood my father decreed it should be restored as a reminder of our more humble beginnings.'

'Humble?' I had yet to meet a Tr'lirian who didn't act as if they were worthy of worship.

'This was early on in our interaction with your kind,' he said, a sneer audible in his voice. 'Father did not believe it seemly for us to lord our superiority over those doomed to a life without wings. He felt it wise to remind us of the distant past, when our ancestors believed in the existence of mythical creatures.' He waved a hand at the carved bricks.

'In our youth, we were required to descend to this level to take instruction in the temple on the proper way to interact with lesser beings. After a time, as the number of young born to our womenfolk dwindled, the practice was stopped and the temple closed once more. Until I found another use for it.' This time his smile was predatory.

I moved away from him again, only to have the Tr'lirians in front of me step forward and block my way. Cade took my elbow as his men parted, forming two lines for us to walk between. Cade's grip was tight as he strode down the aisle, giving me no choice but to hurry along to keep up with him. The stone steps leading into the temple were crumbling in places. Now we were closer, I saw cracks in many of the bricks forming the front, and presumed they were caused by the earthquakes Cade had said were coming with more frequency.

I forgot about the crumbling exterior of the temple as Cade pulled me inside.

Bars as thick as my wrists formed a wall across the entire front section of the temple, turning what had once been a large open space in the back into a cell.

Crammed into this cell were hundreds, maybe thousands, of people. Most of the ones I saw had dark hair, and none of them was winged. I stepped closer, the smell of so many unwashed bodies mixed with a heavy hint of blood hit me with a sickening realisation. I'd found the missing Davilians.

'As you can see, they are unharmed.'

I whirled around at Cade's smug words; hands clenched into fists. 'You've got them locked up in a giant cage, on a level oozing with uncontrolled nether, and you think that's not harming them. You're a monster.'

He shrugged. 'They are alive, something they should be thankful for. As should you. I vowed on my sister's grave to not rest until every single Davilian was dead, and yet I have allowed them to live on in Angellin, showing mercy Liren was never given.'

'What happened to your sister was horrible, and it should never have happened. But to imprison all these people is just as horrible, if not more so. There is no mercy in locking them away like animals.'

His nostrils flared, the muscles in his arms tensing as he shook both fists at me. 'They are animals, and it is my right to ensure they never see daylight again. They will remain here for the rest of their miserable lives, which will last as long as the city does. Then they will die along with it.'

'What are you talking about?'

'You've seen the city. You said it yourself. It is diseased, the earthquakes that beset us a herald of its impending demise. I had hoped for more time to prepare my people but it is no longer safe for them to remain here. It is time for us to leave.'

'Where will you go?' I asked, dreading his answer.

'Easton, of course. Killian has been preparing for this moment since the day I stripped the wings from his back. The exodus has already begun.' He pointed up into the sky where I could just make out tiny winged figures as they circled the silver tower.

One by one they disappeared, heading to Easton, and there was nothing I could do to stop them.

CHAPTER 25

I shook my head. 'How do you expect to hide the presence of thousands of Tr'lirians? No matter how much land you've brought to house them, they're going to be discovered sooner or later.'

'I have no intention of hiding. It is time your precious humans learned they are not the natural rulers of Earth.' Fervour lit his blue gaze, so eerily like Chris's. 'They will all bow before me, starting with the people of Easton. They will be the first to be converted to the worship of Godden.'

'You're going to play God?' I gave a snort. 'If you knew anything about us humans you'd know we don't like being told who to worship. Just because you've got wings doesn't mean they'll automatically fall at your feet.'

His expression brimming with dark menace, he said, 'Those who do not bow before me will die.'

'Humans outnumber you by around a million to one. Not the best odds. There are over eighty thousand people in Easton alone, more than enough to make you regret ever announcing your divinity. You'll be laughed out of town.'

'Humans are weak, mortal,' he said, lips screwed into a sneer.

'Even if they were capable of resisting me, it would do them no good. I own Easton. Land is not the only commodity for sale. People can be bought. The mayor, the Superintendent of the Easton Police Department, your government officials; they belong to me.'

Disdain evident in the arch of his brow, he said, 'Where it was not possible to purchase their allegiance they were replaced with those I engineered for the purpose of infiltrating every powerful organisation on Earth.'

'Engineered?'

'The breeding program I devised has resulted in what you would term sleeper agents. Purpose-bred individuals living outwardly normal lives, securing positions of strategic advantage to Clan Godden, waiting for the time when they will be called upon to act. I myself have participated in the program, ensuring my eldest human offspring was born into a position of wealth and power as a Bradbury.'

I sucked in a breath.

'You seduced Chris Bradbury's mother on purpose, to get her pregnant?'

He gave a nonchalant shrug. 'It was hardly a chore. She was a beautiful woman. Wasted on Alan Bradbury. Not that I accorded the same honour to the other women chosen to bear my mortal children.'

'What the hell?' I rubbed my temples, unable to believe what I was hearing. It was like being stuck in one of those weird movies where the human population were replaced by pod people.

'Many of the rich and powerful in your world discovered their wealth did not guarantee them an heir. When they sought assistance in creating those heirs, it was a simple matter of switching my seed for the father's. None of them were made aware of the switch, of course. That will change now I am ready to claim what is rightfully mine. My children will be brought to Easton, to fulfil their duty to their clan.'

I threw my hands up in the air. 'Listen to you. You act as if there is nothing wrong in this insane breeding program of yours. How can you be so callous? These are people's lives you're playing with.'

'Our numbers have declined over the last few generations, fewer children being born each year.' Cade shrugged, his wings shimmering with the movement. 'That's why I commanded those I trusted to create children with humans. It was either that or face the extinction of our race, which I will not allow to happen.'

'But you're immortal.'

'Only while we have our wings. Take those away from us and we die just as easily as any human. To ensure our race survives, even if it is without our immortality, we need to strengthen the bloodlines, do everything in our power to see our children take control of future generations on the physical plane. Only then can our legacy be assured.'

It all clicked into place. 'That's why you want Rebecca to marry Chris. Your legacy.'

'With Rebecca at his side, Chris will be ready to embark on a political career, one that will see laws passed to benefit the Tr'lirian people.'

'You're crazy. You can't just arrange people's lives to suit your needs. What about what Chris and Rebecca want? Doesn't that count for something?'

'Immaterial. They are children of Clan Godden. They will do their duty, whether they like it or not.' He scowled at me. 'Without you to distract him, my son will bow to my wishes and I'm sure he will find no fault in the bride I have chosen for him.'

'Chris is not your son. Just because you fathered his biological body does not make you his father. He has a soul, and a right to live his own life. So does Rebecca. You can't force her to marry someone she doesn't love.'

Doing that had poisoned Rhonda's life for so many years. It was only since she was free of my father that she was able to live the life she chose and be herself. So many years of unhappiness and anger would have been avoided if she had not been forced to marry my father.

'I won't let you do this.'

Cade let out a loud laugh. 'As if you could ever hope to stop me.' He clapped his hands. 'You will be dead soon enough, and your tainted clan will die with you.'

Four of his men bounded forward, latching on to my arms. I struggled to break free, dredging up every ounce of energy I could to blast them with aether. I managed a small blast, sending one of my attackers reeling. But he swiftly regained his footing. I sagged in the grip of the other three, that one blast dangerously depleting my energy levels. Head lolling on my neck, I was dragged over to the bars.

I heard a click, and the sound of a gate being drawn back seconds before I was tossed forward. I fell to my knees, barely able to stop myself slamming headfirst into the floor of the makeshift cell. The gate clanged shut behind me. Then silence.

Silence filled with the shuffling of many feet and restrained breathing.

'Told you not to trust Cade.'

It hurt to lift my head, my eyes having trouble focusing on Talaom's swarthy features. He crouched in front of me, not offering any assistance as I swayed in place. I longed to sink to the floor, to close my eyes and sleep for a week. A rumble coming from deep below the temple reminded me I couldn't afford to rest.

Not if I wanted to live.

I stifled a groan and forced myself to stand. The Davilians crowded around me took a step back, expressions wary. I scanned their faces, feeling no kinship with the people Talaom had insisted were mine. That didn't mean I wouldn't do my best to save them.

There were no seats or beds that I could see in the cell, though over the heads of those crowded around me I spotted a corner of the room had been curtained off. From the smell wafting this way, it had to be a makeshift toilet area.

'Have they been here the whole time?' Aghast, I looked to Talaom for answers.

He gave me a grim smile. 'Luckily no, or the smell would be even worse. Until last night they were imprisoned in the level above. Guess Cade no longer feels the comfort and wellbeing of his enemies is a high priority.'

Another loud rumble made the floor tremble and many of those surrounding me dropped to the ground. What I saw in the gleaming black bricks at their feet added to the urgency thrumming through me.

Death heads.

Everywhere I looked, they were reflected in the bricks.

I spun in a circle, peering over the Davilians' heads at the temple walls, catching glimpses of more and more death portents as people shifted positions.

I stumbled sideways, clutching hold of Talaom's arm. 'I need your help. Angellin is dying. We have to get these people out of here.'

He barked out a grim laugh, shaking his arm free of my grip. 'In case you hadn't noticed, I'm a prisoner just like you. I've explored every inch of this temple. There's only one way out and that's the front door, which is guarded by a dozen of Cade's men. They would not hesitate to kill every one of us. Of course, to get to them, we'd have to find a way out of this cell first. I may be strong but even I'm not capable of breaking through four-inch-thick bars, and the padlock they've got on the front gate is twice that size.'

'We have to do something. They're all going to die.'

His eyes met mine, pain in the dark gaze. 'I know. I've seen the portents. I've tried everything I can think of, but it's useless.

We're trapped. So unless you've got a miracle hidden up your sleeve, there's nothing we can do.'

Someone called my name before I could answer him, and my knees buckled as I turned to face Rhonda, struggling not to look to see if her death portent was also reflected in the gleaming bricks.

A strong arm around my waist stopped me from tumbling to the ground. I knew who it was even before he said, 'I've got you, sis.'

Tears sprang to my eyes as I looked from Connor to Rhonda. 'How did you get here?' They were supposed to be safe at the penthouse, not trapped in a dying city that could collapse and kill us all at any moment.

'I'm guessing the same way you did,' said Rhonda, with a disgruntled expression. 'Cade's goons returned not long after you left last night. Flew us up here and dumped us in this cage. Seems he's on a mission to destroy every trace of Davila he can, cleanse the Earth ready for the reign of Cade the God.'

I closed my eyes, determined to keep it together. When I was sure I wouldn't break down, I opened them again and indicated for Connor to let me go. 'We are not going to let him win. We will get out of here.'

'How? I hate to agree with Talaom, but this cell is more fortified than most banks. Unless you've got a stick of dynamite tucked away in your pocket, I don't see us getting out of here anytime soon,' said Connor.

'I'll use aether to get us out of here,' I said.

Talaom shook his head. 'If you were in any condition to blast this cell open, you'd have been able to fight off Cade's men and stop them locking you up with the rest of us. I saw the fight you put up. It was pitiful. You're going to have to come up with another way to save us all.'

I resisted the urge to snarl at Talaom and instead said, 'If I can connect with the aether that built this place I can get us out of here. But for it to have any chance of working, I'm going to need your help.'

He stared at me for a long moment, considering my words. 'You really think you can do it?'

'I do, as long as you can get everyone else to cooperate.'

Hope flared in his dark eyes. 'What do you need?'

'I need you to stop hating Cade, and Clan Godden.'

An uproar met my words, the fury they evoked from those Davilians near enough to hear setting the nether swirling. It rubbed against the aether cloak I had wrapped around myself, finding every little gap, forcing its way through, the stench over-whelming. I covered my nose and mouth as I fought to strengthen my defences against its insidious incursion.

I retched behind my hand, not able to stop my stomach from rebelling. With nothing to come up, all the nausea did was drive me to my knees again.

'Tyler, what's happening? Are you okay?'

Connor pulled me to my feet and I rested thankfully against him, breathing shallowly as I forced myself to speak. 'Their anger fuels the nether that is killing the city. They need to stop hating or they'll never be free.'

I knew it was so. They would remain in this cell and die in the city they'd poisoned with their hate, and Connor, Rhonda and I would die with them.

CHAPTER 26

I looked over at Talaom, willing him to understand what I was saying.

His brows met in the middle, but he gave a nod. 'What do you need?'

'Get everyone to back up; get them as far away from me and the gate as you can. Then I need you, Connor and Rhonda to help me break the padlock.'

The angry mutters and dark looks that followed in Talaom's wake as he ordered the Davilians to move to the back of the cell set the nether swirling again, but I was able to ride it out. The farther away from me they were, the less the dark waves of their negativity made my stomach churn.

When Talaom returned to my side I said, 'I need you to give me your aether.' My eyes moved to Connor and Rhonda. 'I'll need to take it from the two of you as well.'

Talaom's expression darkened. 'You're going to drain us of our natural energy?'

'If you want to save your people, this is what you have to do.' I let him process that for a moment. 'There is not enough aether here for me to draw on, and I'm exhausted from trying to blast Cade's men. You want this cage unlocked? I'm going to need to take some from each of you to do it.'

'What about them? Can't they help?' Connor pointed at the Davilians crowded in the back of the cell.

'They've been stuck here so long their spirits are warped. I need to get them out of here, and as close to the tower as we can get, so they can start to heal, and Angellin with them.'

Talaom's eyebrows rose. 'You think it's possible to save the city?'

'It will be up to them. If they can't turn aside from centuries of war and all the hatred and grief that caused, then there is nothing I can do to save any of us. If they're willing to work with me, there's a chance I can stop Angellin from dying. But not from here. I need to get to the tower, to connect with the last bit of pure aether clinging to it.'

'Let's get to it then.'

I stumbled over to the cell door, head spinning and body shaking at every step. I had to lean against the bars to support myself as I shoved my hands through the gap closest to the lock. I twisted until my hands gripped the padlock and then called the others over.

'Put your hands on me, and think positive thoughts.'

'Seriously?' Connor snorted. 'Are we meditating or escaping?'

I huffed out a sigh. 'The nether is doing its best to corrupt every ounce of aether in our bodies. To stop that happening, I need you to focus on good things, things that make you happy. I'll then be able to harness some of the aether inside you and channel it into the lock.'

'So you want me to think about girls with big–'

'Connor, stop being an idiot and do what your sister wants,' said Rhonda.

The reprimand had me smiling, as did the thought of the petulant expression sure to be on Connor's face. It was a rare occurrence for Rhonda to chastise her precious son, and it never happened for my benefit. Guess the threat of imminent death had its perks.

I closed my eyes and waited until they placed their hands on my back and shoulders to feel behind me for the aether stored in their bodies. Talaom's was dimmer than the others, which I had expected considering his role in Clan Davila. What I hadn't expected was the feeling of hope that burned deep within his spirit. For all his dark deeds, and his guilt over taking his nephew's body, he wanted what was best for his people. He wanted me to succeed in freeing them, and save the city, and was willing to do whatever it took to help me achieve those goals.

Rhonda and Connor's spirits may have contained more aether, but their focus was on their own survival.

Whatever the motivations of those helping me, I would put their aether to good use.

As gently and as sparingly as I could afford to be, I drew it out of their bodies and let it pour into mine. With the fresh influx of aether my energy level increased and I straightened up, no longer needing to lean on the bars for support. But I didn't have time to savour my newfound strength. Instead I channelled it out of my body and into the padlock, picturing the inner workings and the best place to strike.

I let go of the lock and stumbled backwards, taking the others with me.

A concussive boom echoed throughout the temple as the padlock split in half, each piece crashing to the ground.

Without the extra aether thrumming through my body, I needed time to rest and recuperate, but a rumble in the ground beneath the temple told me I'd have to wait.

'We need to get to the tower if I'm to have any hope of saving Angellin.' I looked over at Talaom, whose broad shoulders were slumped after having half his energy levels drained. 'This time I'm going to need all of our people to pitch in.'

He gave me a weary smile. 'Our people, huh?'

I gave him a similarly weary smile in return, choosing to remain silent as he started organising the Davilians and explaining what was to come. It was easier than telling him my change of heart wasn't because I thought of myself as being one of them. It was my job as reaper to protect and provide for the souls of my clients. With the death portent appearing for every one of them, that made them my responsibility, even though they didn't reside in Easton.

I slid the cell door open and stepped through the opening, listening for any indication the guards Cade had left behind were on their way to investigate the noise I'd made. Rhonda and Connor followed closely behind me as I ventured to the main door and peeked out.

No one was visible on the steps leading into the temple, and the area in front of it was also clear. I focused my eyes, letting my sight shift into the astral plane to make sure no one was lurking nearby, feeling for the presence of souls. All was still and silent.

'We good to go?' Talaom appeared at my side along with a woman with red-rimmed eyes. With long dark hair and eyes, and a marked resemblance to the body Talaom now resided in, this would have to be Talaom's sister.

Blane's mother.

My heart ached, unable to comprehend how hard it must be for her to see her son's body walking around and know his soul was no longer in it. She flinched when Talaom reached out to touch her arm, moving back a step. I looked away from the anguished expression on his face at the rejection. I peered over the multitude of people waiting on my say so before they left the temple.

'I can't sense any guards, but we need to keep an eye out in case they're still around.' I chanced a look at Talaom, relieved to see he had managed to mask his pain. 'How long ago did the death portents appear?'

'They were already apparent when I got tossed in here.'

I blanched. 'How long ago was that?' I had no idea how long I'd been unconscious, hoping it had been mere minutes.

'Twelve hours ago.'

'Shit. We need to move fast. What's the quickest way to get to the tower?'

'Fly.'

'That is not helping. You get twenty-four hours from the time the portent appears until the time of death. Half that time has gone already, and we have no way of knowing how much time passed before the first one appeared and you got here. This city is on the verge of collapse. We need to get to the tower now.'

Talaom's nostrils flared. 'The earthquakes are bad, but none of them has been strong enough to destroy the city.'

'That's not true,' said a quiet voice.

I turned to the woman accompanying Talaom. 'What do you mean?'

'We've never had more than one a day before. Elder Abanos said soon there will be one massive quake, and when it hits, Angellin will be no more.'

'Let's not be here when that happens,' said Connor.

A rumble signalled the approach of another earthquake, this one lasting twice as long as any of the others I'd experienced so far. 'We need to move,' I said to Talaom.

He shouted out orders to the Davilians and they attempted to flee the temple en masse. Several people stumbled or were knocked to the ground as the crowd swept outside. Talaom waded in among them, pulling those who had fallen to their feet. He was then knocked to the ground himself, and I lost sight of him in the crush of people. I dived towards the last spot I'd seen him.

Rhonda grabbed my arm, pulling me into the open. 'We need you more than we need him. You're the only one who can stop the nether from destroying the city.'

I pulled my arm free, only to have Connor grab the other one. 'Mum's right. These people are counting on you. We're counting on you. I'll take care of Talaom. Mum will get you to the tower.'

Before Rhonda could protest he threw himself into the crush of people. White-faced, lips a thin line, she clutched my arm and dragged me along with her, following the flood of Davilians heading for a wide set of stairs leading up to the next level.

There was no time to talk as we tackled the first set of stairs, struggling to outpace the earthquakes as they rose higher and higher in the ground beneath the city. The sounds of rock cracking below us was swiftly followed by cries of alarm, but we didn't dare stop to see what damage had been inflicted on people or Angellin. We reached the next level and sped to the closest set of stairs.

Thighs burning, lungs screaming, I forced my legs to keep pumping, head down, eyes on the legs of the person in front of me. I couldn't afford to think about what might be happening to Connor or Talaom; I had to block out the screams coming from below after each earthquake.

The rumble of breaking earth and rock appeared almost continuous now, the gaps between each quake shrinking to mere seconds. Nether writhed in the air around me, thickening, stretching its slimy tentacles over every inch of the city. I didn't know what was worse, the physical abuse my body was undergoing, or the gut-wrenching nausea at being surrounded by so much uncontrolled nether. It felt as if someone had their hand down my throat and was trying to tear my stomach out.

I had no breath to spare to scream as I started to climb to the next level. Rhonda kept pace with me, breath coming in gasps that sounded more like sobs. I lost track of time, consumed by the need to keep going, sweat blinding me, hair sticking to my face. I knew if I stopped, took even a second to catch my breath, my muscles would freeze up and I'd be unable to take another step.

The person directly in front of me came to a halt and I careened into them, knocking both of us to the ground. I rolled onto my back, groaning.

I couldn't do it. Couldn't move.

I couldn't save anyone, let alone myself.

CHAPTER 27

'Get up, Tyler. On your feet.'

Talaom loomed over me, looking even worse than I felt. Blood dribbled down his left temple, the eye on that side swollen and bloodshot. Connor leaned past him, gripped my upper arms and pulled me upright.

Fire flared through my body with each movement but I persevered, finally reaching the opening to a huge square. Vision bleary, I searched for the next set of stairs to ascend.

Elation rose within me. We'd reached the highest level. The tower dominated the square.

We'd done it.

Now all I had to do was somehow persuade an entire clan to put aside centuries of hatred to create enough positive energy to refuel the aether that was the only thing keeping the city together.

I stumbled forward, freezing when I spotted the men ringing the base of the tower. A dozen Tr'lirians had their white wings spread wide, feet firmly planted and swords in hand as they faced us.

To reach the aether, to feed it the energy I was going to harness from the Davilians, I needed to be touching the tower that was the city's anchor. The Davilians outnumbered the Goddens, but they were unarmed, half-starved, and exhausted from the punishing climb. They would be no match against a fresh foe who could take to the skies at will and were armed with swords.

I couldn't afford to waste any of the aether wreathing the tower. I would need every scrap of it to have any chance of saving Angellin. That left one weapon at my disposal, and I prayed what I was about to attempt would work.

I stretched out my senses, searching for their souls.

There.

They were fainter than the songs of the souls of the newly mortal Davilians crowded around the square, but there, nonetheless. And if I could hear them, I should be able to call them.

I'd never reaped more than one soul at a time; had never contemplated taking the lives of twelve people in one reaping. But my intention was not to kill them. I just needed to get them away from the tower.

I focused on the song of each individual soul, weaving them together in my head until I had one thread, its beat in time with my heart's rhythm. I gave a tug, exhilaration filling me when their souls answered. The souls slipped free with ease, silvery ropes of light connecting them to the bodies.

Cade's men, faces grey, dropped their swords to clutch their chests, falling to their knees. Agonised groans filled the air, making me wince. Their wings shook, some of their feathers falling out and drifting to the ground, but I didn't let go of their souls. Not yet.

Forbidden ecstasy hovered just out of reach, tempting me with unimaginable fulfilment. All I had to do was complete the transition, sever the souls' connections to their bodies and I would ride out the destruction of Angellin on a sea of bliss.

With a shudder, I released the souls and watched as they sank back into their bodies.

One by one, Cade's rear guard dragged themselves to their feet, fear warring with hate in their eyes. I could imagine the thoughts running wild through their heads. They were immortal, and thought themselves to be untouchable. I'd just shown them how false that illusion of safety was, at least where I was concerned.

One of them scooped up his sword and took several steps towards me before he thought better of the action. He stopped; sword tip pointed at me. 'You will die with the rest of the Davilian scum, reaper.' He waved the sword in a wide arc. 'You are all going to die.'

He lifted into the air, swiftly followed by the others. Within seconds their wings had taken them to the top of the tower. One by one they disappeared from sight, shifting from this plane to the next.

I turned around to get the Davilians into position and found Talaom staring at me. My cheeks flushed at the awestruck expression on his face.

'What are you?' he asked. 'Not even Grimm could take the soul of a winged Tr'lirian. I know this to be true. I saw him try and fail on Almorthanos's orders.'

'Now is not the time.' I said, my words punctuated with a deafening rumble deep below us. The pavers shifted under my feet, making it hard to stay upright. Loud cracks rent the air as the buildings ringing the square shuddered from the force of the earthquake.

Shouts of alarm from behind Talaom had him whirling around. I looked over his shoulder and gasped when I saw the nether mist had crept to the edge of the stairs and begun encroaching on the edge of the square. Talaom turned back to face me, a grim set to his features.

'Get to the tower. I'll get everyone into position.'

I ran, urgency washing away the pain and exhaustion racking my body. I placed my hands flat on the cool, smooth surface of the tower, sighing as the familiar tingle of pure aether wrapped around me, soothing my jangled nerves. Hands grasped my shoulders and I looked back to see Rhonda and Connor were on either side of me. I gave them what I hoped was a reassuring smile as more and more people lined up around them. Soon the tower was surrounded by Davilians, all of them touching the person in front of them, forming a human chain that allowed them to join the connection between me and the tower.

I closed my eyes and concentrated on the aether wreathing the tower, searching for its heartbeat and synchronising mine to it. When I was one with the aether, submerged in its song, I called out in a voice amplified so it reached everyone's ears.

'I need you to close your eyes and let go of every negative thought you have ever had. I need you to picture Angellin as it once was, before the war with Clan Godden, back when the city was vibrant and alive, filled with aether. Picture it in your minds and your hearts. Let love flow back into the streets to wash away your pain and grief. If you want to rebuild your home you have to rebuild your spirits first.'

Slowly, as centuries of war fought to erode the positive message I was broadcasting, images appeared in my mind. Memories from when the Davilians first came to Angellin, a sluggish trickle becoming a flood as I sent each image I received to everyone I was in contact with. As their hearts opened to each lilting note of the symphony sung by their souls I felt the aether respond, strengthening, expanding.

Rhonda had not been exaggerating. Angellin had been breathtaking, a beautiful silver city in the clouds, shining its light over those who lived in it. I only hoped the aether created by the memories of its remaining inhabitants was enough to restore it. It swelled within me, building up until it saturated my pores. The tingle in my skin became a burning sensation as I struggled to hold on to my control. Pain erupted in my body, centred in my back, and I held back a scream at a tearing sensation along both shoulder blades.

Blackness hovered at the edge of my vision as the song the Davilians created with their souls reached a crescendo. I unleased the aether into the tower, screwing my eyes shut when a brilliant light flared beneath my hands. As bright as the sun, it sheared through my closed eyelids and brought tears in its wake.

The ground beneath my feet rocked. I fell to my knees, hands falling away from the tower. I heard thuds and groans from all around me as the Davilians also fell to the ground. I curled into a ball, head ducked into my chest, arms forming a shield to block out the cleansing light still being sent out by the tower.

It seemed an eternity before the light began to fade.

When it reached a level where it no longer brought tears to my closed eyes, I risked a quick peek around the square. Like me, most of the Davilians had formed a ball to protect their eyes, though some were sprawled out as if unconscious. I could no longer sense their thoughts, each soul once again singing its own song, the connection formed by the aether and the tower fading with the light.

People were slowly unrolling themselves and getting to their feet, eyes fixed in wonder on the tower behind me. I got to my feet and looked up at it, tears forming at the sight of so much pure aether. It pulsed and flowed with joyful abandon, turning the tower into a beacon of hope, its light spreading out to burn away the nether mist that had invaded the square.

I walked to the low wall bordering one side of the square, peering over the edge to watch as the light flowed down through the levels. In moments, it had banished the nether and the dark shadows it had created until only remnants of it remained on the lowest level where the temple was.

I felt a presence at my side and looked over to meet Rhonda's eyes.

'You did it. The city is restored.' Tears streamed down her cheeks. 'I didn't believe it was possible. But you did it anyway.'

'There is still nether down there,' said Connor, appearing on the other side of me and pointing down below us.

'No amount of aether can get rid of the darkness completely,' I said. 'It's part of nature. The Davilians are just going to have to make sure they maintain the balance between light and dark to stop the city being threatened again.'

'They will,' said Talaom. 'The elders will make sure no one forgets how close we came to losing the city for good. The temple and the nether that surrounds it will be a constant reminder for them.'

'We saved the city, and that's great,' said Connor, turning around to lean his back against the wall to look over the square. 'But we're still stuck here with no way of getting home. No offence, Mum, but this is not where I want to spend the rest of my life.'

'I'm afraid you have no choice,' said Rhonda. 'Without wings, none of us can leave.'

'I wouldn't be so sure about that,' said Talaom, looking at me with eyebrows raised and eyes wide.

'There's another way out of here?' I asked.

'No, I mean about not having wings.'

'Talaom, it could take years for any young to have their wings emerge,' said Rhonda. 'And years more for them to develop enough to be able to carry another person.'

'Wait, you mean your babies aren't born with wings?' I frowned.

Rhonda shook her head. 'They are born with nubs on their shoulder blades, and usually the wings begin to emerge once the young reach puberty. In rare circumstances the wings never develop, or can take twice as long. It is a rite of passage among our people when the first feathers begin to show.'

'Which is what appears to be happening to Tyler.'

'What?' I spun around and stared at Talaom. 'I don't have wings.' Astral ones, yes, but I certainly hadn't been born with nubs on my shoulder blades.

'Maybe not before, but you do now.' He grabbed hold of my shoulders and twisted me around. Then he grabbed my right hand and guided it to the top of my left shoulder blade, to the spot that had hurt when I'd unleased the aether I'd harnessed from the Davilians.

My fingers found a rip in my shirt and underneath it a hard ridge that had definitely not been there before. I pulled away from Talaom and checked the other side, only to find another rip and a hard ridge. I gulped as I traced the single feather that sprang out of my shoulder blade back at my touch. More and more feathers soon joined the first, and within seconds I was possessed of a full set of silver wings.

My head spun and I clutched the wall beside me when my legs threatened to collapse.

I had wings.

Real wings.

Not the ethereal ones of my astral form.

Oh my God.

CHAPTER 28

'That's impossible.' Rhonda backed away from me, eyes wide. 'Tyler has barely any Tr'lirian blood. She can't just grow a set of wings. Not even a full Tr'lirian's wings develop that fast.'

'Impossible or not, you can't deny she has wings.' A thread of awe laced through Talaom's words. 'Silver wings. Like those Ha'niel are said to possess.'

'Ha'niel are a myth. A children's tale,' said Rhonda, shaking her head.

I flexed the wings in question, curling them around so the tips were in front of me. I stared at them, mesmerised by the way the individual feathers sparkled in the light from the tower. It was an effort to drag my eyes away and focus on Rhonda's next words.

'Malia was obsessed with getting her wings back, searching the world for some kind of power to restore her immortality. I guess she really did find what she was seeking. Restoring the tower must have triggered what was left of the power she'd stored in her necklace.'

Talaom stepped closer, peering first at my wings and then at me. Finally, he shook his head. 'No, this did not come from

Malia. This is all Tyler's doing. I'm telling you; she is Ha'niel. It is the only answer that makes sense.'

'What is a Ha'niel?' I asked.

'It is the name given to those of us who ascend to a higher form of existence after a thousand years of contemplation and sacrifice. Their wings change colour to reflect the journey they have undertaken. Ha'niel are to be revered above all others, so it is said, though no Tr'lirian has ascended in living memory. Until now.'

I shook my head. 'No way. I can't be one of them. I haven't spent a day in contemplation, let alone a thousand years. And I'm only twenty-five.'

'And yet you have silver wings. You must be Ha'niel.' Talaom's assertion was threaded through with desperation.

I could see in his eyes how badly he wanted to believe I was Ha'niel. Perhaps even needed to believe. But I was no one special.

'It has to be the necklace; something I absorbed when it exploded. I should not have wings in the first place. I'm human. When I go back to Easton, how in the hell am I supposed to explain these?' I flexed my shoulders, expecting the wings to respond to the movement.

They vanished.

'What the hell? Where did they go?' Connor waved his hand over my head, meeting empty air.

'They're gone,' I said, a pang of disappointment lacing my words as I felt behind me and found nothing but a ripped shirt. As hard as it would be to explain why I suddenly had wings, my heart had thrilled at the idea of being able to fly for real.

I poked a finger through the rip on my left shoulder blade, frowning when I realised the hard ridges from where the wings had sprung were still there. I smoothed my fingers along it, stomach lurching when a feather once again appeared at my touch. More joined it and soon I had a set of silver wings back.

I spread them out to their full span, unable to contain a grin as with gentle sweeps they lifted me off the ground. I reluctantly stifled the urge to take off, to see just how far and how fast my wings could take me, and planted my feet firmly on the pavers of the square.

Talaom wore a shaky smile as he shook his head. 'I have never heard of anyone whose wings could appear or disappear. Whether you are Ha'niel or not, let's just hope they can be used to open the portal between Angellin and the physical plane.'

'What good are wings that could disappear at any moment?' Rhonda crossed her arms in front of her chest. 'No way am I letting her carry me back to Easton. What if her wings did their disappearing act mid-flight?'

'I don't think they will, not unless Tyler wants them to.' Talaom shrugged. 'I'm guessing, hoping, her wings respond to her wishes. She wants to fly, they appear. She wants to blend in with humans, they disappear. But there's only one way to find out if I'm right.'

I thought about it for a moment, about not wanting to have wings. Gasps from Rhonda and Connor let me know they'd disappeared before I put a hand back to test for myself. This time I didn't touch the ridge to see if the wings would reappear. Instead, I just thought about them returning, smiling when I immediately felt a rippling in the air behind me as the wings spread to their full span.

'Cool. Tyler has wings,' said Connor. 'She gets to return home. But what about the rest of us? The guys who carried us here were huge, and it took two of them to cart me around. Tyler's half my size. No way she'll be able to take off while carrying me.'

'I'm not that small.' I sent Connor a reproving look. 'And I'm stronger than I look. But I don't need muscles to carry you. I can use aether.'

I drew a thread of aether away from the tower, marvelling at the power it contained in its purest form, and wrapped it around

Connor's body. I lifted him in the air, laughing at the cry of shock he let out when his feet left the ground.

'I can easily take you and Rhonda home with me.'

'And me,' said Talaom. 'I'm coming too.'

I gently lowered Connor and stared at Talaom. 'I thought you'd want to stay here, to help your people rebuild.'

He glanced across the square to where his sister stood talking to the oldest Tr'lirian I had ever seen. Talaom shook his head. 'I'm a reminder of all Nadia has lost. Every time she sees me, she sees Blane. It is better for her if I'm not around.'

He forced a grin to his lips. 'Besides, you're going to need my help if you want to stop Cade becoming God.'

I stared at him for a long moment, reading the pain in his eyes, before I said, 'Okay.'

'You're not going to trust this guy, are you?' Connor asked. 'He killed you, and then he double-crossed you. Do you really want to give him the chance to do either of those things again?'

I gave a shrug. 'Trust him or not, he's right about me needing his help. He's a reaper. We can use him. Cade has had years to plan his takeover of Easton. If he really has infiltrated every aspect of government and law enforcement, we are going to be seriously outnumbered. Threatening to reap the souls of his people may be the only advantage we have.'

I shifted until I faced Talaom, hands on my hips. 'But there will be no more torture, revenge killings, or hurting innocent people. You only reap as a last resort, either to save your life or someone else's. If you step out of line I will make sure it is the last thing you ever do. Do you understand?'

Talaom was silent for a moment, gaze steady as he stared at me. 'And when Cade calls our bluff? What then?'

'We find another way.' I swallowed down the lump that appeared in my throat. Killian had already called my bluff. But no matter how outnumbered we were, I would not condone murder.

There had to be another way to resolve the coming conflict without killing. I just had to find it.

First though, I had to get back to Easton.

'Go say your goodbyes,' I said to Talaom. 'I'm going to make sure I can open the portal.'

I spread my wings wide and launched into the air, euphoria filling me at the sensations flooding my body. Flight, true flight, was incredible. Wind whipped my hair every which way, covering my eyes, and I happily let it. I felt so powerful, free. I revelled in the moment. This was so unlike flying in astral form. This was real, every sweep of my wings carrying me higher and higher, until I was at the top of the tower.

I ran my hands through the aether clinging to the spire at the very top, setting it ringing with a joyful tone that rang out through the sky. A shimmer appeared in the air above the spire and I could glimpse thunder clouds within it, a stark contrast to the cloudless blue skies I was currently suspended in.

The portal.

I had found the way home.

I returned to the square, hope brimming in my chest.

I could do this. I would take my family home to Easton and be reunited with Sam.

Then, together, we would find a way to stop Cade and free Chris and Rebecca.

Optimism kept me going as I created a cage out of aether and directed Rhonda, Connor and Talaom into it. Not even the sour look on Rhonda's face as she stepped inside could dampen my good spirits. While she might have doubts about my ability to transport them all safely to Easton, I knew I could do it.

Within seconds I approached the portal for the second time and slipped from one plane to the next, emerging in the astral plane to the north of Easton. The dark clouds I had glimpsed before were all around us, sheets of rain falling, and I kept us in the astral plane as I surveyed the land far below me.

Off to my left, I could just make out the compound, lights blazing to ward off the darkness of the storm raging around it. With luck, all of Cade's Tr'lirians were inside, keeping out of the elements, and there was no one to spot us as I flew towards home. Sam would be going out of his mind, with no idea where I was or what Cade had done to me. I had to find him, and reassure him I was okay.

I was so focused on going home, on getting to Sam, it wasn't until Rhonda called my name, her voice filled with alarm, that I looked down.

We were passing over the northern outskirts of Easton and the streets leading to the highway were filled with cars. But none of them was going anywhere.

A roadblock had been constructed across the highway heading north, two lines of pylons several feet apart. Between the pylons stood soldiers decked out in black uniforms, rifles at the ready as they surveyed the traffic waiting on either side of the roadblock, making it clear no one was getting in or out of Easton.

I flew higher, in case some of those soldiers were Tr'lirians who would be able to see into the astral plane. As I looked for landmarks that would lead me home, I saw hundreds more soldiers on foot, patrolling the streets and turning back any pedestrians or traffic they encountered. I didn't need to fly to the other side of town to realise Easton was now under martial law.

Cade had wasted no time in staking his claim.

Easton now belonged to him, and I feared freeing my hometown could be an impossible task.

CHAPTER 29

$\mathcal{S}$am's car was parked in the driveway of our house when I lowered the aether cage to the front lawn. I shifted us all back to the physical plane before releasing the aether.

Rain pelted me, big fat drops that made my silver feathers sparkle. I flexed my wings, amazed I felt no strain from the flight as I wished them away. Rhonda and the others were already heading for the front door. I raced after them, heartened by the glow from the lights blazing through the windows.

Sam had to be inside. I couldn't wait to see him, to wrap my arms around him and know I was well and truly home.

But no one answered when Connor knocked on the door.

I pushed past him and grasped the handle. It turned easily, setting my stomach churning. Sam would never leave the door unlocked. He was a cop, well aware of the many bad things that could happen in a town the size of Easton. I glanced at the keypad for the security system. It flashed green. Unarmed.

My unease grew. Something was seriously wrong.

Where was Sam?

If anything had happened to him…

I strode into the house, stifling the urge to call out his name as I began to search as quickly and quietly as I could.

The others followed my every move, clearly not wanting to be separated.

After checking each room, and finding nothing, we returned to stand in the middle of the lounge. I moved over to the kitchen counter and picked up the handset for the landline, ready to dial Sam's mobile.

Silence greeted me when I put the handset up to my ear. I looked over at the others. 'There's no dial tone. The lines are down.'

They stared back at me, matching expressions of concern on their faces. I heard a noise from the front door, which was still wide open.

A dark figure stood in the doorway, gun in hand. 'Freeze.'

'Sam?' I launched myself forward, tears of relief in my eyes as I hurried to the doorway and threw my arms around him. 'I thought something bad had happened to you. With the door unlocked and no sign of you... I'm so glad you're okay.'

His free arm wrapped around me, hugging me tight. 'I went next door, to check on Mrs Golinski. Was about to head home when you lot appeared on the front lawn.' He let go, gently moving me to one side. 'Got to take care of something,' he said, leaning down to kiss my forehead. 'Be right back.'

Sam stalked over to where Talaom stood watching him with an uneasy look in his eyes. His dark eyes were riveted on the gun still in Sam's hand, so he missed the fist that came from the right and socked him in the jaw. He dropped to his knees and Sam pressed the tip of the barrel into his left temple.

'Give me one good reason why I shouldn't pull the trigger.'

Talaom's gaze shot to me, a beseeching look in his eyes. 'Tyler–'

'Don't look to her for answers.' Sam gave him a hard shove with his free hand. 'I'm the one you should be worrying about.

You hurt her. You double-crossed her, and you hurt her. That's not something I'm inclined to forgive or forget, even if it appears as if Tyler has. She would never have brought you to our home if she wasn't willing to let the matter go.'

Sam twisted around to look at me, as if checking to see if I was going to interfere. I crossed my arms in front of me, waiting for him to make his next move. I trusted him wholeheartedly, sure he would not kill Talaom, but accepted his need to make his point clear to the Davilian.

He gave me a quick smile before returning his attention to Talaom. 'I'm guessing she thinks, given what we're up against, we need you. But I'm not so sure about that. So, what I need is for you to convince me you're worth it.'

'Or what, detective, you'll kill me? You're no more a murderer than Tyler is. You don't have it in you to execute anyone in cold blood.'

'After watching you hit Tyler, thinking for a moment you'd killed her, my blood is far from cold. Don't you ever doubt I would do whatever it took to protect her.'

'Okay, okay.' Talaom put both hands in the air in front of him, a placating expression on his face.

'I'm sorry. I did what I thought was right, but I was wrong. I know that now. I should never have betrayed Tyler, no matter what Cade was offering. I can't give you a reason not to kill me and be done with it. Any promise I make to you now is not going to hold weight. So, go ahead. Do it. Take me out of the equation and protect Tyler from any future dumb mistakes I might make. It's the only way you can be sure I won't betray her or hurt her ever again.'

For a long moment Sam stood there, gun pressed into Talaom's temple. I held my breath, conscious of the wary expressions on Rhonda and Connor's faces.

Finally, Sam holstered his gun and stepped away from Talaom. Quick strides brought him to my side. His lips met mine and I clung to him, letting his touch, the taste of him, soothe away the tension in my body. I was home, where I belonged, with Sam.

The world might be falling down around our ears, but as long as we were together it would be enough.

'Thank God you're okay. I've been having nightmares, thinking of what that arsehole Cade might be doing to you. I went to the station immediately after they threw me out of the compound, looking to get some backup and more firepower so I could storm the place and get you back. Got fired instead, along with a number of my colleagues. Looks as though my former boss is in the pay of those winged bastards, and she's been cleaning house to make sure anyone left is on their side. And she's not the only one. The mayor called in a private security team first thing this morning. They're basically a personal army made up of mercenaries. He declared martial law and got them to set up roadblocks at every access point in or out of Easton.'

'I know about the mayor and the superintendent. Cade told me. And we saw the mercenaries.' With help from the others, I started filling Sam in on what had happened since I'd last seen him.

'He wants to be proclaimed God, rule the whole world, and make us all bow down to him,' Rhonda said, a sour cast to her features.

Sam rubbed his chin. 'That may be his plan, but so far he appears to be playing it low key. I haven't seen or heard of anyone of the winged variety making an appearance since the shit hit the fan. The official announcement, being broadcast on all local television channels, is that Easton is under quarantine due to a potentially deadly bacterial outbreak. They've cut off any outside communications, including phone lines and the internet, and are advising people to stay indoors until the all clear is given.'

'Easton is his base of operations. He's making sure he has the entire town under control before branching out,' said Talaom.

'He doesn't want to panic the rest of the country before he's ready to seize control completely. That was Almorthanos's plan too, although it appears we had nowhere near the amount of pull Godden does. We were planning on our wings and immortality giving us the edge. Never thought to breed ourselves a sleeper army to do all the dirty work and undermine the current government from within.'

'Speaking of wings,' said Sam, turning to me, 'how come I could see yours when you lot landed on the front lawn? You've never been able to make yourself visible to me while in astral form before.'

'That's because I wasn't in astral form,' I said, a wide smile on my lips as I called my wings forth. 'These are the real deal.'

Sam, an incredulous smile on his face, slowly stretched out his hand and stroked the feathers on my right wing. I grinned back at him, somewhat distracted by the sensation rippling through my body when his caress moved up the edge of the wing to my shoulder blade. His touch was like a shiver, something I sensed more than felt, until his hand reached my skin. I let the wings return to wherever they went when not in use, laughing at his startled expression when they vanished.

'Hey, Sam, you got anything to drink?' Connor asked. 'It has been a hell of a long day, and Tyler growing wings is only half of it.'

Sam shook himself out of his daze and looked at Connor. 'There's scotch in the cupboard above the fridge. Knock yourself out.'

Connor happily took himself off to the kitchen, with Rhonda and Talaom close on his heels, giving Sam and me a welcome moment to ourselves.

Sam wasted no time in taking me in his arms, hugging me tight. 'Thought I'd lost you for good this time.'

'I'm not so easy to get rid of, especially with a few new tricks up my sleeve,' I said, making an effort to keep my voice light.

Without those new tricks, being able to call on the soul of an immortal Tr'lirian and manifest wings, I would not be standing in Sam's arms right now. I'd got lucky. We all had.

But luck was not enough to stop Cade.

He had to be stopped, or the people I cared about would never be safe.

'Cade thinks you're trapped in Angellin,' said Sam. 'You have the chance to walk away from all of this. With your wings, you'd be able to bypass his roadblocks and get far away from Easton, and live a normal life.'

'A normal life, huh?' I huffed out a laugh. 'I'm a reaper. That's about as far from normal as you can get.'

'True, but the option is there. You could even take your brother and his mother with you. Not sure how you managed to fly all the way from Angellin to Easton lugging them and that Talaom arsehole around, but you are obviously capable of carrying heavy loads. You could be far from here with no one the wiser.'

I stretched back until I could see his face. 'Leaving you behind, right? I know you, Detective Sam Lockwood. Fired or not, there is no way you are leaving town when you know people are in danger.'

'Sweetheart, I would give anything to be able to run off with you. But Cade knows me, and he knows I wouldn't be able to get out of Easton without help. I leave and he is bound to send people looking for me. I'm a loose end he can't afford to lose track of. You and the others, you're the ones with a real chance of escaping this mess.'

'I'm not going anywhere. I'm partly responsible for this mess, and I'm not leaving town until I fix it.'

'And how, exactly, are you planning on doing that?' Talaom asked from the doorway, a generous measure of scotch in the glass in his hand. 'I'm all for throwing my lot in with a lost cause, but I'm hoping you have something more planned than just you and me threatening to reap all the bad guys' souls.'

I grimaced, knowing his scepticism was warranted. We had no weapons, limited numbers and no plan.

Stopping Cade was going to take a miracle.

CHAPTER 30

'You know, returning to the scene of the crime is what gets most criminals caught,' said Sam, murmuring in my ear.

I shrugged. 'It's not as if we have a lot of options here. We need to free Chris and Rebecca. Not just for their sakes, but so they can't be used against us. Killian knows me too well. He knows I'd never do anything to jeopardise their safety.'

'Fair enough. Are you going to make another one of those aether baskets to carry us all to the compound so we can break them out?' Sam asked.

I squeezed his hand. 'I'd give anything to be able to take you with me, but to avoid being seen I have to travel through the astral plane. It's the only way I have any chance of getting close to Chris and Rebecca without being spotted.'

'Tyler's right,' said Rhonda. 'Being able to slip in and out of the astral plane is the only advantage she has. You'd just get in her way. Get her caught.'

To soften the blow Rhonda had just dealt him, I gave Sam a crooked grin. 'Besides, it will be much easier for one person to infiltrate the compound.'

'Make that two people doing the infiltrating,' said Talaom, putting his glass on the coffee table and squaring his shoulders as he faced us. 'I'll go with you.'

Sam stared at him, rubbing his chin, not saying a word.

Talaom straightened to his full height. 'Like it or not, detective, I'm the best backup she's got. I have full access to the astral plane and I can reap souls. The two of us can be in and out of there with minimum fuss and noise, and I'll do whatever it takes to make sure she returns to you.'

Sam still didn't respond, and Talaom shifted under the weight of his steady regard. Finally, Sam turned back to me. 'You do whatever it is you have to do, and then you get your arse back here. Got it?'

'Got it.' I leaned in for a quick goodbye kiss, nerves bubbling.

I had to sneak into a heavily guarded compound, find Chris and Rebecca, and spirit them out of there without attracting any attention. The only positive about what I was planning was that Cade and Killian had to assume I was dead. I had to act now, to take full advantage of the situation.

'While you're out rescuing Bradbury and his new girlfriend, I'll see what kind of support I can drum up. Cade's Tr'lirians can't have taken over everything. A buddy of mine is the vice president at the Easton Shooters' Club. He's ex-army and knows a thing or two about urban warfare.'

I winced. 'Not sure I like the idea of civilians running around the streets with guns. That has the potential to make this situation even messier.'

'If Cade doesn't give up on his plan to be God, messy will be an understatement. But I'm not looking to start a war. I just want to be prepared, to have a fall-back position, if we can't come up with a way to neutralise the threat Cade and his goons pose.'

'How are you going to persuade your friend to help you without telling him the truth?' Connor asked. 'The more people who find out about the Tr'lirians, the harder this will be to contain. Once word spreads that winged people are living among us, that's going to set off a panic for sure.'

Rhonda shuddered. 'I've seen firsthand what humans can do when they're riled up about something. Malia took advantage of mob mentality to set her followers on to Liren, and we all know how well that turned out.'

'Relax,' said Sam. 'I'll think of something. Trevor's a good guy. Steady. I'll tell him enough to get him on side without revealing the entirety of the shit storm about to rain down on Easton.'

I heaved a sigh. 'All right then. But be careful. There is no way to tell who is a Tr'lirian supporter and who isn't.'

'Rhonda and Connor can come with me. She can be my Tr'lirian detector, and he can be my backup.'

I gazed at Sam, wishing I could ask him to stay at home and wait for me to return instead of putting himself in potential danger. But that would be just as effectual as him asking me to do the same thing. Besides, his inability to sit back and let bad things happen was one of the reasons I'd fallen in love with him.

'We should get going,' said Talaom. 'The longer we wait there's more chance of Godden finding out we're still alive and that Angellin wasn't destroyed.' His brow furrowed. 'Our people are defenceless; weak. If Godden finds out they survived, he will not hesitate to ensure the complete destruction of our clan.'

'Okay.' I moved into the middle of the lounge, calling on aether as I prepared to wrap it around Talaom so I could carry him to the compound.

He moved towards me, stopping after a few steps. He frowned, a hand hovering over his chest. 'Someone is dying.'

'What?' I placed a hand over the hollow below my throat, feeling nothing but warm skin. 'Are you sure?'

Talaom's eyes went wide. 'Don't you feel it?'

I shook my head and dropped my hand, heart pounding.

'What is it? What's happening?' Rhonda's head swung from one of us to the other, voice rising.

'Talaom is getting the call to reap a soul.'

'And you're not getting the same call,' said Sam. 'But you're the reaper for Easton. Not him.' Suspicion riddled his words, eyes narrowed as he glared at Talaom, clearly suspecting a trap of some sort.

I nibbled at my bottom lip, unsure what to do. I stepped closer to Talaom, acting on instinct to place my hand on his collar bone. I closed my eyes, concentrating on his heartbeat, syncing mine to it.

There. Faint, but unmistakable, the call of a soul to be reaped. I opened my eyes and stepped back. 'It's real. He has to reap a soul.'

'But you don't.'

I met Sam's eyes, aware mine would be brimming with doubt and confusion. 'No. This is not my soul to reap, and I have no idea why.'

Talaom grimaced, a groan escaping his gritted teeth. 'I can't ignore this much longer. The cold…it's getting worse.'

I gave a sharp nod, well aware of how intense the cold could become when a reaper attempted to hold off on the need to reap. 'I'll come with you.'

Sam opened his mouth to say something and I cut him off. 'I have to do this. I have to know why he is called to reap and not me.'

Sam stalked over to Talaom, a hard glint in his hazel eyes. 'Anything happens to her…You know what happens next.'

Talaom gave him a pained smile. 'Got it.'

I put a hand on Talaom's arm. 'Let's go.'

'I can't go like this,' he said, waving a hand over his body. 'I need to be in astral form.'

'Fine. You lead. I'll follow.' I summoned my wings as he took a seat on the couch, Connor and Rhonda jumping up to give him room to stretch out. Within seconds his astral form hovered in the air in front of me.

I quickly slipped into the astral plane and followed Talaom as he led the way up and through the ceiling, questions hammering at me. Why hadn't I felt the call to reap? I was the assigned reaper for Easton. Talaom an interloper here by happenstance. But he had been called, and not me.

I'd been able to establish the validity of the call to reap when I'd touched him, but just because someone was dying didn't mean I wasn't flying into a trap.

The storm had passed while we'd made plans. But the clearing skies did nothing to cheer me up.

My misgivings grew as Talaom flew ahead of me, heading for the northern outskirts of Easton, the direction of travel on the same trajectory as Killian's compound. The ball of dread in my stomach grew heavier, uncomfortably so, as it became clear we were headed to the compound.

Talaom's flight was unwavering, with no attempt at evasion or concealment as he flew over the heavily guarded gate. Instead of heading into the main building, his path veered to the left, around to the back of the building. He reached the back corner and halted, though his astral form writhed as he held himself back from the reaping.

I flew to a stop a short way behind him, calling on aether as I prepared for an ambush. Nothing happened, other than for Talaom's astral form to writhe with increased agitation. He appeared poised to fly forward, yet was holding himself back, the effort to do so taking an extreme effort.

I edged closer, still not sure if this was a trap or not, and peeked over his shoulder.

I swallowed down a gasp at what I saw.

ade stood in the middle of a concreted parade ground, a blood-splattered sword in his hands, with hundreds of stone-faced Tr'lirians lined up in rows facing him. Killian stood on his left, while Chris had his arms wrapped around Rebecca on the right. Tear streaks were visible on Rebecca's cheeks as she sheltered in Chris's embrace.

Twelve men kneeled on the ground directly in front of Cade, one of them with blood pouring from gashes on his bare back where his wings had recently been cut away. His white wings, now splattered in blood, lay discarded on the ground between him and Cade. The men on either side of him still had their wings, but they were patchy, with more feathers falling out to drift lazily to the ground even as I watched.

I held back a cry when I saw their faces. They were the ones who had barred my path to Angellin's aether-wreathed tower. I had called on their souls, causing them to flee through the portal. The one whose wings had been cut from his body was the one who jeered at me before he left, taunting me with the news I would die along with the city and all of the Davilians.

'For dereliction of duty and deserting your post, you are

hereby sentenced to death,' said Cade in a clear and considered tone, showing no pity or remorse as he pronounced his sentence.

The words were barely out of his mouth before he casually ran his sword through the chest of the wingless Tr'lirian. I dug my nails into my palms, frozen in place as I watched the body topple sideways. As if from a distance I heard Rebecca scream. The body hit the ground with a sickening thud. I finally felt the call of the dead Tr'lirian's soul, but I couldn't risk moving forward to collect it even as the chill below my collarbone intensified.

For Talaom it must have been ten times worse, having felt the call for so much longer. His astral form shuddered and he moved forward, obviously intending to go and reap the soul.

Tr'lirians could see into the astral plane.

Cade would be able to see him.

He would know he had not been killed in Angellin.

If he realised the city had not been destroyed, the lives of all the Davilians I had recently saved would be put in jeopardy again. I couldn't allow that to happen.

I used a thread of aether to tether Talaom's astral form in place. Once he was secure, I reached out for the soul of the man Cade had just executed. I called the soul out of his body. It hovered in the air above Cade, the light blazing out of it a mix of black and silver. He stared at it for a long second, before deliberately turning his back on it. Though disgusted by his lack of respect for the dead, I ignored him as I used aether to guide the soul higher into the air.

I was heartened to see many of the formerly stone-faced Tr'lirians broke ranks to crane their necks and watch the soul of their former comrade as it ascended into the sky above them. I whipped it towards the north before pulling it in a circle around the compound and out of sight of the watching Tr'lirians.

Talaom's agitation was worsening when I finally pulled the soul around the last corner and let it settle in front of him. He stretched out a hand, astral features racked with pain and concern.

'As soon as I touch it, I'll be drawn back to my body,' he said in a whisper. 'I won't be able to help you.'

'I know, but you need to do this. Your client is waiting.' And it was his client. Not mine. Although I could now feel the draw of the soul, everything that had taken place told me this was Talaom's responsibility.

I tugged the soul the last few inches so it made contact with Talaom's hand. Light flared around us as it began the next stage of its journey. I released the bands of aether around Talaom and watched as the call of his body dragged him away from the compound.

Only then did I turn back to see what was happening on the parade ground, to see if any of them had noticed the flare of the soul being sent on to rebirth.

I need not have worried. All eyes were centred on Rebecca as she wrenched herself out of Chris's arms and strode up to Cade, violently slapping him across the face.

'Monster.' Her loud cry echoed in the hush following her actions. It was as if no one dared breathe.

Cade roared; bloody sword poised to strike her down.

Chris darted forward and grabbed Rebecca's arm, pulling her to safety a second before the sword would have cut her in half. Cade came after her again, bellowing in anger when Killian stepped in front of him.

'Cade, no, she didn't mean it.' Killian's handsome face was tight with worry, hands held out in entreaty as he begged for his daughter's life.

'How dare she strike me? I will have my vengeance.' Cade made as if to step around his second in command.

'There has been enough killing,' said Killian. 'We need to focus on what is important. We must solidify our position. It is only a matter of time before someone in the national media realises

Easton is in lockdown. We must ensure we have total control before that happens. Right now, the citizens are confused, scared, and malleable, but that won't last. They'll start asking questions, and resisting. It's their nature.'

'They will bow before me or they will die,' Cade said in a low growl.

'Granted, but subduing resistance will take time we cannot afford. Better to strike now, and make it impossible for any of them to organise.'

Cade's nostrils flared, but he lowered his sword. 'Very well. Get the men ready to fly. We take Easton in one hour.' He bent down and wiped his bloody sword on the dead Tr'lirian's pants. 'And get this mess cleaned up.'

Without another word, he sheathed his sword and launched himself into the sky.

I took the first breath in a long time as I watched Chris usher Rebecca towards the compound, shadowed by four hulking Tr'lirians. I wanted to go to them, whisk them away to safety, but had no hope of making a clean getaway with so many of the enemy in attendance.

I watched in silence as Killian dismissed the bulk of his troops. Soon only he and the surviving members of the rear guard from Angellin remained. A deep frown furrowed Killian's brow as he leaned down to close the eyes of the Tr'lirian Cade had so casually run through. He bowed his head for a moment, before ordering the men still on their knees to remove their fallen brethren.

A hard lump settled in my throat as four of them picked up the dead man's wings, while the remaining seven contended with the body. Heads down, eyes averted even from each other, they shuffled off the parade ground with their grisly burdens.

Killian remained where he was, staring down at the pool of blood marring the ground in front of him.

I retracted my wings and stepped around the corner of the building, swiftly making my way to his side.

He gave no indication he was aware of my presence.

'The next blood to be spilled could be your daughter's. Is that what you want?'

He slowly turned to face me, a grim twist to his full lips. 'You're supposed to be dead.'

'Happy to disappoint,' I said with a tight smile. 'I'm here for Rebecca and Chris.'

His eyebrows arched. 'And, what, you think I'm going to just hand them over to you?'

'You will if you want your daughter to live. You can't protect her from Cade forever. He will kill her. You know he will.'

A dark bleakness settled in his deep blue gaze. 'She is safer with me than you. Once Cade finds out you're still alive, he will not rest until you lie dead at his feet. You should never have come back here, Tyler. I don't know how you managed to get this deep into the compound without being discovered, but your luck won't stretch much longer. You need to leave. Now.'

'I won't leave without them.'

He turned away. 'Then you will die here. There can be no other outcome.'

'Yes there can, if you help me. Cade is insane. You have to know that. Help me get Rebecca away from him. I'll make sure she's safe. She and Chris.'

For a brief moment, I thought he would say yes. I saw a lightening of his expression, the slightest hint of relaxation in his tense stance.

'Reaper.'

I spun around at the enraged shout, unable to stop myself taking a step back at the sight of Cade flying towards me at immense speed, dozens of Tr'lirians in the air behind him. Killian lunged and grabbed my arm.

'You should have left when you had the chance,' he said, digging his fingers into my forearm, expression tense.

A cold sweat erupted all over my body at the thought of being caught by Cade, fear fizzing in the pit of my stomach, a rush of acid making for my throat. I pushed it down, swallowing the bitter taste the bile left in my mouth. I would not let him take me.

I pushed at Killian with a wave of aether, calling on my wings as I did so. He released me instantly, eyes wide as he took in my silver wings. He fell to his knees, staring up at me, mouth hanging open.

Another roar from Cade dragged my attention away from the awe in Killian's gaze.

I spun around and launched myself into the air, powerful sweeps of my wings lifting me high and fast into the sky. But it wouldn't be enough. I'd barely had wings for half a day. Cade and his soldiers had been flying for generations. They could probably outmanoeuvre me in their sleep.

Not that I was ready to give up. I still had a few tricks in my arsenal.

I flung a blast of aether behind me, whipping up a whirlwind of power that would, I hoped, take care of some of my pursuers, or at the very least slow them down.

I held back the urge to scream, forcing myself to breathe evenly as I flew as fast as I could for Easton, brain racing to come up with a plan that didn't end with me being skewered on Cade's sword. I couldn't go home. That would only endanger Sam and the others. It would have to be the hockey grounds. With luck, they would be empty at this time of night and I'd have more of an idea of what the hell I was going to do once I got there.

I screamed when a sharp pain ripped through my left wing, just above the shoulder. I twisted in mid-air, right wing flapping furiously to stop me falling from the sky. Gritting my teeth, choking back another scream, I reached up and grabbed the knife jutting out from between the feathers. I wrenched it free, agony dropping me closer to the ground, blackness hovering around the edge of my vision.

No.

I was not going to pass out.

I fought the pain, refusing to give in to the dizziness threatening to swamp me with each sweep of my left wing. The wing still worked, but agony shot through my body with each movement. I had to land, but within seconds the sky above and below me was filled with Tr'lirians. Surrounded, I had no choice but to turn and face Cade.

CHAPTER 32

Cade gave a maniacal laugh, waving his sword in my face.

'I'm going to enjoy watching you die, reaper. You are a perversion that should never have been allowed to live.' He pointed the tip of his sword at my damaged wing. 'An abomination, parading yourself around with what only the most holy of our kind should ever possess. You are no Ha'niel to wear silver wings.'

For once, the thought of reaping an illegitimate soul did not trouble me as much as it normally would. It was him or me.

And I chose me.

I focused on the draw of his soul, calling it to me.

It responded, briefly, but I lost contact with it when I was jostled from the side, pain flaring through my damaged wing. I slipped lower in the sky, narrowly avoiding the outstretched sword of the Tr'lirian who had banged into me.

'Mine.' Cade swung his meaty fist, slamming it into the Tr'lirian's shoulder, forcing him away from me. 'I will be the one to kill her.'

He sneered at me, a fierce light in his eyes. 'I don't know how you managed to carry out this perversion, but rest assured I will pluck each and every accursed feather from your wings myself before I kill you.'

'It doesn't have to be this way.' I said, seeking to distract and delay him as I marshalled my energy to call on his soul again. And not just his. I had to call on those of the Tr'lirians surrounding me as well, to have any hope of surviving this encounter. 'I'm sorry my having silver wings upsets you. If you let me land, safely, I'll make them go away. I promise.'

'Every word that drips from your mouth is a lie. You may have fooled my son, but you will never get the better of me.'

I sucked in a deep breath. 'Then let's get to it.' I reached out my senses and latched on to his soul, spreading my net as wide as I could to catch the souls of the Tr'lirians arrayed around us both. I heard shocked cries as my power was felt but did not take my eyes off Cade.

His free hand clutched his chest, lips curled into a snarl. He lifted his sword, arm shaking with the effort it took to maintain his grip.

Cries of agony echoed in the air around me as I tugged on the souls, seeking to call them forth.

Too many.

I could feel them, slippery within my grasp, but was unable to yank them clear.

We hung in the air, Cade and I, as around us his soldiers fought to overcome the pain racking their bodies. It couldn't go on. I couldn't justify the torture I was inflicting on them. I had to release their souls, knowing the second I did so Cade would carry through on his threat to kill me.

But I had no choice.

My vision blurred, and I shook my head to clear it.

But the blur remained, a shimmer in the sky between Cade and me.

No. Not a blur.

A shimmery oval that undulated in the air, giving me a

glimpse of a black expanse filled with hundreds of sparkling stars.

I gulped down fear as I realised I was looking at the portal into the Underworld.

Cade didn't appear to see it. Killian had said the portal had been closed to them ever since the battle where I had destroyed Jonathon Grimm and freed the Grim Reaper from Almorthanos's taint. But I could see it, more clearly with each passing second.

So, did that mean the portal would open for me?

Even if it did, I would find no refuge in the Underworld.

The Grim Reaper had said he would kill me if ever I were to return.

Still, there was a chance I could slip through the portal and then get back to this side without him ever knowing I had been in the Underworld.

I was facing certain death here.

Fleeing to the Underworld might be my only chance.

I had to take it.

I called on every scrap of courage I possessed as I readied myself to release the souls I held. I flew closer to Cade, grimacing at the pain that tore through my left wing, ignoring the gleeful look in his eyes as I came almost within reach of his sword arm.

I had one shot at this.

I let go of the souls and lunged for the portal, praying it would open for me, dreading what would happen if it did.

Cade's outraged bellow followed me as I tumbled head over heels into the Underworld.

I held my breath and scanned the darkness surrounding me, senses alert for any sign my presence had been detected. I spun in a slow circle, seeing soul lights in every direction, bright and full of promise, songs muted. There was no sign of anything or anyone else.

I let my breath out slowly as I turned to face the portal, squinting to see through it to where Cade and his Tr'lirians searched the skies above Easton for me. They would have to give up eventually, and I would be able to slip back into the physical plane and have another go at freeing Chris and Rebecca. Killian was faltering in his belief in his clan leader. I could feel it. If I could just get him alone long enough I was sure he would agree to help me, for his daughter's sake if for no other reason.

It wouldn't be easy, sneaking back into the compound for a second time. But there had to be a way. Maybe I'd swing by home first, and grab Talaom to act as a decoy. He owed me that, for all the trouble and pain he had caused while following Almorthanos.

Minutes inched by, each one seemingly slower than the next, but eventually Cade and his soldiers began to fly off. I prepared myself to leave the Underworld.

I stretched my wings, grimacing at the pain in the injured one, and moved closer to the portal.

A cold, hard hand gripped my ankles, wrenching me backwards.

I screamed, frantically flapping my wings, uncaring of the pain as I fought to kick myself free. The grip on my ankles tightened, cold leaching into my skin.

I looked down, sure who had hold of me, desperate to deny the truth.

Flames shot out of the Grim Reaper's empty eye sockets as he stared up at me, his cloak billowing around him, revealing and then concealing his abnormally tall skeletal frame. The longer I looked at him the colder the air around me grew, until each breath felt like swallowing jagged shards of ice.

I opened my mouth to beg, to plead, to scream, when he swung me through the air.

Nether mist deadened my screams even as they erupted from my mouth. I was flung at dizzying speeds through the black sky of the Underworld, the souls awaiting rebirth shooting before me like a wave. The wave separated down the middle, leaving a dull black expanse between the two sides.

I careened into it and then stopped, spinning in the grip of the nether mist as all light around me was extinguished.

I felt ground beneath my feet seconds before a heavy weight pushed me to my knees.

A fierce wind whipped around me and I covered my eyes to shield them. The wind died away and when I opened my eyes the Grim Reaper stood before me; scythe raised in his skeletal hands.

'Abomination.' That single word, spoken in a chilling and cavernous voice, sent shudders racing through my limbs, freezing the protest barely formed on my lips.

'It is time to die.'

I could do nothing but watch as he swung the scythe at my neck.

The dark light wreathing the blade flared, blinding me. I screwed my eyes shut, tears leaking from the corners.

This was it.

The end.

CHAPTER 33

'What have you done?'

My eyes snapped open, widening when I saw the blade inches away from my neck. Even more disturbing was the way the dark light reached out to envelop me. No longer blinding in intensity, it had softened as it moved over me.

I did not risk moving anything but my eyes as the dark light flowed behind me. I shivered as it caressed my wings, its touch strangely soothing as it stroked the injury I'd sustained while fleeing Cade.

The Grim Reaper's gaze followed the movement of the dark light as it left my wings and returned to the blade of his scythe. He stretched out a skeletal hand, almost as if he wanted to touch my silver wings himself. The hand withdrew and he drew himself up to his full height.

'What is this trickery?' He shook the scythe in my face. 'Tell me how you did this. I command you.'

Still on my knees, I gazed up at him, not daring to shake my head in the face of his towering rage and with the scythe still so close. 'I don't know what you're talking about. What is it you think I've done?'

'You have the wings of an ascended being, but humans live too short a lifespan to achieve such greatness. It is a perversion for any but the true of heart to wear the silver. You would have had to positively affect the lives of millions of people to qualify for ascension. Not possible… unless–'

He lunged for me, gripping my chin in a punishing grip. He leaned in close, so close I could see all the different colours in the flames dancing in his eye sockets, yet strangely they gave off no heat. His head was so close to mine, my eyebrows should have been singed.

'Look at me,' he said. 'Show me your soul.'

Mesmerised by the dancing flames, I forgot to blink, forgot to breathe, as he held me immobile with his gaze. An eternity later he released my chin and stepped back.

'Your quota is fulfilled. You are no longer required to act as reaper for Easton.'

I stiffened. 'That's impossible. I have thousands of souls to reap before my contract is fulfilled. There's no way I've reached my quota.'

'And yet, this is what you have done. To be truthful, you have more than met your quota. You have exceeded it exponentially.'

'How?'

'This I do not know. All I can see is the mark left on your soul.'

'But I haven't reaped the souls of five hundred people, let alone thousands.'

'A reaper's duty involves more than just reaping souls and sending them on to rebirth. A reaper is responsible for the souls of every man, woman and child in their assigned domain. Something you have done in the time between when you were last in the Underworld and now has brightened the light of every soul in your care, along with many more.'

He waved his scythe and we were no longer in the void.

Instead we hovered beneath the canopy of stars representing the souls awaiting rebirth.

'Think, Tyler Morgan of Easton. What was it you did that prevented these souls from being extinguished?'

I bit down on my bottom lip, shaking my head. 'I don't know. The wings just appeared after I...' I gazed up at the souls shining so brightly above me. 'Angellin. I saved Angellin. Uncontrolled nether was destroying it, and I used pure aether to restore the city, to balance out the light and dark.'

I frowned as I thought it through. 'You're saying I fulfilled my soul quota by saving the lives of the Davilians trapped in Angellin? But there were barely three thousand. I killed over a dozen wraiths, incurring a thousand-soul penalty for each one. It doesn't balance out.'

'Your actions did not just save the Davilians. If Angellin had fallen, the effects would not have been contained to that plane. There would have been a cataclysmic chain reaction, and Easton would have borne the brunt of the storm as the higher plane collapsed. It would have been engulfed within hours. Aftershocks would beset the rest of the country, spreading all over the world, before the balance between the nether and the aether was restored. Millions would have died, if not for you.'

I shuddered to think how close to catastrophe we had all been. If Cade hadn't taken me to Angellin to lock me up with the Davilians, the city would have been destroyed. I choked down a hysterical giggle at the thought he had inadvertently played a part in saving the world.

It was so surreal it was hard to take it all in.

I looked at the Grim Reaper, wary though he appeared to no longer want to chop my head off with his scythe.

'What happens now? I mean, with me.'

'Your contract is fulfilled. You will no longer be called to reap the souls of Easton's dead.'

That explained why Talaom had felt the call for the Tr'lirian guard Cade had killed and I hadn't. Yet?

'But I'm still a reaper, aren't I?'

He nodded.

I thought about it for a moment. 'Chris Bradbury. He fulfilled his quota, but he was no longer a reaper when he was brought back to life. Why am I different?'

He waved a hand at my wings. 'You need to ask?'

A fleeting smile curved my lips before I got back to business. 'What about Talaom? He's the dark reaper who was resurrected in a new body, like I was.'

'The abomination must die. You must kill him when you return to the physical plane.'

I shook my head. 'There has been enough killing. I won't do it.'

He went so still I thought I had pushed my luck too far. After a long and tense moment, when I was sure he was going to punish me for refusing to obey him, he said, 'You are no longer mine to command, but never forget I am the Grim Reaper. I decide the fate of my reapers. You may have ascended to the silver, but you are still an abomination.'

'You're right. I shouldn't be alive, and neither should Talaom. But if we didn't exist, if we weren't abominations, Angellin would have fallen and millions of innocent souls would have died, never to be reborn. That has to count for something.'

'Very well. If your abomination continues to act as reaper for Easton, as penance for his crimes, I will allow him to live.'

'Okay, that's great. He'll do it.' I let out my breath in a rush of relief.

'He must understand only death will free him. Only then, if he has fulfilled his duty as reaper, will I allow his soul to be sent on to rebirth once his mortal body dies. If not, I will rip his soul to shreds myself.'

I nodded fervently. 'Understood. I'll tell him.'

'Go now. And, Tyler, understand this is the last time I will allow you to take refuge in the Underworld. You do not belong here. You belong with them.' He pointed at the canopy of souls. 'The duty of those who wear the silver is perhaps even more onerous than that of a reaper. Do not fail them.'

I had no chance to respond. A great wind swept me up and threw me towards the souls, forcing me towards the barrier between the Underworld and the physical plane.

Just when I thought I was going to slam into the inky barrier, a shimmering portal appeared and I slipped through, blinking against the sudden brightness of day.

How long had I been in the Underworld?

I cast about me for signs of Cade or his Tr'lirians but the skies were empty.

Time to head home, tell Talaom about his new role, and come up with a plan to save the people of Easton from Cade.

The Grim Reaper was right. The weight of obligation I felt to the living was far heavier than what I felt when I'd only been responsible for the dead.

I could only hope I'd be able to fulfil my obligation without any more people dying, but as I scanned the street below me, a sense of doom threatened to bring me down.

Fires burned all over the city, smoke obscuring the sky. Yet despite this I could hear no sirens, see no fire engines or other emergency services vehicles. Instead it was a sea of black as the mercenaries tramped the streets, menacing the locals. All while white winged soldiers hovered above in the astral plane, supervising the organised chaos.

Cade's invasion was underway.

CHAPTER 34

I landed on my front lawn, and received my second shock in as many minutes.

Killian stood at the front door, with Chris and Rebecca a step behind him. They turned at my gasp, all three sets of eyes going wide as I retracted my wings.

Wary, I scanned the astral plane, searching for anything amiss. Was this a trap, or had my impassioned plea to Killian been heard? I could see nothing to alarm me, with the exception of my unexpected visitors.

Killian slipped between the others and marched toward me. I stiffened, still not convinced I wasn't being set up somehow. I was in no way prepared for what happened next.

He halted a short distance from me and smoothly went down on one knee, head bowed. 'Forgive me, Ha'niel, if I had known what you truly are I would never had gone against your wishes. I will accept whatever punishment you deem fit.'

'What the hell?'

My thoughts echoed the explosive comment from Chris.

I hurried forward and latched on to Killian's arm. 'Get up.'

He resisted my efforts to pull him to his feet, but did raise his head to look at me, anguish in his deep blue gaze. 'I am not worthy to stand in your presence. I worked against you, refused to aid you in your quest to free my daughter and her fiancé.' His voice choked up. 'I almost got you killed. Cade told me you were injured, and passed through the barrier to the Underworld. I was sure the Grim Reaper would kill you, as he vowed to do if you ever returned to his domain.'

'Yeah, well, as you can see I am totally fine.' Better than before I entered the Underworld, in fact. I called on my wings and gave them a shimmy, relishing in the feel of them, whole once more after whatever the dark light of the Grim Reaper's scythe had done to the left one.

Killian took in my wings, a sick expression crossing his features before he prostrated himself with a low moan. 'Please, kill me. I deserve to die for what I have done to you.'

'Okay, that's it. I've had enough bullshit to deal with these last couple of days. You do not get to flake out on me, Professor Michael Killian.' I sent my wings away and smacked his bowed head. 'On your feet, soldier. Now.'

He scurried to do my bidding, though he kept his eyes downcast once he stood.

'I get that the idea of me being a Ha'niel means a great deal to you, but it's not true. My having silver wings has nothing to do with any Tr'lirian heritage, or a thousand years of contemplation and sacrifice. Okay?'

When he still refused to lift his eyes, I gripped his chin with both hands and wrenched his head up. 'Look at me, and listen to what I am telling you. This is a reaper thing. I fulfilled my soul quota in a big way, preventing what the Grim Reaper called a cataclysmic chain reaction. In doing so I ascended to a higher level of existence. That's why I now have a real set of wings. Not because I'm some mythical Tr'lirian.'

Killian's eyes widened as he listened. He gave himself a shake, and then brushed my hands away as he took a step back. 'You are not Ha'niel?'

'I'm afraid not,' I said. I flicked a glance to where Chris and Rebecca stood, watching on silently. 'But I'm not sorry if you thinking I was one made you see reason where Cade is concerned. I'm also thinking you believing me to be a Ha'niel isn't the only reason you brought them here.'

Killian stared down at me, brow furrowed. 'You're right. Cade's quest for revenge against Clan Davila these last centuries has clouded his judgement. Still, he is my clan leader, I owe him my obedience.'

'You don't owe him your daughter's life.'

He rubbed at his chin, composure firmly back in place. Though he avoided making eye contact with me or the others as he said, 'I need to get back there, before he finds out what I've done.'

He gave a deep sigh. 'If you are truly not Ha'niel, I can help you no longer.' Now he met my gaze. 'Keep my daughter safe. If anything happens to her, I will kill you.'

I grinned, glad to be back on familiar ground with him. 'Good to know.'

Without another word, he strode to the car parked at the kerb and climbed in. I didn't bother watching him drive away. I turned to Chris and Rebecca instead.

'Are you two okay? You look a little shell-shocked.'

'Honestly, I'm not sure how I'm feeling,' said Rebecca. She gave me a weary smile. 'After everything that has happened in the last twenty-four hours, all I want to do is curl up and forget the end of the world is coming.'

'You look wrecked. Let's get you inside so you can rest up.' I put my hand on her arm and guided her to the front door. I tried the handle. Locked. I peered through the window pane set in the centre of the door. The light was on in the front entrance, despite it now being daytime, and no one came to answer my knock.

'Don't think anyone is home,' said Chris. 'No one responded when Killian knocked earlier.'

I frowned. Sam and the others had been going to look up his friend from the local gun club. But that had been last night. They should have been back hours ago. And Talaom; he would have returned to his body once he'd reaped the soul of the Tr'lirian Cade had killed. Were they all out looking for me? When I failed to return soon after Talaom, Sam would have been worried. But surely Killian would have said something if Sam had come out to the compound looking for me.

I nibbled my bottom lip as I tried to think of where they might be. Perhaps they had returned to Rhonda's, or gone to one of the hotels. Regardless of where they were now, I needed to get Chris and Rebecca inside and out of sight before any of the mayor's hired mercenaries or Cade's people spotted us.

I contemplated the door in front of me. I had to get inside. I needed to find out where Sam and the others were. If something had happened to him...God, just the thought of him being in danger made me ill.

'Generally speaking, doors don't open just because you stare at them,' said Chris. 'I take it you left home without your keys. Want me to kick the door down?'

I let out an unladylike snort, his offer serving to release some of the tension running through my body. 'Thanks, but how about we leave that for Plan B.'

I let my wings return, ignoring the shocked gasps from my companions as I stepped into the astral plane, passing through the closed door with ease. Once inside, I returned to the physical plane, unlocked and opened the front door, and stepped aside so Chris and Rebecca could enter.

Chris's eyebrows were arched as he stepped over the threshold. 'Are you sure you're not one of those Ha'niel types Killian was all hot and bothered over?'

'Positive. I'm just your garden variety reaper, with a few

upgrades.' I smiled brightly, as my wings returned to wherever they stayed when I didn't need them.

He shook his head, blue gaze intent. 'Believe me, Tyler, there is nothing garden variety about you. You are one of a kind.'

Rebecca cleared her throat, a stiff look on her face. 'Hate to interrupt the lovefest, but do you have anything that will get this off? The stupid thing is stuck and I want it gone.' She held out her left hand.

I sucked in a breath at the sight of the huge diamond solitaire on her ring finger. 'Damn, that sure is a lot of bling.'

She grimaced, pulling her hand back and placing it against her midriff. 'Chris insisted I wear it to appease my father and Cade. But as we are no longer their captives there is no reason for me to continue to wear it.'

I looked over at Chris but he didn't say anything, and after an uncomfortable moment I said to Rebecca, 'I have something in the bathroom that might work. It's this way.'

I took two steps into the living room and stopped, gasping at the sight of Talaom stretched out on the couch, in the same position he'd been in when we'd left to go to the compound the night before.

'What is he doing here?' Chris's voice was hard, cold, no doubt remembering the last time he'd seen Talaom, when he'd betrayed us at the hockey hall.

'Is he dead?' Rebecca asked a moment later.

I hurried over to the couch and bent down to lay my hand on Talaom's chest. I closed my eyes as I followed the song of his soul. 'He's reaping.' I frowned, getting a sense of the soul he had been called for. No, not soul. Souls.

I stepped back. 'Dozens of people have died somewhere in Easton. He's reaping their souls.'

Chris's hand landed on my shoulder. He turned me around to face him. 'You can sense that from touching him?'

I nodded, and his eyes narrowed. 'He's the new reaper for Easton? How did that happen, and why is he here in your home?'

'It's a long story, one I will explain once he has returned from reaping.' I grimaced, wondering how Talaom would react to discovering he was going to be a reaper for the rest of his life. 'With that many souls to send on to rebirth, he's going to be gone a while.'

I gave Rebecca a smile. 'In the meantime, why don't we see if we can get that ring off?'

It was Chris's turn to grimace as I led Rebecca out of the lounge. For her part, she loosened up the second we were out of his sight. 'You have no idea how good it is going to feel to get this stupid rock off my finger. It makes me sick looking at it.'

I shot a glance at her over my shoulder. 'Are you kidding? The ring is gorgeous.'

'It's not the ring itself. It's what it represents. Being chained to Chris Bradbury against my will.' She gave a delicate shudder as we entered the bathroom.

I opened the bottom drawer and fished out the tube of industrial strength cleaner Sam used to get grease and oil off his hands after he'd been tinkering in the garage. I squeezed some on Rebecca's hand and watched as she worked it in around the ring.

'I thought the two of you were getting on now,' I said, leaning against the vanity.

'I was forced to go along with this bogus engagement, and play nice with him, to keep my head on my shoulders. Not by choice. That would never be my choice.'

I frowned, surprised by the vehemence in her voice. 'Don't you think you're being too hard on him? Why not give him a chance? You may be surprised by what you find.'

Rebecca didn't look up, too busy tugging on the ring. 'You clearly see some good in him, but all I see is a sycophant looking to curry favour. Not the type of guy I would be interested in.'

'Chris is definitely not a sycophant.'

She raised her head, lips pursed. 'He made a deal to marry me in return for being my father's right hand man. What is that called if not sucking up to the boss?'

'He didn't agree to marry you because of that. He did it to save me. To give me a second chance to live my life. It had nothing to do with wanting to get ahead in the new world order according to Cade. He didn't even know what Cade and Killian were planning.'

Rebecca stopped tugging on the ring. 'What are you talking about?'

'I know Chris told you how I died and ended up in my cousin's body. What he didn't tell you is that I couldn't handle it. I planned on dying, for good this time, as soon as I'd made sure those I loved were safe from Almorthanos and Malia. Chris knew this, so he made a deal with Killian to get my real body out of the Underworld. Marrying you and taking on the role of Cade's son was the price they demanded for doing so.'

Her eyes dipped. 'He agreed to sign his life over to Cade and my father, to keep you alive.' Her words were slow and measured. 'Yes.'

There was silence for a moment, before she said, 'Wow. He must really love you.' Her gaze met mine again, shock wreathed over her pretty features. 'But you ditched him for Sam. He gave up his freedom to get you your body back, and you let him do it and then walked off with another man. That must have broken his heart.' The shock in her eyes was replaced by pity. 'The poor man.'

'No. It wasn't like that. I didn't know about the deal until the other day. And Chris knew Sam was the man I loved, before he made the deal. He didn't make it so he and I could be together. He made it so I could be happy. The same way he agreed to Cade's demands so you can have a chance to be happy.'

Her eyes widened, and she shook her head. 'You think he has feelings for me, don't you? But that's crazy. You are the woman he loves. You're one of a kind, that's what he said not five minutes ago. I'm second best. A consolation prize.'

I gave her a gentle smile, realising where all her anger was coming from.

'Believe me, Chris wouldn't be signing his life over to Cade for someone he didn't care deeply about.'

'That's impossible. He just met me. Anyway, even if I did believe he had feelings for me, or I have feelings for him too, I couldn't do anything about it. That's exactly what my father and Cade want, a Tr'lirian dynasty with both their bloodlines. After everything they've done, the last thing I want to do is go along with their plans. All the manipulation, the threats, it's all so wrong. I won't condone that by giving them what they want.'

'What about what you want? You and Chris deserve the chance to be happy, on your own terms. If you truly do have feelings for each other, then there has to be a way for the two of you to be together that doesn't require you to sign your lives over to Cade and his plans for world domination.'

It felt strange to be using such words, but that was Cade's ultimate plan. Take over the world, one town at a time, starting with Easton.

Unless I came up with a way to stop him.

CHAPTER 35

Rebecca and I returned to the lounge area, and I quickly checked on Talaom. He was still sprawled out on the couch, reaping. A chill settled in the pit of my stomach at the thought of how many souls he was tending to. Relief he had been called to deal with them instead of me clashed with guilt for feeling that way. Even though the Grim Reaper said I was no longer required to act as reaper for Easton's dead, I still felt a measure of responsibility for them.

My hand hovered over his chest. I could follow him; follow the trail left in the aether by the dying souls. Help him. I glanced up, gazing at the canvas print on the wall above the couch. Sam and me, dressed to impress, for a charity ball.

I stepped away from the couch and looked over at Chris. 'We need to find Sam.'

Talaom would have to handle any reaping by himself for a while longer. My priority had to be the living.

'I wouldn't worry. Lockwood is probably at work,' said Chris. 'They're sure to have called in every available officer to help handle the current situation.'

'Sam was fired, along with every other police officer who isn't aligned in some way with Cade.' I filled him and Rebecca in on everything that had taken place since they'd been kidnapped at the hockey hall, including Talaom's involvement.

Chris ran his hands through his dark blond hair, shaking his head. 'Unbelievable. You single-handedly saved Angellin, and millions of lives. No wonder Killian was so willing to bend knee to you. He would have laid down his life for you, if you'd let him continue to believe you were a Ha'niel.'

I shifted, uncomfortable with the reminder. 'I'm not going to pretend to be something I'm not. And I wasn't alone in saving Angellin. It took all of the Davilians, with their positive memories, to restore the aether. I was just the channel they flowed through.'

'Why are you so sure it would be a pretence? What if you truly are a Ha'niel?' Rebecca asked.

Chris looked at Rebecca's left hand, and the ring that refused to budge despite the huge amount of hand cleaner she'd poured over it. A faint smile curved his lips as he said, 'That's a good question. Who's to say Killian's Ha'niel and the Grim Reaper's ascended being aren't the same thing?'

'I am not some mythical being. I'm just me.' I lifted my chin. 'Anyway, we've got more important things to worry about. Killian can't be the only one doubting Cade's decision. My God, the man executed one of his own men in front of them. He would have killed Rebecca if Killian hadn't stepped in. We don't have the manpower to go up against him on our own. We need to discredit him, and show his people he can't be trusted, that he will sacrifice every one of them in his pursuit of glory.'

'How are we supposed to do that? He controls everything. The police. The town council. The media. How can we counter that?'

'I don't know. But there has to be a way.' I moved over to the television and turned it on, grimacing when I flicked through all the channels and found only static.

I turned back to Chris. 'We need to get communications working again. Cade has cut Easton off, so he can solidify his position here before he branches out. If the state and federal governments knew what was happening, they'd send help. Cade can't have infiltrated the whole country.'

'I wouldn't be too sure about that. He's been planning this takeover for a long time.'

I shook my head. 'No, he wasn't prepared to move so soon. The rapid decline of Angellin caught him by surprise. He thought he had more time to make sure you and the other purpose-bred individuals were in positions of power. We can take advantage of that.'

'How?'

'When Talaom and I left here last night, to rescue the two of you, Sam was planning to visit a friend of his who is a member of the local gun club. He had Rhonda and Connor with him, and they were hoping to drum up support and weapons we can use to fight back. We find Sam, get the local gun owners organised, and take over the television station. If we can broadcast an S.O.S. to the state authorities, we can call in reinforcements and stop Cade before he gets too powerful.'

'I'd scratch that plan, if I were you.'

I spun around to see Talaom struggling into a seated position on the couch, one hand holding his head. 'Man, my head is pounding,' he said, his voice a rasp. 'Never knew being a reaper was such strenuous work.'

'Rebecca, can you grab a bottle of water from the fridge?' I asked, well aware of how the intense cold from being called to reap, not to mention being in the astral plane for an extended length of time, dried out the throat.

Talaom leaned back, head resting on the back of the couch, humour dancing in his dark gaze despite the gravity of the situation as he surveyed the three of us. 'Considering the number of times I have witnessed you achieve the impossible, I shouldn't be surprised you managed to free these two. But I've got to say, when you didn't return last night I thought you were dead for sure.'

He accepted the bottle of water from Rebecca and chugged down half of it in a few gulps.

Worry for Sam kept my smile brief as I said, 'I very nearly was dead. And I didn't free Chris and Rebecca. Killian did.'

Talaom choked on his next mouthful, water spraying over his hands as he coughed and spluttered. When he recovered, he stared up at me. 'Killian would never go against Cade. Never. It has to be a trick. Unless...' His eyes went wide. 'He saw your wings.'

'Damn straight he did. Kneeled down before her and everything,' said Chris. 'I'll bet if she hadn't told him she wasn't a Ha'niel, he would have done whatever she asked him to.'

Talaom's eyes narrowed. 'Bradbury is right. Killian is old school. If he believed you to be Ha'niel, he would lay down his life for you. I bet he'd even kill Cade if you commanded it.'

I shook my head vehemently, hating the thought of using someone's faith against them in that way. 'I would never command someone to kill another person. Never.'

'Not even if it would save the world?' Chris arched an eyebrow.

'Weren't you listening to a word Tyler said?' Rebecca rounded on him, hands at her hips. 'I've only know her a few days, and I already know she is not the kind of person to throw away someone's life like that. She would die herself before she would let anyone suffer because of her actions.'

'Believe me, sweetheart, I know exactly how self-sacrificing Tyler is. All I'm saying is it would be one way to end Cade's plans once and for all. Not that I believed for one second she would go for it.' He gave Rebecca an ironic smile. 'Still, Killian can't be the only Tr'lirian to hold so much faith in the idea of a Ha'niel.'

He looked over at me. 'If thinking you were one had such a

profound effect on Killian, imagine what it would do to the rest of Cade's soldiers. You could take away half his fighting force, all by standing up and letting yourself be seen. You wouldn't even have to say you were a Ha'niel. Just let them see your silver wings and come to their own conclusions.'

'He's right. The idea of a Ha'niel would be a powerful draw for any Tr'lirian,' said Talaom. 'Your very presence would sow doubt about the validity of Cade's rule in the hearts of most members of Clan Godden, especially the older ones.'

'No. I've already told you I won't pretend to be something I'm not.' I shook my head. 'To twist a person's faith like that, to lie to them about something that means so much. It's wrong, and I won't do it.'

'What if it's not a lie? I'm not exactly sure what a Ha'niel is, but I do know that you, Tyler Maree Morgan, are something special. Something this world has never seen before. I've been ready to lay down my life for you from the moment I laid eyes on you. If a Ha'niel means to any of the Tr'lirians half of what you mean to me, then I say we use that to our advantage.'

My eyes flicked to Rebecca during Chris's impassioned speech, heart aching to see her face blanch at his declaration and hurt brimming in her eyes.

'I said no.' I glared at Chris. 'We stick with my original plan, getting communication with the rest of the country back on line and calling for help.'

Talaom shook his head. 'Your boyfriend already tried that. Didn't work out so well.'

I sucked in a deep breath. 'Is he okay?' Oh God, was he one of the souls Talaom had just been reaping?

'He's fine, last time I saw him. If you count fine as being locked up with a hundred or so other people.'

I strode over to Talaom. 'What happened?'

'He went to visit his friend, as he planned, only to find himself in the middle of a raid. The cops have a list of every registered weapons holder in Easton, and they spent the last twenty-four hours confiscating as many guns and as much ammunition as they could. With phone lines cut, there was no way for members of the club to warn the others about what was happening until it was too late.'

Chris stepped forward. 'Surely they couldn't have got them all? In a town the size of Easton there would have to be hundreds, if not thousands, of registered gun owners.'

'Plenty of unregistered owners too, I'll bet,' I said, nibbling at my bottom lip.

Talaom nodded. 'That was the detective's thinking as well. He and his ex-army mate took off to see if they could find anyone who hadn't been raided yet. They sent Rhonda and her son back here to wait for us to return, to let you know what had happened. The plan was for everyone to regroup here before heading to the television station to get word out.'

He grimaced. 'When I returned without you, I had a hard time convincing your little brother I hadn't betrayed you again.' He rubbed at his jaw; a bruise visible from when Sam had hit him earlier. 'We fought until your stepmother stepped in and walloped the both of us. Then we settled in to wait for you and the detective to return.'

I resisted the urge to throttle him. 'We don't have time for this. What happened to Sam and the others?'

'Okay, okay. Long story short, I got called to reap again, and when I returned to my body I was alone. Nothing happened for hours until a short while ago when I got a call to reap so intense I thought for sure I'd be frozen for life. I've got to say, when I realised I was heading to the television station I was not thinking happy thoughts. Even less so when I saw half the building was on fire and a gun battle was going on in the car park. Seems your detective and his mate managed to round up a hundred or so pissed off gun owners and they were trying to break into the television station to broadcast that S.O.S. you were talking about.'

His voice lowered, gaze sombre, he said, 'The mercenaries the mayor hired to guard the place opened fire on them, shooting them down like...' He swallowed several times. 'They didn't stand a chance, not up against superior numbers, weapons and an enemy that did not hesitate to shoot to kill. Your detective did the only thing he could. He surrendered. Last I saw of him was as he and the other survivors were being shoved into the back of a couple of paddy wagons and driven away.'

He shrugged. 'I finished up reaping the souls of those who didn't make it, and came back here. Figured we were all done for, that maybe I should have stayed in Angellin, and then I saw you. What do you say, Tyler? You got another brilliant plan to save the day up those sleeves of yours? Because the way I see it, if you won't use your being a Ha'niel we are all royally screwed.'

CHAPTER 36

I moved away from Talaom and the others, needing time to think.

Sam was alive.

That single thought sang through my heart, drowning out everything else. He was alive, and it was up to me to make sure he stayed that way.

I turned back to Talaom. 'You said the television station was on fire. How much damage do you think was done?'

He let out a harsh laugh. 'Face it, Tyler, you can't get the message out. Cade's not stupid, and neither are his people. If there was a way for anyone to broadcast an S.O.S. they have shut it down. We're on our own.'

'All right then. It's up to us.' I glanced around the room, meeting their eyes one by one.

Rebecca gave me a watery smile when my gaze met hers last of all. 'What do you need us to do?'

'We have to track down Cade so I can finish this once and for all.'

Talaom gave a snort. 'Finding Cade is easy. He's set himself up at the showgrounds, surrounded by his loyal subjects.'

I narrowed my eyes. The Easton Showgrounds was a sprawling complex on the Southside. It boasted an enormous centre ring with covered grandstands all around, as well as over a dozen pavilions, and plenty of space for large numbers of exhibitors to camp out during the many events held there. The perfect place to set up a command post for Cade's forces.

I excused myself to go get changed out of my ripped shirt. I put on black jeans and a silver halter-neck top that would allow me to call my wings forth without causing further damage to my clothing. Not that I consciously planned to coordinate my top with my wings. It was the only item of clothing I owned that would suit, other than a skimpy black dress. That was not what I wanted to wear to a showdown with Cade.

'Okay then, let's get going,' I said as I stepped back into the lounge and scooped up my car keys.

The others crowded at my back as I headed to the internal door that led to the attached garage. I had no idea what I was going to do once I got to the showgrounds and confronted Cade. I only knew I had to do something. Chris, Rebecca and Talaom were close behind me as I stepped into the garage and unlocked my Corolla.

I pushed the button to open the garage door and handed the keys to Chris. 'You should drive, in case Talaom or I need to go astral.'

It felt strange to sit in the back seat of my own car, but considering Talaom was almost a foot taller than me it made sense to let him have the front passenger seat. It wasn't often my little car was made to carry four adults, but even with the front seats pushed back to accommodate the guys' long legs, Rebecca and I had plenty of room to move.

Chris backed out of the garage, and used the remote attached to the dash to close the roller door behind us before making his way onto the street.

Silence filled the car as he navigated his way towards the bridge. Ours was the only car on the road for the first few blocks. It was eerie to see the streets so empty, and it wasn't just the lack of traffic that made it so. There were no people out on the footpath, or visible in their front yards. Curtains flicked furtively in some of the houses we passed, the occupants drawn to the window to see who would dare to be on the streets after martial law had been called.

Three blocks from home, two blocks back from the bridge, a black van shot out of a side street and started following us. In less than a minute another van joined them. It crossed onto the other side of the road and accelerated until it was beside us, matching our speed. The windows were tinted, making it impossible to see who was inside, while they would have a clear view of the occupants of our car.

After a quick glance their way, I kept my gaze focused on the road ahead, stomach clenching as I tried to ignore our escort. For whatever reason, they made no attempt to halt or hinder our progress as we turned onto the main road and approached the bridge.

'Shit!' Chris's exclamation came a split second before he slammed on the brakes.

The seat belt gripped tightly across my body as I was flung forward, connecting with the still healing bruise from the car accident three nights ago. I screwed my eyes shut, pain driving the air from my lungs. The amount of cursing coming from my companions echoed my own thoughts.

When I could breathe again, I opened my eyes and felt like letting off a fresh round of cursing.

A roadblock stretched across all four lanes in the middle of the bridge. Mercenaries in black combat gear stood in a line in front of the roadblock, with what looked like automatic rifles in their hands. And all the weapons were pointed at us.

One of them stepped forward, a megaphone held up to his

mouth. 'Get out of the vehicle, and keep your hands where I can see them.'

Chris swivelled around to look me in the eye. 'Go,' he said. 'Get into the astral plane and go.'

I shook my head. 'I can't just leave you guys.'

'Yes, you can. You need to get to Cade. I can handle this lot.' He gave me a confident grin. 'I'm a Bradbury. I handle tougher situations than this on a daily basis. I'll have them eating out of my hand quicker than Talaom here could rip out their souls.'

I knew he was right in at least one respect. I couldn't stop Cade if I was being interrogated or imprisoned by the mercenaries under his command.

I gave a quick nod. 'Be careful. Don't get too cocky. Talaom might be able to reap souls and slip into the astral plane to avoid a bullet, but you and Rebecca can't.'

Rebecca laid a hand on my arm. 'We'll be fine. Go finish this.'

I sucked in a deep breath, and slipped into the astral plane, calling on my wings as I did so. I lifted up and out of the car, hovering in the air above it as the mercenary with the megaphone spoke again.

'You have three seconds to comply or we start shooting.' He held his free hand in the air, fist clenched, ready to give his men the order to fire. 'Three...two...'

Chris opened his door and slowly got out of the car, as Talaom and Rebecca did the same. I waited as the three of them put their hands in the air and moved to stand in front of the car, not ready to leave them in the hands of the mercenaries until I was sure they were going to be okay.

The mercenary frowned, lowering his hands as he stared at them. 'Where's the other one? There was another woman in the car with you.'

'You're mistaken,' said Chris, his voice light. 'There's no one else in the car.'

The mercenary raised one eyebrow, lips quirking. 'Really?

Then you won't mind if I do this.' He dropped the megaphone to the ground and pulled a gun out of the holster strapped to his right thigh. He aimed it at the car, grinning fiercely as some of his men grabbed hold of Chris and the others and pulled them away from the car. Then he opened fire.

The side of my beloved Corolla was peppered with bullets, most of them centred on the side I had been sitting.

'Okay, that's it.' No way was I leaving the others in this psycho's hands. I flew forward, returning to the physical plane as I came to a halt in the air in front of him. 'You owe me a new car.'

He stumbled backwards at my abrupt appearance, lifting his weapon and aiming it at me. I used a thread of aether to rip it out of his hands and send it flying over the side of the bridge, hearing a satisfying plop as it landed in the murky water below.

'What the hell?'

'Exactly. What the hell gives you the right to shoot my car?'

He regained his composure, glaring up at me. 'Listen, lady,' he said as his gaze slid over my wings, 'or whatever you are, I have full authority to enforce martial law on any and all citizens of Easton.'

I put my hands on my hips as I let my feet touch the ground. 'I don't care what authority you think you have. Martial law is over. I'm in charge now.'

His eyes narrowed. 'Just because you have wings doesn't make you boss. I answer to the mayor. You want to take charge; you need to take it up with him.'

I reached out and latched onto the song of his soul.

The colour leached from his face and he fell to his knees when I gave his soul a tug. 'Are you sure about that? Because, from where I'm standing, it looks as though I hold your life in my hands.'

A loud click sounded in my ear and I looked up to see another mercenary had come up beside us and was holding a gun to my head.

'Let him go,' the mercenary said, hard voice at odds with her surprisingly delicate features.

I smiled at her even as I used aether to form a barrier between us. 'He'll be dead before you can squeeze the trigger. And then you'll join him.' I let the smile slip from my lips as I used aether to augment my voice so all the mercenaries arrayed around us could hear my next words.

'It's over. This campaign, coup, whatever you want to call it, is done. You are going to pack up your gear and get the hell out of my town.' As I spoke I used the songs of their souls to weave a symphony in the air around me, linking them all together until they felt everything their commander did. As one, they fell to their knees, guns dropping from hands gone limp as their souls answered my call.

Faces pale, breath coming in gasps, horror welling in their eyes, they stared at me.

Sure my point had been made, I released my hold on their souls, though I kept in tune with the song they created in case any of them decided to do something stupid.

I looked to where their commander still kneeled at my feet, not at all fazed by the black look he was aiming at me. 'You have one hour to get your people out of Easton, or I will finish what I started here. Do you understand?'

'I'm not going anywhere, bitch. We're owed a lot of money for this operation.'

'Not my problem. You can't spend your money if you're dead.' I reached out and gave all their souls a little tug. Just enough to remind them what I could do. 'You need to make a choice. Your wallet. Or your life.'

'Screw this,' said the female mercenary beside me as she retrieved her weapon and holstered it. She turned to her commander. 'If you don't call the retreat, I will. We are not getting paid anywhere near enough to warrant going up against this shit.' She waved a hand at me. 'Let the winged freaks fight it out. We can send a bill to whoever wins for the rest of our money.'

She looked back at me, one eyebrow arched. 'One way or another, we will get our money.'

I smiled at her. 'Good luck with that.' I turned my back on her and walked over to where some of the mercenaries were guarding my friends. I didn't have to say a word. They took one look at their commander and backed off, hands well away from their weapons.

Within moments the roadblock was dismantled and they had piled into their black vans, leaving us standing beside my bullet-riddled Corolla. I stifled a pained sigh at the sight of it, and then deliberately turned away. I could deal with that later. I had far more important things to worry about.

CHAPTER 37

I heard the loud murmur of hundreds of voices as I neared the showgrounds, with Chris and the others suspended in an aether cage below me.

The noise level swelled the closer I got, using what little cover the surrounding buildings offered to hide our arrival. Soon there was nothing to obscure my view of the showgrounds, or to hide me from any of the Tr'lirians who cared to look my way. None of them were in the skies above the complex. I was able to exit the astral plane and land the cage on the empty road closest to the main entrance.

The gates were wide open; unguarded. I unravelled the aether cage, letting the remnants of it blow away as I retracted my wings and peered into the complex. Chris, Rebecca and Talaom joined me, all three of them casting suspicious glances around the area.

'They must all be in the centre ring,' I said.

Chris ran a hand through his hair. 'Sounds like that's where all the noise is coming from.'

'Where are the guards?' Talaom asked, a frown creasing his brow. 'They'd never leave it unattended. Something's wrong.'

'You think it's a trap.' I cast my senses forth, searching for any

232

souls in the vicinity. I could detect a large number of them, able to distinguish the difference between a human and a Tr'lirian by the way the souls called to me.

'Chris is right. They're in the centre ring. All of them.' I turned my head left, staring at the small pavilion nearest the entrance. 'But there are three humans in there.'

Talaom cocked his head, eyes slitted as he concentrated on the pavilion. 'Mercenaries?'

I shook my head, still staring at the pavilion. The large roller doors on the end and those along the side were all down, giving no clue as to who was inside. I sifted through all the sensations coming to me through the aether.

'No. There's something about them.' I closed my eyes to allow me to concentrate better, trying to separate the songs I could hear. One of them called to me, setting my heart racing at its familiarity.

'Sam.' My eyes snapped open and I set off at a run towards the pavilion. I reached the closest roller door, hunting for the way to open it.

A large padlock secured it to the ground. I wanted to tear the padlock off and wrench open the door, but I took a moment to focus on the other two souls I sensed were also in the pavilion with Sam. A relieved smile curved my lips and I formed a thread of aether to break the padlock open.

Before I could open the roller door, Chris grabbed my shoulder and pulled me back. 'You don't know who else is in there.'

'Yes I do,' I said, using aether to force the roller door up.

The interior of the pavilion was in darkness, filled with muted rustling noises. I stepped inside, allowing my eyes time to adjust to the gloom, the only light coming from the open doorway behind me.

Sam, Connor and Rhonda were chained to a support pole in the centre of the pavilion.

Sam's familiar easy smile set my heart racing as I quickly scanned the rest of the pavilion to confirm what my senses were telling me. They were alone.

I ran over and hugged Sam as tight as I could. 'Thank God you're okay. I was so worried. Talaom said you were in a gun battle at the television station.'

'I'm fine too, sis, in case you were wondering. So is Mum.'

I looked over at Connor, a huge grin on my face. 'Glad to hear that.' I let go of Sam and used aether to break the chains around their wrists.

As soon as his hands were free Sam cupped my face in his hands, eyes searching mine. 'Where have you been? God, Tyler, I thought you were dead again.'

'It's okay. I'm okay,' I said, relishing the feel of him, the scent that was uniquely his.

I pulled back slightly, smiling as his gaze steadied. 'I'll fill you in later. Right now we need to find Cade.'

'That shouldn't be too hard,' said Rhonda. 'I heard Killian ordering all his soldiers to assemble in the centre ring once we were secured. It appears Cade wants to deliver a final pep talk before they go out and inform the citizens of Easton there is a new God in town.'

'Want to help me burst his bubble?' I asked. 'It's time Clan Godden found out the truth about their leader.'

'And what truth would that be?' Rhonda's eyebrows arched.

'That he's not fit to lead them, let alone declare himself God.'

Sam gave me a searching look. 'What's your plan?'

'Show his people who he really is. Without them to follow his orders, he's nothing. To defeat him, I have to get his people to turn their backs on him.'

'And how exactly do you plan on doing that?' Chris asked.

I resisted the urge to shrug. 'Not sure yet. I'm just going to have to wing it.'

Family and friends at my side, I marched towards the centre

ring. As quietly as we could, we made for the large gate that allowed livestock to enter the main arena.

At any moment, I expected an alarm to sound, but as the murmur from the centre ring quietened down, I realised all their attention was focused on the imminent pep talk from Cade. We reached the gate and I crept forward with Talaom to see what was happening.

Cade and Killian stood in the middle of a large raised stage situated at the end of the arena closest to us, alongside the livestock gate. Almost filling the arena, arrayed in neat lines facing the stage, were thousands of Tr'lirians. Each one was arrayed for war; swords sheathed on their backs so only the hilts were visible above their heads. They were all winged, the men bare-chested and the women in tight-fitting vests. All of them had their eyes fixed on Cade, awaiting his words.

I waited too, wanting to see what he said, hoping I could use his own words to my advantage. An expectant hum filled the air as Cade stepped closer to the edge of the stage and raised his hands in the air.

'Today is the day we take our rightful place as rulers of this world. No more will we have to hide our existence from humans. After today they will all learn to worship us as the gods we are.'

Okay. This was it. Time to step up and prevent a war.

'Gods?' I said, letting my voice carry across the arena, trying not to show hesitation when every Tr'lirian present spun around to stare at me.

I put on my best smile and stepped forward, motioning for Sam and the others to remain where they were. 'Don't you mean God, Cade? As in, you? From what I've seen, you're not the type to share the limelight with anyone.'

'You.' Cade's mouth curled into a sneer.

'Me.'

'I thought the Grim Reaper would have ripped your soul to shreds by now.'

'Yeah, well, he's nowhere near as crazy as you are.'

'I am not crazy. I am a God.'

'Ha.' I let my derision show as I moved even closer to the stage. 'You're not God. You're a pathetic wannabe who can't stand it when he's not the centre of attention.'

'How dare you.' His handsome features twisted into a grotesque mask of rage.

'Oh, I dare plenty.' I lifted my chin and glared at him. 'Easton is my town, and I'm not going to let you ruin it like you did Angellin. You poison everything you touch. You are not fit to lead Clan Godden.'

'Kill her,' Cade roared, his order swiftly followed by the sound of hundreds of footsteps as his soldiers ran towards me.

CHAPTER 38

I waved Sam and the others back when it looked as though they were going to interfere. I had to do this on my own. With a steadying breath, I turned to face the Tr'lirians and set my wings free.

Those in the front stumbled, shock on their faces, sword arms falling to their sides. Many stopped running and dropped to their knees, in danger of being trodden on by those behind them.

'Ha'niel.' The one word, uttered by dozens of voices, filled the air.

Frozen mid-attack, the Tr'lirians looked from me to Cade, seeking direction.

'I ordered you to kill her.' Spittle flew from his lips as he roared at his people. He pointed at a woman who was closest to me, sword forgotten in her left hand. 'Do it. Now. Or I will cut you down myself.'

She took a step forward, confusion on her face as she stared at my wings.

'Is that what you want? A leader who kills those who won't obey him?' I shook my head. 'That's no way to lead, and you know it.'

'Do not listen to her. It is all lies. She is no Ha'niel. It's a trick.'

I twisted around to face him, shaking my head. 'I never said I was Ha'niel. I don't even understand what they are, and I would never claim to be something I'm not.'

As he glared at me, hatred coming off him in waves, I realised what I had to do.

I lifted my chin, and met his enraged glare with calm certainty as I said, 'I may not be a Ha'niel, but I am a reaper. I was there, last night, when you murdered one of your own men. To do that, to run him through for what you perceived as a slight against you; you're a madman. It's time your people see you for the monster you really are.'

In my peripheral vision, I could see Sam and Chris taking up position on either side of me. I could sense Connor, Rhonda, Rebecca and Talaom behind them, but couldn't afford to let the thought that everyone I cared about was here to distract me from my purpose.

I focused on Cade, on the emanations coming from his soul, and my knees threatened to buckle at the vile flood of emotions he was broadcasting. I forced myself to endure as I reached out to all the souls crowded behind me, seeking to link with every member of Clan Godden. When I was sure I had them, I allowed them a glimpse of what I saw when I looked into their leader's soul.

The feel of his hate was a tangible presence in the air, along with a deep-seated contempt for every other being, winged or otherwise. Viscous and rank, it poisoned his soul as surely as it had the home he claimed to love. Tears streamed down my cheeks as I delved deeper inside the psyche of a man who would not hesitate to kill anyone who got in the way of his pursuit of divinity.

Unable to take it any longer, I severed the connection and turned my back on him. I faced the assembled Tr'lirians, hardly needing to read their souls to know they were afraid, and confused; hearts battered by what they had just experienced.

Time to offer them hope.

'You came here because your city was dying, poisoned by the same hatred and anger that warped Cade's soul. But Angellin was not destroyed. The Davilians saved the city by letting go of all that corrupted it in the first place.'

I let my words sink in before continuing. 'I know you're scared, unsure of what your future holds, but this is not the way. You have a choice. You can follow Cade, and allow him to lead you farther on this dark path, or you can return home and help rebuild Angellin with the Davilians.'

'That's not possible. Uncontrolled nether cannot be contained. Not even a Ha'niel could do that.'

I looked back to see Killian had come to the edge of the stage, hope warring with disbelief on his face.

'You're right. Uncontrolled nether can't be contained, but it can be pushed back. The Davilians opened their hearts and their souls, cleansing them, allowing the remnants of pure aether still clinging to the tower to regenerate. That is what saved the city. They will never be able to banish the darkness completely, but as long as they continue to embrace the light the city will endure.'

I met his troubled gaze. 'You can help them to do that.' I waved a hand behind me to indicate the rest of the Tr'lirians. 'Take your people home, where they belong, and make Angellin whole again.'

'Enough.'

I jumped when Cade bellowed, and was sure I wasn't the only one. I watched him warily as he drew his sword and jumped off the stage. He strode towards me, features twisted.

'You will not escape death this time.'

'Cade, no.' Killian jumped down from the stage. 'Didn't you hear her? She said we can go home.' He ran after his leader and reached out to grab hold of him.

Cade swung around with his sword poised.

I flung out a hand, reaching out to grab his soul.

Too late.

The sword pierced Killian's chest.

'No!' Rebecca's scream sounded behind me, but I had no time to worry about her.

Cade pulled the sword free, no mercy in his eyes as he gazed at the man who had stood at his side for hundreds of years. I latched onto his soul and tugged as hard as I could.

His body shuddered as I stripped away his immortality. Feathers fell from his wings, but I didn't let up.

He would never stop, never see reason. Cade had to die or this would never be over.

Even now, despite the immense pain he had to be experiencing, he fought to raise his sword arm once more.

He gripped Killian's shoulder, holding the wounded man in place as he got ready to plunge the sword in again.

Killian flung up an arm to block him.

I caught a glimmer of something silver in Killian's hand as Cade's body stiffened. He staggered backwards, dropping his sword to clutch at his chest where a knife was buried hilt deep.

I felt it the second his soul let go. It sprang free from his body, which dropped to the ground and was still. An unearthly silence filled the centre ring as his soul hovered in the air, blackened, its light tarnished.

Trembling, I stepped forward and tapped Cade's poisoned soul, wiping away tears as I sent him on his way to rebirth.

My action appeared to shatter the paralysis that afflicted those around me.

Killian fell to his knees with a groan, head bowed over Cade's body. Rebecca ran to his side, face streaked with tears of her own, Chris only a step behind her.

A loud rustle of movement had me spinning around, mouth falling open as I saw all the Tr'lirians had assumed the same position as Killian, heads bowed as they farewelled their leader.

'We need an ambulance.'

Rebecca's cry snapped me back to the present.

'We take care of our own,' said a new voice.

It was the Tr'lirian Cade had threatened to cut down if she didn't kill me. She motioned behind her and two men ran forward. Unlike all the others, they carried backpacks instead of swords. They shucked them off as they neared Killian.

One of them firmly but gently ushered Rebecca aside as the other inspected the wound.

Sam came up to stand beside me, while Chris moved to put his arm around Rebecca as we watched the Tr'lirian medics work on her father. After long drawn out minutes they stood and indicated for several men to step forward with a stretcher.

'He'll live,' said the one who appeared to be in charge. 'But we need to get him back to the compound to treat him properly.'

I gave a nod and within minutes Killian was borne away on the stretcher. Another stretcher was produced for Cade's body, and the rest of the Tr'lirians formed a funeral procession and followed him out. Soon my family and friends and I were the only people left at the showgrounds.

'Chris,' I said, to get his attention.

He turned to look at me but did not move away from Rebecca, who was crying quietly into the front of his shirt.

'I'll take her out to the compound. She'll want to be with him,' he said.

I gave him a smile and a nod as he ushered her back to the gate. Once they had left the centre ring I turned to face Sam and the others.

'Now what?' Connor asked, scratching his head. 'Is that it? Cade's dead so the invasion of Easton is over?'

'I guess so,' I said, giving him a weary smile.

I took Sam's hand and walked out of the centre ring, taking

my first easy breath in days. Only time would tell what the future would hold, and not just for me. For the Tr'lirians as well.

Not that everything was tied up in a nice little package. There would be fall-out from Cade's failed attempt to take over Easton and pronounce himself God, but we would deal with it, together. Of that I had no doubt.

Whatever happened, I had Sam on my side and my family at my back. With their support, I could handle anything.

EPILOGUE

$\mathcal{I}$ pushed open the doors to the Southside office of the Easton Police Department, smoothing down my black skirt. Not that I was nervous.

Why would I be?

It wasn't as if I was embarking on an entirely new career path, one that at first glance was the complete opposite of my lifelong goal to become a journalist. My decision to go to university to study journalism had been prompted by a desire to make a difference, to help people and uncover the truth about issues affecting the wider community.

I had set that goal aside to take on one with more of a local focus but no less important. Easton was now home to a number of Tr'lirians who had chosen not to return to Angellin. Davilian or Godden, with wings and without, they were adapting to a life free from Cade's tyranny.

Killian, perhaps as punishment for his role in Cade's death, had chosen to exile himself to the physical plane. Then again, it could be his desire to stay connected to Rebecca that had been the deciding factor. She had returned to Sydney with Chris, and the two of them were cautiously dating to see if the ties formed during the chaos in Easton were real.

Whatever reason Killian had for staying here, it made my job easier to work with someone I knew. As Cultural Liaison, my official job description was to liaise between the Tr'lirians and the authorities. Given my mixed heritage and unique abilities, the mayor and the superintendent in charge of the Easton Police Department had decided I would be perfect for the roll.

Of course, the only reason they knew anything about me and my unique abilities was because they had been purpose-bred by Cade. With him out of the picture, his plan to rule the world in tatters, they had been forced to reassess their commitment to the people of Easton.

That was where I came in.

With so many Tr'lirians unwilling or unable to return to Angellin and choosing to settle in Easton, it was only a matter of time before the general population found out about the winged beings they now shared their hometown with. Clashes would undoubtedly occur. Killian may have been wrong about many things but he hadn't misjudged the reaction his people would receive once their presence became known, and we couldn't keep them sequestered away at Greenlakes forever.

But having them out and about, intermingling with the general population, could cause a few headaches and it was my job to help sort them out.

That took care of the standard job description, relying on my ability to manipulate aether, manifest wings and travel through the planes.

It was the unofficial job description that made me take in a deep breath as I stepped inside Sam's office.

While Talaom had taken over my role as official reaper for Easton, as penance for his wrongdoing in his previous life, I was still a reaper. I could still reap the souls of those who died and send them on their way to rebirth, but as a freelance reaper, with silver wings, I was able to read the signs the souls left behind with their empty bodies. As such I was in a unique position to assist the police in their homicide investigations.

Starting now.

Sam's welcoming smile soothed the worst of my jitters.

'Howdy, pardner,' he said, tipping an imaginary hat.

I laughed as I walked over and plonked myself down on his desk. 'Really? That's how you want to commemorate our first ever case. By pretending to be a cowboy?'

He shrugged. 'Seemed like a good idea at the time.'

'Yeah, well, I don't need a cowboy. Not when I have Easton Police Department's best detective as my partner, pardner.'

It was his turn to laugh. 'Fair enough. This is what we have so far. Someone broke into the Southside branch of the Easton Credit Union last night, and they somehow managed to get in and out of the vault while it was still locked, without setting off any alarms or appearing on CCTV.'

He slid a manila folder over to me. 'There is no sign of forced entry, and the logs confirm the vault door, which operates on a timed lock, had not been opened. Yet a large sum of cash is now missing. Considering how much was taken, it would appear there is more than one person involved, possibly as many as three.'

I looked up at him, frowning. 'You think it was one of the Tr'lirians who stole the money. They'd have been able to use the astral plane to get into the vault without being detected. But that's robbery. Not homicide.' And it would involve my role as Liaison, not reaper.

Sam opened the manila folder, revealing a crime scene photo of a young man, sprawled on the ground. 'Looks as though the thieves were surprised by the arrival of a security patrol.'

I sucked in a deep breath as I gathered up the folder and met Sam's steady gaze. 'Okay then, I guess it's time for a visit to the morgue, and for us to solve a murder.'

ACKNOWLEDGMENTS

Writing can be such a solitary past time, but getting a book published takes a team effort. *Silver Reaper* would never have been published if not for the very generous support of my family and friends.

My husband and children have been cheering me on every step of the way, even when I lock myself in my writing room and get lost in the writing. My mother continues to be my number one fan and Donna and Jael, as always, are ready to listen to me talk on and on about my characters as if they were real people.

Special thanks have to go to Sandy Curtis, Kris Sheather, Sue-Ellen Pashley, Helen Goltz and Sally Odgers, for providing wonderful advice and helping to make Silver Reaper shine.

Lastly, thank you to the readers who have continued to wait patiently for the next instalment in the Reaper Series, with a special shout out to DD Line for her continuing enthusiasm for my stories, and for the gentle encouragement (not nagging) for me to hurry up and get this particular book published so she can read it.

ABOUT THE AUTHOR

Shelley Russell Nolan is an avid reader who began writing her own stories at sixteen. Her first completed manuscript featured brain eating aliens and a butt kicking teenage heroine. Since then she has spent her time creating fantasy worlds where death is only the beginning and even freaks can fall in love.

The first two books in her debut adult urban fantasy series, *Lost Reaper* and *Winged Reaper*, were published by Atlas Productions in 2016, with *Silver Reaper* published in 2017 to complete the series. 2018 saw the release of her *Arcane Awakenings Novella Series*, and Odyssey Books will be publishing the first book in a new post-apocalyptic series in 2019.

Born in New Zealand, moving to Australia with her family when she was seven, Shelley currently lives in Central Queensland, Australia, with her husband and two young children. They share their home with two wrecking ball kitties, a deformed budgerigar and two dogs that are fairly normal as dogs go.

Shelley loves to hear from her readers so feel free to contact her on Facebook or leave a review on Amazon or Goodreads or on her website - shelleyrussellnolan.com